BOOK TWO
CHANGERS
ORYON

T COOPER &
ALLISON GLOCK-COOPER

ATOM

ATOM

First published in the United States in 2015 by Black Sheep,
an imprint of Akashic Books
First published in Great Britain in 2016 by Atom

1 3 5 7 9 10 8 6 4 2

Illustration on page 23 by Alex Petrowsky

A CIP catalogue record for this book
is available from the British Library.

ISBN 978-0-349-00244-6 (paperback)
ISBN 978-0-349-00245-3 (eBook)

Printed and bound in Great Britain by
Clays Ltd, St Ives plc

Papers used by Atom are from well-managed forests
and other responsible sources.

MIX
Paper from
responsible sources
FSC® C104740
www.fsc.org

Atom
An imprint of
Little, Brown Book Group
Carmelite House
50 Victoria Embankment
London EC4Y 0DZ

An Hachette UK Company
www.hachette.co.uk

www.atombooks.co.uk

...al to a broad demograph... . Teenagers, after all, are ...ng experts on trying on, and then promptly discarding, new ide... ...es'
— *New York Times Book Review*

'"Selfie" backlash has begun: The Unselfies project wants to help people quit clogging social media with pictures of themselves and start capturing the intriguing world around them'
— *O, The Oprah Magazine* on the We Are Changers Unselfies project

'This is more than just a 'message' book about how we all need to be more understanding of each other. The imaginative premise is wrapped around a moving story about gender, identity, friendship, bravery, rebellion Vs. conformity, and thinking outside the box'
— *School Library Journal*

'A thought-provoking exploration of identity, gender, and sexuality ... An excellent read for any teens questioning their sense of self'
— *Publishers Weekly*

'An excellent look at gender and identity and the teenage experience'
— *Tor.com*

'Everyone should read this, regardless of age. The book discusses important topics about growing into your skin (literally and physically), and gender identity ... Go get a copy of this right now'
— *Huffington Post*

'Changing bodies, developing personalities, forays into adult activities — where was this book circa the early 2000s when I needed it? But something tells me my adult self will learn a thing or two from it as well'
— ... *Book Blog*

For Dixie and Matilda

And for anybody who has looked in the mirror
and not recognized the person s/he sees

Before she became the one she was meant to be, before she lived through those four years called high school, those four years where everything she ever knew evaporated into air, where the ground dropped away, and she fell in love, and she lived through hate and violence and cheerleading, and saved lives without even knowing how, and she was rescued by a girl and a boy and words and music, and she did everything wrong until she got a few important things right, before she questioned what it meant to be special, what it meant to be anything, and harnessed her power, the power she didn't believe she had, the power others tried to take, before that and a hundred other awful, wondrous, ruinous, magical things happened, she was just a kid in Tennessee named Drew.

SUMMER

CHANGE 1—DAY 365

Won't sleep.
Will. Not. Close. My. Eyes.
*Don't do it, Drew. Don't do it. Don't sleep, don't sleep, don't
sleep.*
Will. Not. Go. To. Sleep.

I've been chanting to myself for the last hour. What is
it, two a.m.?

God, I'm so tired. I am so so so so so so . . . tired. All I
want to do is sleep. But I can't sleep. Okay, of course technically I *could* sleep, I am physically *able* to sleep. But I don't
want to. No. I am going to be fully conscious when I change.
The millisecond I turn into somebody else. Again.

My lids droop against my will. I can actually feel the
muscles in my eyelids twitching. Wet face, clammy skin. My
bedroom is going fuzzy, and everything blurs—the glow-in-
the-dark constellation poster; my dusty skateboard propped
in the corner, untouched since Tracy gave it back to me on
the last day of school; Snoop-Dogg down at the foot of my
bed. He seems to have had no problem drifting off, curled
into his customary ball, nose tucked under paw, snoring
away. Probably because *he's* not going to awaken as a totally
different animal, like a fur seal or a hoot owl.

Dogs are so lucky not to feel dread. He has no clue what
a momentous transformation is about to take place for me

sometime in the next five hours. To him, even after 365 days as Drew, I'm probably still Ethan. Well, Ethan with longer hair and a nicer smell, that is.

KNOCK-KNOCK-OPEN. Mom's trademark maneuver, plowing into my room.

"Hey, sweet pea," she whispers softly. When I stir, she adds louder, "I can't believe you're not asleep yet."

"Really?" I shoot back, my sarcasm hiding the fear I feel about having the snow globe of my universe shaken up, leaving me lost and shivering under some plastic dome with Rudolf the Social-Message Reindeer yet again. My heavy lids flicker, and I peer in Mom's general direction, somewhere between the doorknob and the light switch. She slowly sharpens into focus: pink tank top, plaid pj bottoms, tortoiseshell reading glasses swinging on a beaded chain around her neck.

"I'm staying up all night," I announce.

"Not advisable," she says. "But best of luck with that."

"You can't stop me."

Mom smiles, looks at me with a hint of pity. "You're really embracing your oppositional streak tonight, huh?" she says, all shrink-like, which I get is her day job, but I kinda wish she'd leave work at the office for one freaking minute. "Does that make you feel more in control? Because I get it, I really do—"

"Do you swear you don't know who's next for me?" I interrupt.

"I swear," she answers, wrinkling her forehead. "I would tell you if the Council told us. But they don't."

I give her my best, *For shiz?* look.

"Okay, I wouldn't tell you if I knew and they told us *not* to tell you," she corrects herself. "But I wouldn't lie about not knowing."

I stare her down, my eyeballs stinging like they're floating in bleach.

Will. Not. Sleep.

After a few seconds more of twilight, Mom asks, "Baby, are you okay?"

And then, yay, a whoosh of waterworks. As if the last week hasn't been filled with enough crying. Crying because my period is due, crying because summer is over and I know what's coming next, or more accurately because I don't know *who* is coming next. Crying really mostly because I'm going to miss Audrey—even though of course I'm going to be able to see her, but it's not going to be remotely the same as it was freshman year. Because I'm going to be dead to her. As in, I might literally be dead to her. I don't even know what feint I'm getting from the Council to explain to Aud (and everyone else) where Drew went. Where *I* went.

This sucks. No matter who I am, I'll never be able to tell her that I'm the person she let into her life so completely last year. That I was her best friend. I mean, whomever I am when I wake up in the morning is not necessarily even somebody Audrey's going to dig at this point in her life.

Even though I'm going to be the same person (I think), I'm still going to be me (whoever that is), but Audrey won't know that. Or will she? I don't freaking know, *The Changers Bible* says nothing useful to prepare us for this: *Life changes everybody, Statics and Changers alike . . . The whole concept of control is ultimately an illusion . . . You are and will always be the same honest and true core, regardless of the aliases you don . . .* My head is spinning, and I start hyperventilating, and now Mom has swept me up in a hug, which makes me wail even more, the snot starting to ooze out pitifully with each shoulder shrug, like my nose is a frozen yogurt dispenser.

"I'm so tired," I manage between sobs.

"I know, love," she purrs, brushing the sticky hair off my face, adding, "I completely understand."

"No you don't!" I shout. "You've never changed into somebody else!"

She takes a deep breath, exhales slowly and steadily. "I might argue that assertion, but that's a conversation for another time." She holds me tighter for a few beats.

"I'm sorry," I snuffle.

"It's okay. You're right, I've never actually woken up as a new person like you and Dad have," she concedes.

"I don't want to be a loser," I whine.

"You aren't a loser, Drew. You're just a confused kid like every other—"

"I mean, *turn* into a loser," I blurt.

Mom suddenly pulls back and gives me her "severely disappointed" face. I know, I'm not supposed to feel that way; being a Changer means I should know better than to label, or at least know how superficial labels are. But I've seen how the freaks, geeks, and forgotten get treated at school.

Being a Changer is hard enough. I don't want to do battle on every front. If I have to be someone else, I want that someone to be appealing and popular and confident and good at stuff and . . . OMG, I'm writing a personal ad for *myself.*

"Beauty is as beauty does," Mom says evenly. "I know a lot of so-called winners who are toads underneath. And it always shows through. What matters is what is on the inside."

"Have you *been* to high school, Mom?" I ask, dragging the back of my hand across my drippy nose.

She chuckles. "You have a point."

And then I drop the bomb. "I don't want my outside to be a boy," I pop out, trying to gauge her reaction from the corner of my eye. Nothing. She doesn't respond. The therapist reflex. Unshockable. Makes me want to tell her more. How for so long I hated being Drew and would've done anything to bring Ethan back, but now that I've been living as Drew for a year—well, now that I *am* her—I'm realizing it hasn't been the worst, and I've grown accustomed to being in high school as a girl. Well, a girl like her.

"Who do you think you want to be?" Mom asks.

I consider the question for a few seconds. Then a few more. "I want to be myself," I finally say, uncertain even as I'm saying it.

"Well, ain't no getting around that," she laughs, kissing my head and standing up. "Now go the eff to sleep."

Mom hits the light and pulls the door shut behind her, and then I am alone again. Well, me and Snoopy, who groggily cuts an eye toward me.

Blink-blink. Blink-blink. Blink.

He lowers his head, seems to fall back asleep instantly. Show-off.

It's so damn quiet in here. No choice but to return to focusing on me, myself, and I, I, I. At least the unbridled fit of hysteria has begun to wind down to a low, somewhat manageable hum. *Breathe. Breathe.* Inhale five, exhale eight. I can actually hear the oxygen whispering through my trachea with each breath. Weird. Does that mean I have something? Like asthma, or maybe emphysema from hanging out and talking to Aud last year on the school steps where all the burners sparked up.

Speaking of, I wonder what Audrey might or might not be doing right now on the eve of her sophomore year, whether she's thinking of me, what she's wearing. (I don't mean that in a creeper way.) She sent three e-mails after getting back from Camp Killjoy (no Internet, no electronics, no music besides spiritual hymns permitted). Which I could only bear to respond to in the most cursory fashion and with, necessarily, more lying. Lying about being excited for the first day of school. And about being psyched to see her on the first day of school. Well, the latter being not *technically* a lie, because while *I* am not looking forward to the first day of school (emphasis on *I, Drew*, am not looking forward to the first day of school because *I* am going to be A COMPLETELY DIFFERENT PERSON on the first day of school), I am, however—whomever I'll be—looking forward to seeing *Audrey* on the first day of school. That part is not a lie. *Le sigh*.

Okay, back to [not] sleep. I clap twice, and the overhead light magically comes back on. God, I love the Clapper I bought on eBay this summer. I wonder if a Changer invented it. Clap twice, you're a ninth grade girl! Clap two more times, hey, you're a boy again! Or something else entirely!

That's stupid.

Speaking of, the last time I saw him at ReRunz, Chase told me he heard around RaChas central that there was actually some homeopathic way to influence who you change into. That the Changers Council doesn't want us to know about it, but there's something about a crystal and having somebody you love gently swing it from a string over your head in an oval pattern while you visualize your intended V just as the clock strikes midnight on the last full moon before your change. He made me swear not to tell anybody (like who am I going to tell?), but Chase said that he was going to try it, and did I want to come with? I guess that meant he still cares about me. Or maybe he only wanted company, like a reasonable, nonsuperstitious friend to shine a light on the three-ring circus of all those culty RaChas swinging rocks on fishing line around their heads in hopes of controlling the uncontrollable, the way we all grip arm-rests on airplanes during turbulance.

I told Chase he'd obviously been reading too many teen werewolf sagas, and to get a freaking clue. Those idiots'll do anything that their leader Benedict tells them to do over there at the RaChas compound, but how ignorant can they be? Like the Council's going to leave anything up to chance like that. Besides, those crystal deodorants don't even work. If they won't stop you from smelling funky, they sure as shite aren't going to stop you from fulfilling your destiny.

I. Can't. Deal. My head is hot, palms sweaty. I get up again to look at Drew in the mirror for probably the last time. I look pink. Puffy and pink. I think I have a fever. My body must be gearing up for the change. I remember feeling sort of sick last year about this time. Stupid me thought I was just coming down with a little cold. Instead, I came down with a raging case of the ladies.

So, das Chronicles, Dear Diary in my head, here I am, Drew Bohner, in her final hours. What are my deep thoughts? What would I like all of Changer posterity to know about what's going on in my addled brain space on this last night of Change One? Wait, you know how really devout Jewish men wake up every morning and in their first prayer they have to thank God for not making them into women overnight? And how Jewish women are supposed to thank the Almighty for making them as they are? Besides the fact that that whole noise is totally messed up,

9

and makes my brain get logic cramps when I try and work it through, I still can't help but wonder which little prayer I'll be muttering soon as my eyes pop open come daybreak.

"Bye, then," I say into the mirror, "later." Then zombie-walk-collapse back into bed, and . . .

Clap-clap. Lights out.

FALL

Where do I start?
Wowzers.

Uh, so hey, future self: This is, uh, Oryon Small, reporting in fresh off the Change boat. I'm probably about 5'8", a buck-fifty, brown eyes, black hair. A guy. African American. Cute. Cute *enough*. Slim. Promising. Maybe. I've been a dude again for about ten hours now, and so far . . . so good?

Not really. It's actually rather discombobulating, blank you very much. I wonder if it ever won't be.

Okay, I'll start at the Quonset hut, where I met Tracy this morning before school. She was dressed in a rose-colored tweedy-looking suit straight from the Blush and Bashful collection, with coral lipstick to match.

"I know it feels like old news, but I want you to try to Chronicle every experience you can remember, especially these first days as this new V. You're going to want to record every detail and nuance. The idea is to not forget the who you were while on the path to becoming the who you're meant to be," she rattled off from *The Changers Bible*, more rote than seemed possible, even for Tracy.

I hadn't seen her in a week or so, which was a rarity; she'd periodically checked in on me all summer long. But today, of all days, she was completely distracted, consumed with brushing a tiny pink thread off her lapel.

"What's up with you?" I ask, suspicious.

She looks up, cocks her head. "Who? Me?" Acting all confused.

"You're being weird," I say.

She smiles, mouth shut.

"If anyone should be acting weird, it's me."

"I'm not acting *anything*, Drew—" She stops herself. "*Oryon*."

"See, not so easy, right?" I tease.

God my life is bizarre. I'm standing in front of Tracy, looking as different in pretty much every way possible from who I was when she last saw me, and her brain still slips and calls me by another name. She still sees the old me, who I *was*. It's mind-blowing is what it is. Like when you really start thinking about life on this planet, pulling up, up, and away from the city you're in, then the state, keep going up past the country and the earth and solar system, then universe, and you keep coming back to what an infinitesimal speck you really are when it comes down to ALL OF TIME. And yet, we cling to these ideas of who we are, *what* we are. We make decisions like they matter.

"Turn around," Tracy barks at me while fumbling with something inside her purse.

"Uh-unh, not this crap again," I say under my breath while taking a step back, fighting rapid-onset post-traumatic stress disorder as I flash on the last time my brand-new touchy Touchstone Tracy mercilessly jabbed me in the back of the neck with a needle the size of a pencil and injected me with my big-brother Chronicling chip. God only knows what the Council requires the second time around, a "painless" *spinal fluid* tap?

"It's not invasive this V," she says, manhandling me.

I resist. "No. You're telling me what you're doing before you do it."

"Wow, control freak much?" she snaps.

"Pot meet kettle."

Tracy sighs. Like she doesn't have time for this.

"Just tell me," I insist, holding my ground and standing up a little straighter.

Tracy stares me down. Another giant sigh, but she relents: "It's just a little magnetic fob I'm required to wave over your chip to reboot and initiate Y-2, so you can start transmitting your Chronicles."

"No needles?"

"No needles," she promises, producing and pressing her thumb on what looks like a Barbie-sized camping flashlight. It beeps, glows red, then flashes blue. "Now turn around already."

I finally comply. No hair to hold up this time (not the worst). I shift my weight back and forth and stare at a toppled stack of old tires in the corner of the hut, when I feel Tracy placing the metal fob against the back of my neck. It beeps again, and I sense a faint *click* at the base of my spine, a mini zap to the bone.

"Done," she chirps.

"That's it?"

"That's it."

"Thank G," I say, genuinely relieved.

"I told you to trust me," Tracy chides as I turn back around. She puts her hands on my shoulders, studies me closely, seeming more present than before. Her eyes get glassy. "This is going to be a big year for you," she says, suddenly maternal.

"Nah, it's just . . ." I reach for the right words. "It's just another year."

"You've already come so far," Tracy adds, and I can sense her pride in me.

I think back to last fall, when I stood here with her, wearing Mom's frumpy khaki shorts, torturous jog bra, my crazy long hair all knotted up, flopping around in Ethan's giant Vans—shout-out to Mom who had the presence of mind to hold onto them for me in case I turned into someone who could wear them this year (I stand in those very shoes now). Back then I was a terrified lemur, petrified of taking those last steps up the dirt path to school to begin my new life. I tear up, and I'm expecting to just start bawling, but . . . nothing. Just a little dampness pulling on my bottom lids.

"When I was C2-D1 like you, it was about right now I had a strong sense Tracy was the *one*," Tracy says, full of nostalgia and hope.

"I know the story, I *remember*—"

"No pressure if you don't feel the same way now!"

Of course, no pressure, never any pressure from Tracy, queen of all things pressurized, a walking, talking diamond sprung from her own overachieving butt.

She dabs at a tear in the corner of her eye, continues, "I'm just saying, it's an exciting year, and I want you to get everything you can out of it. Now, I know you're an old pro, but I'm going to try to be here just as much as I was last year, and if there's ever anything you need, literally anything comes up, I want you to come to me, and we'll get through it. Together. Like last year."

"Okay," I concede, because I don't know what else to say. "Should we fist bump or—"

She suddenly pulls me into a hug, and I'm stiff, don't know where to put my arms, so I just sort of encircle her and let her do the hugging. She seems so small now.

Tracy releases me, steps back, and takes a good look, the corners of her lips curling up. "You're, what? Like a hipster this year or something?"

"It's only 'cause my clothes are tight," I say.

"Well, you're definitely too cool for *me*, much less TV."

"Mom saved a few of my old . . . Ethan's old, you know, my old things, I guess so I would have something to wear if I woke up as a boy this year."

"I love your mom. Thank goodness I remembered to give you back your skateboard last year, huh? You're going to need that, just to carry around and look *fly*," Tracy says, trying out a word she's likely never employed outside of describing what birds, planes, and pigs do.

"Do I look *fly*, Trace?"

"Hella," she says, laughing with me, then seems to remember something and checks her wristwatch. "Ooh, you have to get going, you need to get registered. Let me know if you want to meet up at ReRunz later."

But it doesn't seem like it's me who's supposed to be somewhere. Tracy slings her purse over a shoulder and heads toward the door, the early-autumn sun filtering in through the marred plastic window behind her.

"Hey!" I call after her, and Tracy stops. "Did you know I was going to be Oryon?"

"I didn't," she replies somberly. "Nobody knows, really."

I nod like I agree, but I keep feeling there's got to be somebody steering the ship, some massive design or pattern to why we Changers are who we are every year.

"Maybe there's no reason," Tracy continues, obviously reading my mind. "What are you worried about?"

"What am I *not* worried about?"

Tracy, knowing better: "Tell me. Is it Audrey?"

"I'm scared she won't want me in her life," I mumble, holding my arms out, like *Look at me.*

"Maybe," Tracy says. "But maybe not. Audrey's a good person."

"But—"

"And so are you," she cuts me off.

I'm quiet.

"YOU are a good person," she repeats with some serious emphasis. "And you're the same person. Oryon, Drew, Ethan . . . you're *all* good."

I shrug, even though I know she's trying.

"So then, I have to be somewhere to meet someone about a thing," Tracy says awkwardly, not quite pulling it off. I cock my head at her, and one hot tear drops onto my left cheek just as she budges through the rain-swollen door.

"Thank you," I whisper, my throat thick, but I don't think she hears me.

Okay. I should backtrack. First of all, I can't believe how much I hated Chronicling a year ago this time, and how nowadays I'm all like, *Dear Diary this . . . Dear Diary that . . . Ooh, poor me, it's so hard to be a Changer.* Like I can't survive without blabbing on and on about my Changery adventures every second. I guess I've sort of gotten used to it, and it feels like something is missing if I don't get stuff down.

Over pizza dinner last night, Mom and Dad were all trying to have a "talk" with me about sex and the "added responsibility" that goes with suddenly being a young, bigger, and stronger person in the world.

I was like, "Check out my legs: they're limp soba noodles," but Dad just directed me to where he keeps the condoms in the bathroom linen closet.

I am going to assume he bought them solely for me in the event I became a guy for my second V, even though any talk or activity like that is strictly premature (not to forget "premarital," ha ha!)—as well as frowned upon by the Changers Council, the place where all natural instincts go to suffocate and die. Never mind that any thought related to prophylactics and my dad, and why he would have them in the house he lives in with my mom, is something I'd rather not consider. Only now, *ew*, I can't stop thinking about it. I can't. The more I try not to think about it, the more I think about it.

GROSS.

Okay, where was I? Right, back to this morning. I guess I'd finally fallen asleep despite all my efforts to stave it off, but the first thing I'm conscious of is Mom bursting through my door, with Dad right behind, and I jump up out of bed fire-drill style. I'm just wobbling there bleary-eyed, and Mom is there on tenterhooks, clutching the thick envelope from the Changers Council in her hand, and Dad appears behind her, a little out of breath, and then we're all standing there staring at each other, like they do in old Westerns, right before the shooting starts. Snoopy casually sniffs toward the three of us and scratches his neck, the jingle of tags on his collar the only sound in the room.

I'm looking back and forth between my parents' eyes, barely coming to, desperately trying to discern who I am, what I am, just from studying their faces. But there's nothing in them to tip me off. They are both giving "complete acceptance of your child no matter what she is or does" realness, tinged with maybe a dash of political correctness/condescension, like they do with the waitstaff when we go to the Indian all-you-can-eat buffet in Nashville and they leave a giant tip even though it's a buffet and nobody waited on us at all. As I'm thinking about the duality of that, how it's simultaneously sweet and patronizing, I suddenly realize my Hello Kitty underwear feels really tight and binding, as does the tank top I wore to bed the night before.

"Good morning," Mom and Dad say in unison tentatively, as their eyes can't help but tumble down my body so that my hands instinctively, instantly cover my crotch and I go bounding into my bathroom and slam the door behind me so I can be alone with the mirror.

I take a deep breath. Exhale. *Here goes* . . . I slowly turn to my reflection above the sink, but before I can get a look, I suddenly ascertain that I'm actually palming a handful *down there*. Hello Kitty indeed. How soon I forgot what it's like to have so much going on "down there" in the mornings. I sneak a glance in the mirror. I'm a little scrawny, but I look sort of, I don't know, like an almost-man. So, instant puberty. That happened.

Okay, maybe I'm not supposed to be wasting time Chronicling about what's going on in my nethers, but honestly, I can't really ignore it because I'm remembering all over again what it was like when I was Ethan. Wrangling girl parts was rough in so many ways, but at least I never had to deal with the "control issues" boys have around their anatomy, especially in the a.m.

I notice my reflection in the mirror, slowly catching up to reality, and I'm . . . wait . . . *What?*

That's me?

It's so different than anything I imagined. I don't know why I didn't picture this, but I didn't. I tilt my head. He tilts his head. Tongue in. Tongue out. Yep, it's me all right.

I know it shouldn't be one of my first thoughts, but: I

guess if I'm being honest—which is supposedly what we're doing here—you could say my most immediate sentiment is, *Phew, at least I'm okay-looking.*

In the mirror it looks like I have a black eye where a smudge of eyeliner was never completely cleaned from the glass surface. In a fit of despair about Audrey after I wasn't allowed to spend time with her anymore, and after the whole horrific thing with Jason went down, but before I told my parents what he did to me, I'd dramatically scrawled in dark brown eyeliner on my mirror, *Love is a four-letter word!* It stayed up there for months; I guess Mom must've finally taken some Windex to it, because I never wiped it clean myself, and one day it just wasn't there anymore.

Audrey.

What is Aud going to think of this dude who's presently staring back at me in the mirror?

The thought is interrupted by Mom frantically barking vitals through the door, "Oryon Small. Fifteen. Birthday: October 17. You are a foster child from Atlanta. Your biological parents died in a car crash on I-75 when you were really young, so you don't remember much about them. Passed around various family members and temporary homes until you were placed in foster care with a family—well, us . . ."

So that'll explain the lily-white parents. The Council, it seems, thinks of everything.

I'm gazing at "Oryon" in the mirror. He looks like somebody I'd think was too hip to want to be friends with me. A hip nerd type. A kid who flipped the script and made his nerdiness the source of his hipness. I notice my pecs peeking out of my tank top and can't help but smile. Whoa. I have some serious dimples too. And long, ropey muscles, like a professional runner or rock climber. I peel off the tank top,

21

let it drop to the floor. I spin around admiring my bare chest. Now *that's* a feeling I missed.

"I have a shirt out here I think would work," Dad is calling through the door. "And some boxers."

"And I saved your old Vans," Mom adds nervously.

"It's cool. Just leave everything there. I need another minute alone," I say, for the first time hearing his, *my*, voice. Which is, what? "Testing, testing. One, two, three, um, twelve?" I say quietly into the mirror, just to hear the voice again. It's sort of raspy. A little breathy. Deeper than Ethan's was. Not a trace of Drew.

"And, uh, honey?" Mom warbles. "The Council also sent the, uh, the—"

"What?" I shout through the door.

"Your emblem?" she says apologetically. "Do you want me to do it again this time, or help you—"

"I got it," I say flatly. "Just leave it out there, please."

I listen at the door for a while. Then a little longer to make sure they're gone. Finally, a minute alone, so I crack open the door and reach my hand out for the clothes they left on the floor, and the little lipstick tube of death that Mom assaulted me with last year when I bent over completely unawares that I had to be BRANDED with a Changers logo before I could be allowed to leave the house.

I close the door, lock it. Double-check it's locked. Pick up the tube, pop off the top, and there, like a cigarette lighter from an old car, is the cheesy Changers emblem I guess I'm supposed to sear onto one of my butt cheeks right now. I take a deep breath. Then another one. I eyeball the device a little bit closer. How does it get hot? How bad did it hurt again? Funny how you can forget something like that. We always think physical pain is what will stick with us, but it never does. Emotional pain—now that's the stuff that gets branded on you for life.

I prop my foot on the toilet, twist my torso and look at my butt, firmly grasp the tube in my fingers like a highlighting pen, which, it kinda is. I take another deep breath and press the tip into my flesh. At first I don't register what's happening because I'm the one doing it. But then the searing starts, plus a tiny puff of electrical-smelling smoke, and I have no control over the reflex to pull my hand away. I jerk and drop the offending weapon into the toilet bowl. Great.

The emblem maker gives off a *pssstt* sound as it hits the water. I've obviously killed it. And, just as obviously, I'll have to retrieve it, because the Council isn't going to be down with their technology finding its way into some filtration system and getting discovered by the dude whose job it is to clean the waste-trapping grates at the sewage-treatment plant. I reach my hand into the bowl and splash around trying to grab the tube.

"Everything okay in there, honey? You sick?"

Fantastic. My mom thinks I have diarrhea.

"I'm fine, Mom!"

(I can't believe I'm going to have to do this two more times in my life.)

After I fish out the brander, I try to look at the brand itself. From what I can tell in the mirror, one of the feet is missing:

I don't care, I have to get this freak show on the road, so I start unfurling the clothes my parents left for me: big-ass blue-striped boxers and a plain white T-shirt. I have a moment where I think, *Bra!* but I don't need one. Gracias, Changers Council.

I quickly pull on the clothes, then dig around my closet for a plaid button-down that was left over from Ethan days. I shrug it on, and it feels like my shoulders are going to burst through the fabric, *Teen Wolf* style. Never mind. It's late, and I don't want to be calling additional attention to myself by sprinting into school so tardy that everybody has a chance to ogle me.

I quickly brush my teeth, run a palm over my short hair. I splash some water on my face, and check myself in the mirror once again. Oryon. Damn, my butt burns. This is really happening.

Okay, let's do this.

When I get out to the hallway, Mom assaults me with a giant hug. I'm now at the height where I can put my nose into her hair. It smells fruity like Drew's shampoo. I hand her the dripping-wet branding tube. "Don't ask."

Dad lopes over from their bedroom door and gives me a quick and awkward embrace as soon as Mom releases me.

"I need pants," I say to him.

I scan Dad's clothes on his side of the closet, but nothing jumps out at me as ideal. Then I spot some old-man green polyester golf pants. "Can I cut these?" I ask over a shoulder to neither of them in particular.

"Of course not, what are you—"

"*Sure* you can," Mom cuts Dad off. "Those'll be cute."

I turn around and look at her. "Cute" is not exactly what I'm going for, but they will definitely look better than they currently do if I cut them just above the knees and leave the hem ragged. I look to Dad, who's wincing slightly.

"Go ahead," he relinquishes, and Mom gently rests a hand on his forearm.

"Thanks," I say, heading out to the kitchen to find a pair of scissors.

My parents trail me back down the hallway, so I stop, swivel back toward them—and they both slam into me, then each other. It's like a Wile E. Coyote and Roadrunner chase up in here.

"I got this," I add, then keep going. I slip into the bathroom and shut the door behind me just in time to keep them out. I hold the nerdy green pants up to my waist in the mirror, consider for a minute, then pinch where I want to cut. I do one leg, then the other at approximately the same length, and once I step into them and cinch them up with a preppy belt with lobsters on it (also courtesy of Dad), I stand in their full-length mirror like I did a year before (in tears), stare at myself for a few good seconds, and think, *Yeah, much easier for a dude.*

I open the door and casually grab some blue-and-pink argyle socks from Dad's top drawer, while Mom starts digging around on her side of the closet, and soon she pulls my old Vans from a top shelf and presents them to me. I take them and kiss her on the cheek before sitting on the ground and trying to jam my feet into them. They're way too small, but when I crush down the backs, I can sort of make it work.

Andre 3000 retro swag. Not the worst vibe to pop on my first day.

Of course I am late for registration at Central. In the office, ol' Miss Jeannie is shutting down the ID line when I blow in, breathless after sprinting up the hill from my meeting with Tracy at the Q-hut. I didn't notice a single other person on the way in; I just kept my head down and hurried through the hallways, taking the stairs two at a time.

"You're too late, son," Miss Jeannie warbles, sweet as cobbler, soon as I make it to the front desk.

"I'm so sorry," I say, surprised anew to hear this croaky voice emerging from my throat. "Is there any way you can fit me in? I got lost on the way here."

Miss Jeannie stares at me. Thinks about it for a few seconds. "Well, I was just going to turn off this computer until tomorrow, but I haven't pushed the button just yet."

"Thank you *so* much," I say, as she pokes at the same old console that looks like a television set from the '70s, a *Too Blessed to be Stressed* button jangling from her floral blouse. "Oryon Small? Tenth grade?" I offer, lilting at the end. When I do, Miss Jeannie perks up her head like she's sensing a disturbance in the force. Why am I doing that? Reflexively up-talking? Oh, right. Because girls do that. Because we, I mean *they*, are taught to intuitively doubt everything they say. Which is solid B.S., but not something I can remedy in this moment. I make a note to self not to do it anymore, and to concentrate on ending my sentences flat, man-style, like I don't give a damn.

"Small, Small," Miss Jeannie says, scrolling. "Smaaaall."

I wait at attention with my elbows propped on the desk. The first period bell rings out in the hallway, and I startle. There are just a few stragglers in the office, mostly doped-out-looking kids who don't seem to care about getting registered—or anything, really. One kid with his long ratty hair pushed back in a plastic headband looks up and makes eye contact with me; he gives a sleepy-eyed version of the universal nod meaning, *S'up?*

I nod back, *S'up?*

"Here we are, *Small, Or-ee-on*," Miss Jeannie says after a few more seconds. "I gotcha. Hmm. Looks like you're all set." Then she seems surprised. "I see you're new in town from . . . Georgia! You like peaches?"

"I guess," I say. "But I'm more of a nectarine girl."

"And do you play football, hon'?" she asks, completely unaware of my blunder.

My face is burning. "Uh . . ."

But she doesn't wait for an answer, seems scarcely to be listening, instead just pushes a blank blue 3"x5" file card across the counter and tells me to fill it out with name, date of birth, any medical conditions, and emergency contact information—which I do, carefully trying to recall everything that was contained on the first page of the packet on Oryon Small that the Changers Council sent over this morning.

Peck-peck. Punch. Peck-peck-peck. She silently works the keyboard, hair as turtle-shell shellacked as ever, jowls vibrating as she mindlessly completes each step in the process of making Oryon Small official at Central High. She's not as TMI as when we did this freshman year while I scrawled Drew's emergency information on a bright *pink* file card. Not that she'd remember, but Miss Jeannie was more than happy to let Drew in on the menopausal hot flashes she'd been dealing with this time last year. I mean, we were such instant girlfriends she practically styled my student ID photo shoot like it was for *Teen Vogue*.

Maybe she's just having a bad day. Or her husband just had a hip replacement and everything's falling to her. Or times are tough, and she's supporting a grandchild with diabetes on a crappy Tennessee state salary and Medicaid.

"Okie dokie," she says when ready. "Stand over there on the tape and take a gander up here at this camera." She taps the eyeball lens atop the giant beige monitor with a long acrylic fingernail painted like a ladybug.

I do as I'm told, even smile.

"That's a big grin," Miss Jeannie says, snapping the shot and pressing *Enter* on the keyboard. The printer starts humming, and after it spits out my schedule, she presses another button and my ID slowly follows. All I can see are my dimples and teeth in the tiny square photo. "Almost done. You're going to have to hightail it to homeroom, Mr. Or-ee-on."

"Yes ma'am," I say, as she separates my ID along a perforation and feeds it into the laminator.

"You'll get your new student handbook in homeroom" (*I don't need it*, I think). "There's a used-book exchange in the gym after school today and tomorrow" (*Do I look like I can't swing new books?*). "And other than that, welcome to Central High; not that we hope to see you in here often," she winks (*Do I look like the kind of kid who winds up in the principal's office?*).

My ID comes out crooked and bent inside the laminate, but she's not gonna do it over, just cuts it out and hands it over to me, still warm.

"Thank you," I say, and head out of the office. I know exactly where homeroom is.

When I get to the door, I take a sharp breath and push through: Mr. Crowell is half-sitting on the front of his desk in midsentence, blabbing on and on (*I* might change, but some things never do), something about Sancho Panza from *Don Quixote*. He stops talking when I walk in, looks over at me.

"Sorry," I say. "I think I'm supposed to be in here?" Ergh! *Just say it, don't ask it!* I yell at myself in my brain.

"Yes, yes," Mr. Crowell replies, a curly dark chunk of hair flopping down over his forehead as he refers to his roll sheet. "You must be . . . Nina Jackson." He looks up hammily, and the class starts laughing. "Of course not. You must be . . . Mr. Small?"

I nod yes, feeling every eye in the room on me. I don't return any contact, instead spot a free chair toward the back of the room hailing me like a beacon.

"Why don't you have a seat?" Mr. Crowell gestures toward the same chair. "Anybody know Ms. Jackson?" he asks the class.

"*Sorry, Ms. Jackson,*" a familiar voice sings from the corner of the room, "*I am for reccal!*" It's Jerry, who appears to have grown something like three inches over summer. I give a giant knowing grin when he looks over at me. But there's no recognition in his countenance—even though he seems as genial as ever.

My pulse pounds in my ears as I weave through the rows toward the empty seat. I notice some girl's bare legs dramatically move out of my way when I pass, like I have bubonic plague or something. I surreptitiously follow the legs up to the short-shorts, to the tiny tank top, to a veritable Technicolor palette of eye shadow, to an absurd curtain of perfectly blown-out bangs, to . . . Chloe. Of course, who else would it be?

"Thank you for the musical interlude, as always, Jerry," Mr. Crowell says, and then to himself, "We'll give Nina a little more time before we get started in earnest," and checks off something from his clipboard.

I finally plop into my seat, and everybody stops staring. I glance around the room, trying but unable to identify every student.

"So as I was saying," Mr. Crowell continues, "we're trying out a new homeroom system where you will be stuck with me—and I stuck with you—throughout all four years here at Central."

"More for some people," Chloe snipes, cutting her eyes at Jerry.

"We feel like this will build a sense of both continuity and community," Mr. Crowell says, ignoring her, "where you always feel you have a trusted advocate on the faculty, and we can really mature with one another over the years."

"Or not," Chloe snickers, again at Jerry, as her partner-in-petulance Brit giggles and slaps Chloe's hand across the aisle. A couple heads from the front row turn around.

"Give it a rest, it's day one."

I recognize that world-weary voice from the first syllable. *Audrey*. At the recognition, my heart clatters in my chest like dropped china.

"Okay, okay," Mr. Crowell raises his voice, keeps talking about how the schedule's also different this year and begins scribbling his office hours and e-mail address on the board.

Hard as I try, I can't quit staring at Audrey. She's tan. She got a short haircut, the kind where it's super short in the back and much longer in the front. She looks good. Really, really good.

"What's your drama, mullet head?" Chloe hisses to Audrey.

"A mullet is pretty much the exact opposite of this haircut," Audrey answers coolly. "You know, party in the *back*?"

"Whatever, carpet muncher," Chloe spits, jerking her head back and forth to see who's laughing along.

Audrey sighs. "Now *that* would be a party in the *front*."

I sputter hard, and noisily, at Aud's comeback. She turns toward me, as do Chloe and Brit and a handful of other students, and suddenly it's clear I've laughed far too loudly.

I smile wide at Audrey like I did two minutes earlier at Jerry. Knowingly. But she just turns back around, a little creeped out, if I had to guess. I mean, I would be if I were her and some random new kid was staring at me and grinning like he knows me intimately.

"Ooooh, burn. Too bad your boring little girlfriend isn't here to watch and applaud," Chloe taunts Audrey. "I guess even *that retard* couldn't stand being around you anymore. Did you chop off your hair after the break-up?"

"Okay, okay, okay," Mr. Crowell says in that composed, neutral voice authority figures are taught to use when they need to calm down crazy people. "Please try to be kind."

It suddenly lands on me: Chloe is talking about me. I'm the retard. Well, *Drew* is.

I know the Council wants us to feel what it's like to be treated differently based on our outsides, but it's starting to seem downright sinister—schadenfreudey at best—to watch as my friends wrestle with me being MIA, and to see and hear what they really think about me. It's like being alive at my own funeral. To all those folks who wish they could be a fly on the wall, I'm here to tell you: no, you don't. Nothing good comes from being the fly.

"Oryon?" Mr. Crowell is prompting. "Oh-rye-on?"

Crap. That's me. "Present."

"Indeed. Go ahead, stand up," he says.

I can't move my legs.

"Or sit," he adds mercifully. "But introduce yourself. Who are you, what do you like? What's your relationship to the Bard?"

"Uh . . ." I start. I struggle to keep my voice monotone. "The Bard is dope?" Crap. Another question.

"What's your favorite play?"

I look at Audrey, who's intensely studying her fingernails. "*Romeo and Juliet*," I loudly proclaim. She doesn't flinch, still scarcely registering me.

"A perennial favorite," Mr. Crowell says. "Too bad you weren't here for your freshman year—we covered that play from ruff to merkin, wouldn't you all say?"

Chloe nods self-importantly. "I was Juliet."

"I was Romeo at my old school," I venture, eyes trained on Aud, willing her to look at me, but there's no reaction. Is she thinking about me? I mean Drew? How we kissed in this very room when performing the party scene from *Romeo and Juliet*? She has to be thinking about it. I would be. Am.

I wonder what she's heard happened to me. Where I am, if not sitting here in homeroom and starting our sophomore year together, fighting the good fight against Chlo-Jo and the Queen Bees. I feel awful for dropping out of her life, but I didn't know what else to do besides disappear. Seemed like that would maybe hurt less.

"Okay, Romeo, share something else about yourself," says Mr. Crowell, not letting the Q&A go. *Dude, give it a rest*.

"I'm new here," I try.

"Yes, that is imminently clear. And . . . ?"

"I like skateboarding," I say. Now Jerry is looking directly at me. Chloe and Brit are looking. Mr. Crowell is looking. Everybody, it seems, *but* Audrey is looking. I hesitate, stutter, hesitate some more, and finally a curious Audrey rotates just enough to catch my eye. What can I say to let her know we like the same things? My brain hurts. "I like reading. Daft Punk. Potato chips, track . . . cheerleading!"

Everybody laughs.

"Me too, bro," Jerry yells raunchily. "Cheerleaders are *everything*." Everybody laughs even harder, except Chloe, who rolls her eyes like it's her job.

"And where do you come to us from?" Mr. Crowell continues.

"Atlanta. Georgia. I, uh . . ." *I can't freaking remember.* "I, I'm . . . my parents died in a sudden accident when I was young. I bounced around a bunch of situations and now I live with a foster family," I blurt rapid-fire.

The room goes silent. Pre-hurricane, air vacuum-suck quiet. Great. I've single-handedly killed any swag I might've started with. Not to mention, big thanks, CC, for giving me what suddenly becomes clear is a racist backstory. I couldn't be a genius math scholar from another country, or a piano prodigy, or even just a normal foreign exchange student? I gotta be "the sad kid of color"? At least they didn't put my pops in federal prison or make my mama a dope fiend.

All of my classmates are now unabashedly rubbernecking the train wreck that is the new pitiful orphaned foster kid in the back row. Even Chloe is looking at me with slightly kinder eyes. And Audrey. Audrey is compassionate, perfectly sensing what someone might need in this situation and focusing her gaze elsewhere.

"So yeah, that's the 4-1-1 on me," I say, clearing my throat.

People slowly start pivoting back around in their creaking seats. Somebody drops a pen and it rolls on the linoleum.

Mr. Crowell coughs a couple times. "Thanks for sharing, Oryon. We're happy you're home now in the Central community. I'm sure your classmates are eager to get to know you better. As am I."

A few students nod uncomfortably in agreement while Mr. Crowell shuffles his papers, pretending to look for something on the top sheet secured to his clipboard. More creaking seats.

"Okay, so," Mr. Crowell chirps, trying to move past the tragic Dumbo in the room, his timbre nervous, hesitant. "As you all know, you'll be enjoying my company every morning when the first bell rings. I presume you all have your schedules, but if you don't, please see me; I have copies up here. If there are any problems, conflicts, dramas"—here he looks up at Chloe—"please come to me first. I'm still teaching ninth grade English, so I won't be seeing you fine people in class, but I would love for all of you to join me on the *Peregrine Review* lit mag. I've even arranged with the English department for your participation on the *Review* to count as extra credit this year."

Blah blah blah. After that point I have essentially no clue what else was said for the rest of class. All I can remember after my "Little Orphan Oryon" speech are random images: the angry mosquito bite on the back of Chloe's left calf, and how she anxiously bounced her crossed legs for the remainder of homeroom; Brit's new aqua-colored contacts that seemed to be bothering her because she applied eyedrops every three minutes; the coffee stain on the ankle of Mr. Crowell's retro-striped socks. (How does that even happen?) But mostly, obviously, overwhelmingly, what I recall is the contour of Audrey's shoulders, the precise tilt of her head from behind, her hidden expression clear in my mind, having gazed into her face so many times before, her features as familiar to me as my own. Well now, more so.

After the period was over, I bolted out of there as quickly as possible and slipped into the same boys' bathroom I almost mistakenly went into last year when Audrey first touched me, grabbing my forearm and informing me I was going into the "wrong" bathroom, *silly*.

I stepped into a stall and pulled the door shut behind me. (There was no lock, of course; finding a secure stall in the boys' bathroom is like finding a shark tooth on the moon.)

I stood there staring at the beige rectangular tiles behind the toilet. Something foul was smeared across the back of the porcelain with toilet paper stuck to it. It was like a monkey house crammed into a port-a-john. And school had been open less than an hour.

I turned around and tried to breathe through my mouth while catching my breath. Not an easy task. I noticed some graffiti scrawled in black Sharpie above the toilet paper holder: a rudimentary sketch of girl with frizzy hair labeled, *Rhonda Suck-You-In-Your-Honda*, to which somebody else had added with an arrow, presumably, her cell number. Man. Boys are assholes.

I hurriedly exited the bathroom feeling bad for *Rhonda-Suck-You-In-Your-Honda*, who probably had never even been in a Honda, let alone done what she was rumored to, when I smacked right into Audrey, now standing so close I could smell her (sesame body oil, by the way). It seemed like she might've been waiting for me, although she quickly made it look like she wasn't.

"Are you okay?" she asked.

"Aud—" I started.

She looked confused, a little horrified even, at what sounded like a complete stranger knowing not only her name, but my nickname for her.

"I'd . . . I'd . . ." I quickly corrected myself. "I'd . . . be wondering where my first class is if you weren't fortuitously standing here in front of me. Chem lab?"

She thought about it for a sec but then seemed placated. *Aud* sounds enough like *I'd*. "Upstairs, two down on your right," she said, and then: "I'm sorry about how that was in there earlier. People don't really know how to deal with anything."

"Oh, it's okay." I wanted to hug her.

She studied me.

"Anyway, I just wanted to say hi and introduce myself." She nodded her head a little, offering a hand like we were at a job interview. "Audrey."

I took her hand. It was warm.

"Oryon," I said quietly. Firmly. Not a question. "Like the constellation," I added.

"Orion the Hunter?" she asked.

"Something like that."

I didn't want to let her go. But I could tell it was verging on strange how long I was clinging to her hand, just rocking it slightly back and forth in the otherwise empty space between us.

"I think it took a lot of courage to say what you said," she told me, prying her hand away. "I guess I just wanted to let you know."

"Not really."

The cliché about getting shot through the heart is not such a cliché when you actually feel it: a literal stabbing and twisting in my chest as I stood there so impossibly close to her. Thankfully, any anguish I betrayed on the outside could conveniently be played off as deep sorrow over my supposedly tragic start in life.

This was Audrey. *My* Audrey. And she had no idea whom she was talking to. I felt like a complete ass-hat and considered taking her aside, as I had so many times before, and spilling all. She could be trusted and would probably understand. Maybe not at first. But if the movies are any reflection of reality—and of course they *are*—she would come around, and we would fall in love anew, and the credits would roll as we skipped along the seaside, hand-in-hand, heads thrown back laughing at this crazy, wild, wonderful life. But then an imaginary figment of Tracy popped onto my shoulder like the fairy godmother she fancies herself, chiding, *Against the rules, cupcake,* and the first period bell shrieked over my head, and there was no time to say anything, much less betray my entire Changer race to a Static.

"Chem lab!" Audrey hollered over the loud bell, pointing me in the direction of class.

"Chem lab," I echoed as the bell wound down, and she hurried off in the opposite direction.

I watched her go for a few impotent seconds, then Jerry blew by on his way to class and punched me on the shoulder, hard. "Trust me, bro, you have NO chance with that chick," he declared, then continued running down the hall, his right skating sneaker squeaking with every other step.

I guess I never noticed how much high school cafeterias are like federal prisons. When I was Ethan I went through an MSNBC *Lockup* stage. Well, feverishly watching any show related to incarceration, really. Documentaries, dramas. In all of them, there's meaning behind which tables the inmates self-separate into after they come inside from their hour in the yard. (You know I know a lot about prison when I know it's called "the yard.")

Anyway, in prison there's the white table. Which I'm mentioning first because until now I've been raised as one of these people who would mindlessly be sitting at the white table while never giving it a second thought.

After the plain white table, there's the white *supremacist* table. Lots of face tattoos over there. The Latino table, the mixed table—and the black table. It's always like that. Rarely are there exceptions. I mean, sometimes there's some intersection and conflict among the white tables, as in, if you're white, you're either with us or against us, so you better be all white all the time, as in Master Race White— or you might as well sit with the blacks because you must love them so much if you don't hate them. One white inmate at San Quentin said in an interview that he was now considered black "inside" because he would not admit to hating blacks, so the whites shunned him, and the blacks took him in and protected him from the white supremacists who were always trying to shank him for being a race traitor. (And I thought Changers' lives were bewildering.)

While nobody's getting eyelid and inner-lip tattoos of swastikas in high school (nobody at Central anyhow, except possibly Aud's deranged brother Jason, in his dreams), and the "protection" offered by affiliating with a particular group is more emotional than physical, it was made crystal clear for me today at lunch how much people stick to their tribes. I don't know why I didn't notice before. Oh right, because I'm passively racist, and I had the luxury of not *having* to notice such things. Obviously a failing that I, as a "Changer of color," am now supposed to learn from, and I've been given this V so I can spend the year figuring it out, instead of wasting all my time fretting about whether Audrey still likes me.

Last year, as an apparently empirically "cute" Caucasian freshman girl, I never found myself in the predicament I found myself in today: standing alone at the end of the food line clutching my beige fiberglass tray, looking left, then right, then left again for somewhere to sit, watching all the already-best-friends clustered together, cutting up, sharing tater tots, spewing chocolate milk at stories about stupid crap that happened over summer that's nowhere near funny enough to inspire sprayed milk.

Last year it was like I had an instant soul mate in Audrey, and we sat together at lunch from the first day of school onward. But this year, while she certainly reached out to me after "Homeroom: the Remix," it wasn't like, *Hey, there you are, standing awkwardly like a giant dufus in your dad's green polyester cutoffs and yet another white undershirt, so stop looking so unfortunate and come over and sit with me and my girl-friends from JV cheerleading.*

Aud did glance up at me with a flash of pity and gave a

little pageant wave before transitioning that hand into pushing a strand of hair out of her eyebrow, but then she went right back to talking with Shuba and Em about who knows what. All the rollicking times she had at the restrictive, possibly Abiders-affiliated summer camp her parents forced her to go to with her psychotic brother? It was clear it would've been odd for me to plop down next to her and the girls I used to be on the squad with. Well, odd for them at least.

So I just craned my neck around, surfing the din and chaos of the cafeteria, eyes lighting on the various segregated sets and subsets of groups until I found a mostly empty table. I took a lonely seat and hunched over, shoveling in my gluey mac 'n' cheese. Before I knew it, a few other kids (none of them white) started sitting around me, saying, "What's up?" and, "Hey," and not even bothering with, *Yo, is it cool if I sit here?* like it was simply where The Black Table was located today, and they'd obviously missed the memo.

I nodded back, spearing salty, soggy green beans with a spork, intermittently eyeballing Audrey who was sitting four tables up and one table down.

"Yo, Erkel," I hear after a couple more soggy bites.

I look up.

"I heard you're from the A-T-L." It's a guy about my height, though buffer, with glasses and a crooked snapback Braves cap, sitting right across from me. I guess word about the new kid travels fast.

I don't recognize him from around school last year, but then I probably wouldn't, given he wasn't on the girl's cheer squad. I nod, a little scared he's going to start quizzing me on all things Atlanta, and I'm going to have to bluff or be outed as the guy who pretended to be from a city he wasn't from, which is almost as sad as my heartrending dead-parents backstory. Mercifully, he doesn't wait for an answer.

"I was born there," he says. "We moved here when I was three."

I still don't say anything, just chew my runny, metallic beans.

"We go back once or twice a year to see my grandparents in Stone Mountain," he adds. "It's hot. I'm gonna go to Morehouse. Or GSU."

I nod my head like, *Oh, of course, GSU.*

"You don't talk much, huh?"

"No, I do," I protest softly, still lilting up like a loser.

He furrows his brow, skeptical. I don't really know what to say to this guy. Most of me can't stop reflexively thinking he's flirting with me—why else would he be so nice? I can't help but operate like I'm still Drew. *When will that stop?* I wonder.

I try to think of something to ask, but I don't really want to know anything. I just want to keep it simple, get my bearings, eat these beans, reconnect with Audrey, and then and only then maybe worry about other people.

I try, "So, uh, you like the Braves?" *Weak.*

"Yeah," he says, swiveling around his cap so the *A* logo faces me. "I. Like. The. Braves."

Now he's making fun of me. I glance over toward Audrey, her table getting more crowded with a fresh round of girls juggling trays.

"What's your name?"

"Oryon."

"I'm DJ. Junior." He sticks out a hand, I shake it quickly.

"DJ Junior," I repeat.

"No, I *am* a junior," he corrects.

"Oh. I'm a sophomore."

"I *know*." He frowns. And then after a second: "No offense, Oryon, but there's like 20 percent of us at Central—and you're sporting more of a D-Wade shade, so it's not like you're gonna slip under the radar like some high yellow. Do the math, that's like, not a lot of black folks, so if you want to have some allies, and if you can manage to stop ogling that white girl over there for a few seconds, then maybe I can show you around a little if you want."

My cheeks flare. I feel so busted. I make a theatrical disgusted face at him like, *I am* so *not staring at any white girl*. But it's obvious I am. Luckily someone sits down next to DJ right then, blocking my view. "S'up, Deege?" I recognize the voice and instinctively light up. Then tamp it down.

"Hey girl," DJ says, scooting over a little to make room for her tray. "This is Oryon. He's new. Quiet. Maybe slow. Jury is out."

"Hey you," I say to Kenya, regretting the *you* as soon as it slips out of my mouth. Her braids are pulled back into a thick bunch resting on the back of her neck. She stares kind of through me, telegraphing instant *not interested*, unconscious of the fact that we were on the same track team last semester.

"Hey you?" she says coolly, unfolding her napkin on her lap, as DJ chuckles.

"How was training camp?" I pop out. Before I can help it. Again.

Her eyes narrow like, *Excuse me?*

"Excuse me?" Kenya actually says then, highly suspicious and a little peeved. I know she's private about her life on account of what her family's been through with losing her brother and all.

I frantically backpedal, "Yeah, DJ was just looping me in on how you're this huge track star, and how you're getting a scholarship to Florida or somewhere, so I just—"

"Hold up," Kenya interrupts, grave-faced. "Are we friends? Do I know you? Why are you talking about my future plans?" DJ is mugging next to her, making a crazy face, sucking in his cheeks and cocking his head at me. Kenya turns to him. "I thought you said he was quiet."

DJ erupts with laughter, grabbing his belly for effect. "She's killin' you, man. DOA."

I decide to change tack. "So, actually, DJ was going on and on about how you're the hottest girl in school and how much he's always been in love with you," I say, turning the beat around, "but he knows he'll never have a chance because you're so focused on track and never have time for anything like a boyfriend, and besides, look at him. But he said he'd do anything if you'd go out on a pity date with him, just once."

"We went out two years ago," DJ snaps flatly, crossing his arms. "But by all means, keep spinning."

I'm looking back and forth between them, and the tension is mounting, and mounting . . . and suddenly Kenya's face breaks out in her infectious, welcoming smile, and she reaches across the table with a fist awaiting a tap.

"I'm just playing," she says, giving a goofy wink. My heart is fluttering again, but I manage to pound it out with Kenya, and then DJ, and then I quickly pile my trash onto my tray and decide to get out of there while I still can and while everybody's cutting up and forgetting how the hell I know stuff about Kenya no new kid should know.

I stand up and glance over at Audrey's table one more time, but she's already gone.

"You run track?" Kenya asks, bringing my attention back to our table.

"I used to," I say. "One season. Hurdles."

"We do some fall training if you want to come out, get your jump on."

After getting close with Kenya from all of our hours practicing, competing, bouncing in the last rows of janky buses to and from track meets, I know that she would never say something she didn't mean. And I am flattered that somebody—that two people—are being cool with this new me, without my even really trying.

"Yeah," I say. "That'd be fab."

"*Fab*," DJ echoes.

"Rad," I throw out, too late. "I was also thinking of maybe trying out for football," I add. See? I'm a dude. A totally normal, football-playing man person.

"You play football, Erkel?" DJ asks, but not really asking at all. "That why you're so jacked?" He strikes a bodybuilding pose.

Kenya takes a bite of salad, suddenly engrossed by it. Dang. I should have walked away ninety seconds ago. I'd forgotten how quickly the atmosphere shifts from hot to chilly in the high school ecosystem.

"I'll see you guys around," I say, slinging my backpack over a shoulder and heading toward the tray-drop area. Neither Kenya nor DJ says goodbye.

I knew I was going to need something to rock besides green cutoffs, white undershirts, and too-small Vans every freaking day. So after school I ran home, choked down a cup of all-natural soy-gurt. (*Note to Mom: this body is a rental. Stop fretting about hormones and GMOs, and buy yogurt that doesn't taste like medical waste. Also, a pizza-pocket wouldn't kill me.*) I grabbed a couple trash bags from under the sink and trolled the apartment, scooping up the entirety of my old Drew wardrobe and jamming the clothes inside. I took the bags down the elevator—one over-a-shoulder Santa-style, the other propped in the middle of my skateboard to let it bear some of the weight.

The doorman tracked me as my board *ca-cook ca-cooked* across the shiny marble tiles in the lobby. I smiled sheepishly, though he didn't return the sentiment.

When I got to ReRunz, there was a long, deflated-looking line for selling, as usual. The listless, double-cheek-pierced attendant behind the counter robotically pawed through some poor girl's formerly beloved ensembles, picking select skirts and blouses up by her fingertips as if they were radioactive, then dropping them to the floor like the garbage they now were. Every so often the girl selling would whine in a high-pitched voice, "But that was from Abercrombie," and the attendant would laboriously turn the garment inside out, eyeball the label, and then drop the piece of clothing to the floor again in a gold-medal display of passive-aggressiveness.

Clearly this was going to take awhile, so I shoved my bags in a corner out of the way and sat down to wait to be called. Kurt Cobain growled from the tinny speaker over my head, "*Come doused in mud, soaked in bleach. As I want you to be. As a trend, as a friend . . .*"

"Next!" a guy behind the register shouted out after about fifteen minutes, nodding in my direction. Deep voice, thick eyebrows, stocky, like "The Rock," pre-'roids, when he was still a touch doughy and wasn't starring as ancient superheroes no one's ever heard of in all those movies my long-lost buddy Andy always wanted to see on opening night.

I hefted the first bag onto the counter, just as it gave way and Drew's clothes exploded through the rip in the seam, bras and lacy leggings on full display. Rock Junior eyed me suspiciously.

"This yours?" he asked, holding up a pink camisole with *JUICY* written on the front.

"No. Yes. I didn't steal them or anything. They're my sister's things. She's going in a new stylistic direction."

"Whatever, man," he shrugged, and began sorting through my old wardrobe with the pronounced disdain I was starting to suspect was a job requirement for the Re-Runz staff. I watched as my entire past year flashed before me in this guy's square hands: Drew's first pair of cheetah-print jeggings; an (I thought) ironic vintage *Choose Life* oversized T-shirt from the '80s; a white sweater with a giant pink heart on front; the retro purple ruffled shirt I wore to prom when Audrey kissed me and I saw a flash of her future; and then the gray Converses on which I'd scribbled The Bickersons' band logo with a black Sharpie.

I was starting to get misty watching it all go when Baby Rock suddenly jerked up his head and snapped, "I can't accept this," pointing to the tuxedo shirt.

"Okay," I said. *You're the boss, dude.*

"Or this," he said, tossing aside another T-shirt.

"Fine." This jerk was full-on hostile. Maybe I was wrong about *pre-*'roids.

"Or this," to a pair of jeans, "or this or this or this," he went on, tearing through Drew's wardrobe like the Tasmanian Devil, clothes flying everywhere.

"What's your issue?" I asked, wincing as my whole freshman world fell into depressing, rejected piles around him.

"My *issue* is . . . these dingy kicks? No freaking way." He sniffed at them, wrinkling up his nose theatrically, before flinging them at my chest. "Your sister? Is *basic*."

I looked around to see if anybody was paying attention to how this idiot muscle-head was carrying on. I realize it's very powerful to be the decider who tells people whether their clothes are "cool" or not, but this was freaking re-dic-ul-ous.

Mr. Adrenal started stuffing the clothes back into the ripped bag, and pushed it across the counter toward me. "We don't buy from *your kind* here," he hissed under his breath.

I almost shat my pants. Was he suggesting what I thought he was? How did he know? Maybe he was an Abider. Where was Tracy when I needed her? I thought ReRunz was supposed to be a down-low Changers establishment or something. The freak just kept hate-eyeing me, nostrils flaring, smelling what I got cooking.

And then, suddenly, he starts laughing his ass off like he's goddamn Ashton Kutcher on *Punk'd*. I'm still cringing there, worrying he's a Changer-hater who's clocked me and wishes me and my entire lineage dead, when he unexpectedly launches half his substantial body over the counter and swoops me into a giant man-hug.

"It's me," he whispers into my ear while he has me in a headlock.

I am barely catching up to what just happened, and not a little alarmed by the fact that this guy, in his newfound affection for me, is collapsing my trachea like a pancake when it hits me: *Chase*.

"Oh my god, man, look at you!" he says, finally releasing his vice grip on my neck.

"Look at me? Look at *you*," I counter, grasping for a shred of composure, all too aware that people are starting to stare.

"*Man*." He's taking me in, really gulping me down. It's

making me nervous. I try and check him out too, only less obviously.

"I guess the whole crystal-ritual identity McGyvering didn't pan out," I say, chuckling, then adding, "You are big. Like, Olympic dead-lift big. Like-you-could rip-my-head-off-and-crap-in-my-neck big."

Chase comes around the counter then, and we just stand there gawking at each other for what seems like a decade. He smiling. Me sort of smiling. *This. Is. Weird.*

"This is major-league awesome, right?" Chase says, karate-chopping the air between us.

"I guess," I exhale. "I mean ..."

I have so many questions. Where's he living? Is he back in school? Is the Changers Council off his back? Did he really knock up some RaCha girl? Does he have a RaCha baby in a BabyBjörn somewhere? I don't even know where to begin, and maybe I shouldn't even bother, because we aren't the same people anymore. Even if we hadn't changed into new Vs, we'd be different. Older, *changed*. Summers do that. Experience does that.

I decide maybe the thing to do is to start as friends who just met. Pretend the past belongs to somebody (some *body*) else, even as we are publicly gazing into each other's faces like long-lost lovers, the shards of our former intimacy on full display.

Chase embraces me again, less tightly this time. "What's your name supposed to be now?" he asks, loud enough so I shrink, anxious somebody has heard him.

"Oryon," I answer quietly. "You?"

"I'm keeping my name," he announces proudly.

"You can't keep your name," I chide, and he looks at me like, *Poor stupid rule-follower.* And we are right back to where we were the first time Chase disappeared into the Radical Changers "lifestyle." Him knowing-it-all. Me blindly and prudishly doing what I'm told by *The Changers Bible*, marching to the beat of the Council drum. Him judging. Me getting overly upset being judged by him. Fun times. How had I forgotten?

"My body may change, but I don't have to," he continues, working up an indignant froth—for whose benefit, I have no idea.

"I'm fairly certain that's the complete inverse of our mission," I snort.

"You're oversimplifying it. We don't have to live by their rules if we don't want," he says, zeroing in on me, pupil to pupil, trying to dominate me like a trainer does a dog. "You know that, right?"

I don't even want to answer. "Why are we fighting?"

"Who's fighting?"

"Well, it went from down-home week to opening bout in the Octagon pretty quickly."

"You frustrate me, Drew."

"I'm not Drew anymore."

"You sure about that?" he asks, then grins real wide like, *Checkmate, beyotch.*

I have nothing to say. I just gaze at him, and as I do, I notice that his smile is different, transformed, toothy. I think about the first time I saw him smile, here in this stupid shop, and how it made me feel like I'd fallen down a well. I loved him for that smile. And now that smile is history. And, likely, so are we.

Makes you wonder, if it is so easy to lose who you cared about, what's the point of caring in the first place?

I want to cry. But I don't. I don't even have to fight that

hard not to. Which fills me with an ache far worse.

"So. I was thinking of going street-skate-nerd-steez this year," I finally say, changing the subject, opting to skip all the drama entirely, to do the manly thing and compartmentalize. "What do you think?"

Chase knits his brow, unwilling to relinquish his fortifying righteousness. He's obviously been spending too much time with the RaChas' top gun Benedict, drinking that particular brand of ego-stoking Kool-Aid.

"Should I get someone else to help me shop?" I ask, half serious.

Chase, for once in his lives, doesn't know what to say or do.

"How'd you get this job, anyway?" I push. "I know you're not all about the fa-fa-fa-fa-fashion." I give my best help-me-out-here-bro face.

"Tom had to *go away* for a while," Chase coughs up, softer. "Bad Changer."

"Damn. Seriously? What'd he do?"

Chase gives his me his *Not here* shake-off. "He asked if I could fill in for him while he's gone—I need to keep a job anyway, or my folks won't let me homeschool."

Now it's Chase who seems a little glum. But he isn't about to cry either. "I'll hook you up with a mad credit, yo, for your old clothes," he pops out, snapping free of whatever hole he was digging us into, and then busily gathers the piles of Drew's clothes into one huge, girly mass, and dumps it into an institutional-looking laundry cart behind the counter. (Compartmentalization, meet deflection. God, my mom would have a shrink field day with this.)

"Thanks, man," I say. "And if you could point me to the varsity jackets, DCs, and maybe a fly bucket hat, I think I'll go get my shop on."

Chase starts wrestling a three-sizes-too-tight fluffy yellow sweater over his enormous barrel chest. "You 100 percent sure you won't be needing this again?" he jokes, model stomping and flashing a Blue Steel face.

"That's a solid NFW. Looks better on you, anyway," I quip back, both of us doing the BS banter thing, just a couple dudes hanging out and acting dumb, pretending nothing hurts, or matters, or lasts. I don't know about Chase, but I think I just felt the best part of Drew draining away from me like spilled sand.

Back home, I'm unpacking, folding, and putting away two full bags of new threads. (Despite all the unease, Chase refused to take any extra money from me, even though I far outspent my trade-in credit for Drew's clothes.) I decide somewhere between stacking my tank tops and coiling my black punk-rock three-row studded belt to create a new e-mail account and send a note to Audrey.

Yes, I know it explicitly says not to do this in *The Changers Bible*. Sue me.

Dear Aud,

I've been putting off writing this for a long time. It's only because I didn't know what to say. I still don't know what to say. Or maybe I just didn't know how to say it. Anyway, here goes:

Basically, my folks ran into some financial problems that were out of their control. Really bad ones. And we had to move out of state under the cover of night, like those polygamists on TV. They (my parents, not the polygamists) wouldn't let me tell you anything. And I'm not supposed to tell you where we are now either. I'm not even supposed to be writing you. I know it sounds crazy like a B-movie, but it's what happened, and it was probably the hardest thing I've ever had to do, just leaving you without a word like that. But I didn't want you starting a new school year thinking I'd totally bailed. Or that I don't care about you and think about you all the time. Which I do. A lot. An effing ton. In fact, over summer I think I figured out that I love you.

But you probably knew that already.

Anyway, how was camp? How's sophomore year at Central? Did you change much over the break? Please don't hate me.

Love,
Drew

It bears repeating that one glaring advantage I've noticed about this V is how little I worry about how I look. Just like that. Magic. Sure, I wash my face and pump on some body spray. I don't want to smell like a yeti. And yes, I wanted some threads so I didn't have to rock Dad's middle-aged suburban *meh* every day, but I have to say, it's a been pleasure waking up and just throwing on whatever and not worrying what anybody will or won't say about my hair or what I'm wearing. In fact, it would be really jarring if DJ or any of the other guys I've sort of gotten on "hello-nod" terms with said *anything* about my looks. I mean, what would they say? "Your hair looks so cute today." "You are *so* skinny, I hate you!"

Outside of DJ bragging about how dope his style is, or the guys taking note of some girl's *lack* of clothes covering certain areas—a.k.a. "nipple alerts," a.k.a. "her Rihannas are out"—I haven't yet heard a single guy utter a single word about appearances, mine or theirs.

Giant exhale.

Anyway, today.

Basically consisted of me trying to get Audrey's attention in homeroom, then again in History, and then again on the field after school, when she and the JV squad were practicing near where I was trying out for football because . . . well, I don't exactly know why I'm trying out for football, other than to refer myself back to my Chronicles from last year when I suddenly, inexplicably, wanted to try out for cheerleading. Because I can?

Granted, cheerleading also had something to do with Audrey—okay, everything to do with Audrey. Which if I'm honest, this football business also has to do with Audrey because I know from last year's experience that she and the other girls will be practicing when football practices, decorating our lockers, cheering at our games, baking us brownies, riding the bus with our team, dating (etc.) some of us, and so on. Wack sauce on the women's equality front, but good for me, now that I'm no longer representing that particular gender.

All of that said, here is the more detailed Day Three Audrey Report:

Homeroom: a half-smile as I walked past her desk after the bell rang, while she seemed absorbed with something in her planner. She didn't even notice it was I who held the door open for her before we all headed to first period, though ever the polite girl, she did say "Thank you" rather sincerely as she and about ten other students walked through while I stood there propping it open for them.

History: Uncomfortable moment when Dr. Hodges introduced the question of how the European conquest of North America transformed indigenous civilizations and institutionalized African slavery, and all the white kids in class couldn't help but sneak glances at all the nonwhite kids, which I didn't realize included me until the second or third kid made sketchy eye contact with me before quickly looking back at Dr. Hodges. It reminded me of fifth grade when we had to watch a video about puberty, and when the narrator got to the part where he said that some girls develop breasts, get their periods, and grow pubic hair as early as age ten, everybody in the class, including me and Andy, immediately whipped our heads around and ogled Melinda Iacocca, who promptly burst into tears and ran out the door to the bathroom, seeing as she was the only girl in class with boobs and hair under her armpits.

Football tryouts: When Coach Tyler told me to "run as fast as you can, touch the *50*, and come back," I did so, my helmet bobbing around my face to the point that I couldn't see the ground in front of me. So when I saw the *35, 40, 45*, and what I thought was the *50* beneath me, I reached down to the grass to touch the only white line within view, quickly ascertaining it was possibly the other *45* yard line I was gripping a handful of wet chalk from. I promptly tried to correct myself and find the *50*, but instead ended up tripping over my own feet and face-planting in the turf, my helmet torquing completely sideways to the point that I probably looked like the girl from *The Exorcist*.

"Ooof!" A choral response from the guys who were waiting their turns behind me, plus a couple of girl voices thrown in (followed by giggles), which, when I managed to climb onto my hands and knees and straighten my helmet, I noted one of which was Audrey.

I tried smiling at her in an obviously self-deprecating way through my face mask, but I'm pretty sure she couldn't see. Coach Lois strolled between me and Aud then, barking something at the squad, at which point Audrey turned around and gave full attention to her splits.

I stood up, straightened the pads in my pants, and brushed the dirt off my knees, and was just about fully composed—when I felt I hard, sharp slap on my ass as somebody blew by me.

"Much easier to run without pads, boo!" It was Kenya,

who flashed a friendly smirk before returning to the track.

I turned and jogged toward Coach, peering behind me to find Audrey a couple times, but she was busy observing Chloe demonstrate back handsprings for the group.

"Son, you look like you should be faster," Coach Tyler chided me, before telling us all to take a cool-down lap and then stretch it out. "Tomorrow, let's see if you can catch a ball."

Skating home after football this afternoon, I headed to the ReRunz parking lot to reacquaint myself with a few tricks I used to know, back when I was Ethan, and before I'd become Drew—worst skater since Ryan Sheckler. I had just landed a perfectly executed hippie jump over a low rail and was really digging on my reinvigorated skating skills, when I darted past Michelle Hu, the Stephen Hawking of Central, nearly rolling my board over her Chacos.

"Sorry!" I shouted, jumping off and landing on the pavement.

She just smiled and gave me a peace sign. I quickly retrieved my board and skated back toward her to (re)introduce myself.

"Oryon," I say, extending a hand. "Apologies about the near guillotining of your toes."

"Michelle," she says, taking my hand and giving it a hearty shake. "No worries. Sweet trick."

"Thanks. It's nothing, really."

"Actually, it's the physics of projectile motion—where the vertical component of velocity is the only one that changes, since gravity only works in a vertical direction. You know, your basic parabolic arc."

"Wow, I'm more awesome than I thought," I say, not even trying to decipher her deGrasse Tyson–speak. "Do you skate, or—"

"Die?" she interrupts with a cute grin. "Nah. I just like

knowing how the universe works. I find it comforting."

"I'll take your word for it."

"Science will set you free, man," she says, completely sincere. "You should join our physics club—The *Fun*-damental Particles. We meet every Thursday at seven thirty before school."

"You meet at the crack of Christmas to talk about science?"

"Yes! It's super stimulating. Better than coffee. I bet you'd dig knowing the how behind the action," she says, gesturing toward my board. "Science is the reason for every season."

It occurs to me that in my entire last year of school, Michelle Hu spoke probably twenty words to me when I was Drew. Or perhaps it was I who spoke just twenty words to her.

"The how behind the action?" I ask, rolling my board back and forth under my shoe.

"Yes," she says, not quite sure whether I'm serious or mocking her. "Take a front-side 180," she starts, at first hesitantly, before allowing her excitement to bleed through. "You can only land one by rotating your upper and lower body in opposite directions. It keeps your angular momentum at zero. Basically, you're controlling the way you interact with the laws of nature."

I keep nodding with absolutely no understanding of what she's talking about.

"Which is to say," she continues, "sometimes to move ahead, you have to split yourself into two entirely separate people."

Now *that* I understand.

"Anyway, I gotta bounce," Michelle says. "My moms are waiting at the climbing wall. But it was most awesome meeting you, Oryon."

"Same," I say. "See you around school."

"Not if I see you first," she jokes, sounding like an old-time, take-my-wife comic. My immediate thought is that I want to call Audrey and tell her how great and goofy Michelle Hu is, and how we should totally start hanging out with her (not necessarily in the physics club or anything—let's be real). But before I even finish this interior monologue, I realize again that I can't call Audrey, because Audrey and I aren't friends anymore, and I feel the hopeful air *whoosh* from my body as I drop my backpack and sink onto the curb, deflated all over again.

In a fit of desperation, I start rooting around my bag for my *CB*, feeling it at the very bottom. I pull it out, look around to make sure nobody's nearby, and then flip it open to a section I remembered spotting in the index called: *Change Two: Adjustments.*

I laugh a bitter "Ha!" at the word *Adjustments*, like being breathed into a whole new person is some tiny lifestyle tweak, like buying a push-up bra or cutting out dairy, but I read on nonetheless:

> *Be aware of the colliding systems of motivation and emotion. As your unique biology intersects with the chemical changes of ripening adolescence, you may feel restless, exuberant, intense, desperate. Resist the urge to be reckless, both physically and emotionally. Year Two Changers tend to underestimate risks and overestimate rewards. Especially social rewards.*

Tell me something I don't know, *CB*.

> *Life in our community is a long and varied one. Bear in mind the consequences your actions will bring to others.*

59

Becoming an adult means becoming accountable. De-
layed gratification is the hallmark of the mature. Your
Touchstone will model this maturity for you.

It is precisely then that I glance up and across the largely
empty parking lot and spot none other than my very own
model Touchstone Tracy blowing a giant, bright pink bubble
of chewing gum. She is giggling, her be-ribboned head bobbling when none other than my favorite homeroom teacher
Mr. Crowell pops the bubble with the tip of his index finger.
Ah yes, the pinnacle of maturity.

I finish the section:

Remember, your journey is not about you. Your journey
is not singular. No Changer walks alone. In the many,
we are one.

I am just shutting my as-ever-useless *CB* when Tracy
practically skips over sans Mr. Crowell, the spring in her
step rivaling a kangaroo's.

"Most excellent," she beams, straightening the giant
plaid bow in her hair with a flourish. Her head looks like a
holiday gift basket. "Now *that's* what I like to see."

"What? Abject despair? Paralyzing confusion?" I snot back.

She waves her hand in front of her face. "Noooo, silly.
You reading your *CB*, digging into the mission."

"I'm just looking for answers," I say flatly.

"Exactly," she replies with a smug nod. "Any luck?"

"Nope."

"How do you know?" she presses, chirpy, even for her.

"What do you mean, how do I know?" Even as I ask, I
regret taking the bait.

"Sometimes an answer doesn't reveal itself until you ask the right question." Tracy is practically erupting with self-satisfaction.

"Really, Iyanla: Fix My Life?" I look for Mr. Crowell, who seems to have disappeared into the sub shop. "Here's the right question: what is going on between you and my homeroom teacher?"

Tracy's face fills with light, her smile nearly cracking her jaw in half. "Nothing."

"Never play poker, Trace," I say.

She tilts her head, as though a distant alarm has started sounding. "Dinnertime!" she declares, glancing back at the sub shop. "You should get home too. I bet your folks can't wait to hear how day four went."

I look up at her skeptically, but she doesn't notice, just swivels on her little flats and merrily click-clacks away.

Mom and Dad somehow talked me into going to see a movie with them this afternoon, some optimistically lit, schmaltzy thing about rich white people with gigantic, rich white-people kitchens (which are, incidentally, also always white) getting a second chance at life and love and other invented first-world problems. I was, shocker, the only young person, not to mention the only black person, in the audience, which of course Mom wanted to "process" with me on the ride home. The whole conversation was wearying, and I found myself already getting tired of white-people guilt a mere week into my new identity. Like, is it my job to make you feel better about feeling bad? I'm not a shame mirror.

When we got home, I fled to the sanctuary of my room and opened up my laptop. No e-mails. So I logged onto my secret account, where one message popped up, subject line reading, *So . . .*

I was afraid to click on it and read, but knew I could never resist:

Drew,

Thanks for writing. I'm sorry for what happened with your family. That sounds bonkers. And awful. Which I get. Lord knows my family can be both of those things too. I mean, my brother? Yuck. But OMFG your problems seem beyond. Leaving town like fugitives? Are you going to get arrested? Or end up in jail? Makes all that crap we stressed over last year seem fairly stupid, right? I'd heard that you ended up at some hippie boarding school and were abandoning everyone from your old life in favor of a spiritual rebirth or something. That's what they're saying around Central anyhow.

I want to tell you about my summer but it hardly seems worth going into given the circumstances. Let's just say, camp was creepy. I survived. Not everyone was terrible. There were marshmallow roasts every night. So that was cool. But some of the counselors were so into the mission they seemed possessed. Like those girls in the old Beatles footage where they scream and shake and shred their clothes. Epic hysteria. That, I didn't love. But I'm home now and it all seems funny in retrospect. I guess.

What else? It was nice to "read" your voice. I don't hate you. I never could. You are my best friend. I DO hate that you've left me on my own this year to do battle with Chloe and her moronic minions. Now I have to deal with her at church and school by myself. Stellar.

I . . . This is hard. I feel like I sound fake. I don't know how to talk with you without talking with you. In my head the words are pouring out, all messy and jumbled like a swarm of bees. But when I type, all that comes out is this dopey stuff. Like I'm talking to an aunt I haven't seen in five years. There's too much to say. So why say anything, you know?

I just reread your letter.

Do you really love me? I wonder. Not about you. But about why.

Write me again, okay? I feel so alone. I'm not trying to make you worry, especially since you are now on the lam (lamb? Whatever. I'm picturing you in a bonnet, riding a wooly little lamb. Joking is still okay, right?). But I do feel like that polar bear floating on the iceberg. Remember that poster? The one in the Bio lab that almost made me cry every time I caught a glimpse of it.

I'm sorry. This is turning into a bummer letter. I just miss you. I miss us. I miss the me I was with you around. Does that make sense?

Okay. I'm going to stop now. Before I become so pathetic you wonder why you ever liked me in the first place.

Write me again. Okay? I want you to. Even if it sounds like I don't.

Love,
Aud

P.S. Oh yeah. I cut off my hair. I wonder if you'd think it looks pretty.

CHANGE 2—DAY 10

Second week of school in effect. I'm in homeroom watching Audrey, because that's what I do in homeroom. Mr. Crowell is giving yet another pitch for the *Peregrine* literary magazine, trying to cajole us into signing up by making writing and talking about writing sound like more fun than skating, band, chorus, football, or, I don't know, picking your nose.

"Fiction is the lie that tells the truth," he proclaims, his eyes lit up the way teachers' eyes do when they taste inspiration. "It is how we share ourselves. How we get to know each other. Stories are, by nature, intimate."

When he drops the word *intimate*, a few heads do perk up, but not for the right reasons.

"So, any takers?" Mr. Crowell asks, surveying the class, eyes eager.

I'm mumbling, "Hells no," under my breath when I spot Audrey's hand among the few in the air. "I'll do it!" I shout, thrusting my arm above my head like I'm some tween pop star during the fireworks finale of her concert.

"Enthusiasm! Marvelous to see," Mr. Crowell says, clearly thrilled as he jots down my name, Audrey's, and—after he mentions yet again that those who join the lit mag will earn extra credit in English—the names of a few other students, including phony Chloe, who obviously just wants another extracurricular for her college application portfolio. (Speaking of the lie that tells the truth.)

"Will poetry be a part of the *Pelligrino*, Mr. Crowell?" Chloe coos, her tone reflexively solicitous, even at eight forty-five a.m. "I'm an *amaaaa*-zing poet. I find poetry allows me to reveal my inner parts."

From the back Jerry says, "I thought that was vodka."

"Yes, Chloe, the *Peregrine* will feature poetry, and we look forward to your many revelations."

I watch Audrey's head shake slightly. If anyone in this class is poetic, it's Aud. She must have asked me to read *The Bell Jar* a dozen times last year. I never got around to it—it seemed a little too close to home then. Maybe now I will. I can already hear DJ's comments when I whip that book out at lunch.

Aud lowers her hand slowly once she's sure Mr. Crowell has put her name on the list. I can't help but notice what seems like an air of sadness emanating from her. Well, from the back of her neck, anyway. Of course, I could be projecting. At the very least she seems anxious, like she's waiting for the first first-period bell to sound so we can all get out of here and on to the next thing. I can relate.

I can't stop thinking about the letter she wrote responding to mine with the lamest excuse in history about why I was gonzo from her life. I wrote her back again, which I know is verboten, yadda yadda yadda, because we're not really supposed to maintain the relationships our former selves created *as* our former selves. But this is different ... Okay, it actually isn't. But I don't want to stop corresponding with Audrey. I don't want to let her down. She needs me. Well, Drew. She said as much. Really, I'm doing it more for her than myself.

Finally the bell rings and homeroom ends, so I hop up, jamming my planner into my backpack sideways and making a pronounced (some might say clumsy) effort to catch up to Audrey. Mr. Crowell hollers at me on the way out: "See you at the first meeting!" I grunt back affirmatively, and it takes me a few seconds while fast-walking down the hall to remember what the heck he was talking about. Right, the *Peregrine*. I agreed to do that.

"Hey, Sylvia P.," I say to Aud, finally catching up to her and hoping she doesn't wonder how I "guessed" at one of her favorite authors.

"Is that supposed to make you Ted Hughes?" she asks, not missing a beat. "'Cause that would not be a good look."

"More like *Langston* Hughes," I say, proud of myself.

"Do you have any idea what Ted Hughes did to Sylvia Plath?" she asks, like anybody knows who Ted Hughes is anyway.

I get the distinct feeling I've royally effed up. Why didn't I read that stupid book when she asked me to? I reach back into my memory palace and can only come up with a fuzzy image of the cover, a wilted red rose stem or something. I got nothing. I shrug and try to smile so my dimples show, which Mom has repeatedly pronounced "adorable" and says will allow me to "get away with murder" if I ever need them to.

"Well, look it up," Aud says, impervious to the smile. "It doesn't end well for her."

"Noted," I respond, trying to maintain our walk-and-talk.

She suddenly slows, seeming to decide not to be so hard on me. "Anyway, I'm going the Joan Didion nonfiction route," she announces, "so we can leave the adolescent suicidal poetry to Chloe."

"If *only*," I try. Audrey shoots me a that's-too-far look, but then eases into her quiet wicked laugh. I join in. It feels good. To laugh, to have made her laugh.

I chat her up on the way to her next class, which is in the opposite direction and floor from mine, but I don't care if I'm tardy. Just before we get to her room, I push my luck and try to cement our fledgling bond, and like every instance in all of history when one person *tries* to bond with another instead of allowing it to happen naturally, it is a tsunami of awkwardness the minute it starts coming out, but there's no use trying to stop the spinning gyre of *doh*.

"You know, Aud—REY! *Audrey*. I'm here, if you ever need a *homie* to roll with." To which she gives me the same look she gave me on the first day when I called her by the same nickname.

She stops short, frozen like a Pompeii ash relic, ironically, just outside History class. I was only trying to drop a throwback term, a subtle inside joke from her favorite movie, *Clueless*, which Audrey's memorized like the Pledge of Allegiance. Something I now see from the startled look on her face was a bad play. I try dimple-smiling again. She doesn't smile back. Instead, she sort of cocks her head at me, and I realize my inner Drew is perhaps showing a little too explicitly.

I remember when I was Ethan and how most teenage dudes don't talk this much, at least none that I knew. And never about feelings. And even more never about another person's feelings. And sure as shazam never about freaking *Clueless*.

A couple bodies pass between us into class, and Audrey clearly wants to go in too, but knowing her, she's trying not to be rude while also trying to figure out what the eff I'm talking about. I'm emo-ing up the entire hallway like cigarette smoke, and I can tell by her knit brow that I need to stop this emotional upchuck like yesterday, or I will never have a chance at getting this girl back in my life.

"So I saw you checking me out on the field yesterday," I throw out suddenly, switching gears and channeling my idea of smooth, which is a cross between Justin Timberlake and every starter in the NBA.

"It was hard to miss your epic face-plant," she answers, "if that's what you're referring to." The hint of a smirk.

"Well, I made the team," I counter. "I can't be all bad."

"Nobody said you were," she replies, the second bell shricking above our heads.

"Nobody said I *wasn't*, either," I call over it, as she slips into History, and I think I see her shoulders twitch with some sort of satisfaction as she turns the corner and disappears out of sight.

Progress!

Even if it did make me tardy for Chemistry.

Oh, one more thing: when I was changing in the locker room, I saw this freshman acting all bizarre while he was getting dressed. He was covering himself with a towel and seemed unnaturally nervous given no one was paying him any attention, except me, I suppose. Which of course you DO NOT do in boys' locker rooms. So we locked eyes for a beat, both of us apologetically, but then he kind of bared his teeth for a flash, like a cornered rodent.

It's probably nothing, but I had the distinct sense that he could be "in the club." I'm going to ask Tracy if she knows if there's another Changer at Central (like she'd tell me). That is, if I can pry her away from her DL love interest, Mr. Crowell. *Ew.* Brain, please stop going there.

The images, they burn, they burn.

The end zone is in sight. I'm running top-speed (well, as fast as I can wearing a full uniform with pads and helmet). I glance left, glance right: path clear. I keep pumping; it's going to be the first touchdown I've ever scored, who cares if it's just in a practice drill?

But then, jaysus jiminy cricket, I'm plowed down. From my right side, totally unexpectedly, something clobbers me high up in my shoulders/neck area, my whole person flattened by what feels like a speeding bus. Then the crisp crack of plastic and the rattling of every bone in my skeleton from traveling in one direction to *BLAM*, snapping in another direction entirely, some awful, unnatural body physics I'm sure Michelle Hu would know just the right terminology for. And like that, I'm roadkill on the grass, five yards short of the goal line.

My ears ring, and wait, what? I can see sky. Where'd my helmet go?

"Sorry, holmes," I hear from somewhere above and behind me. Jason's voice. *Of course.* He sniggers. Someone else joins in. Like a pair of evil gridiron twins. "Gotta get you toughened up for the big-time Friday," he says, walking around to survey his work. "No weak links," he adds, stretching his jersey out enough to tuck his floppy shoulder pad back inside. He glares at me on the ground, the sun behind his head, while his hype-man Baron clutches my helmet in a gloved hand and dangles it above me.

"Get up, bitch!" Baron hollers like he's a Marine drill sergeant.

Now I'm seeing stars. (FYI: those little white flashes don't actually go in cute birdie circles around your head like they do in *Tom and Jerry* cartoons, but actually shoot in every direction inside your eyes like barbecue skewers trying to find soft tissue to pierce.)

"I'm thinking a football scholarship's not in the cards," Jason snarls. "Maybe soccer? Lotta homos play that." He nudges up his face mask enough to spit on the turf beside me. Baron drops my helmet, and it bounces twice, rolls to a stop against my head.

Which I can't move.

"What the hell are you doing?" I hear distant screeching from the other side of the track.

"Uh-oh," Baron says under his breath, "it's Mother Teresa," and starts jogging away.

Jason stands up even taller. "What?" he asks, petulant.

It's Audrey. Her face bright red and glimmering, practically in tears, like she just witnessed an animal being abused.

"I saw what you did," she snaps. "Even if Coach didn't. You think he'd want you injuring someone from your own team, genius?"

Jason eyes me, then Audrey, thinks for a few seconds, something suddenly occurring to him. "Oh, hell no, this is *not* happening."

"Are you okay?" she asks me, but I'm afraid to nod my head. In case I can't.

"No, uh-uh, this is not gonna happen," Jason continues, even though the coach has blown the whistle calling everybody back into the huddle. "Being a lezzy last year wasn't enough? Now you have to find another way to feel special?"

71

The whistle blows again, this time longer, seemingly more insistently. Jason snaps to and Audrey bends down toward me as I slowly sit up.

"Hey, she's only using you to piss off our parents," Jason says to me. "You know that, right?" He jogs off, his springy athletic trot underscoring why he's the captain of the team however many years running. Probably since he started toddling.

"I am so, so sorry about my idiot brother," Audrey coos sincerely, her sympathy almost splitting my heart into all of its individual chambers.

"We can't help who we're related to," I manage, the torturous stars subsiding some now that I'm fully upright.

She looks so sad. The way Jason always makes her look. Now I start trying to stand up because I've had just about enough of being down here below everybody.

"Here, let me—" She grabs my elbow, but I shake her off. She lets go. "We've got to stop meeting this way," she tries.

I can't believe I'm saying this, but right now I want Audrey to leave me alone. I'm barely managing not to puke, feeling like the entire school's eyes are on me again, thoroughly embarrassed, ashamed, my face burning hot, even though I know I shouldn't be feeling any of those things. There's no logical reason. It was an unfair, dangerous hit, and Jason wasn't even running the same drill as me. He was just asserting his dominance. Again.

And yet I can't help feeling all those things. And Aud being there only makes it worse. Before I can stop it, last year comes flooding back—when Jason got wasted and forced himself on me, how instantly I felt like everything was my fault, that I'd asked for it somehow or, worse, *deserved* it, because I was weak, or naive, or simply too stupid to see it coming.

"Are you okay?" Audrey says again, jolting me back to the now.

"Whatever, it's all good," I say lamely, and sort of harshly. "I have to get back."

She just waits, now on the verge of tears. I try to jog back to join the team, but every step sends shooting pain into my head and neck, so I have to slow-walk in order to bounce less. I don't bother turning back to see if she is watching me go.

"Mom has a late group session," Dad says, soon as I push through the door into the kitchen. "Looks like it's just going to be you and—what's wrong?"

"I don't want to talk about it," I announce, dropping my backpack and gym bag by the door and blowing past him, causing the newspaper he's reading to flutter to the tile floor. Snoopy jumps off the couch and runs to greet me, but I knee him out of the way too.

"Okaaay," I hear Dad exhale, but nothing after that because I slam my bedroom door behind me and dramatically hurl myself onto the bed like a frigging teenage cliché, not that I care.

I lie there for a few minutes, too filled with, what—I don't know, a whole all-the-emotions-you-can-stuff-in-your-face buffet—to fall asleep. All I want is for the day to be over. I'm feeling a little bad for both the newspaper and kneeing Snoopy (though not bad enough to do anything about it), when my laptop dings. It's DJ:

Yo Erkel, wanna come to Nash this weekend? I got a spoken word thing on Saturday, then we're gonna get some pizza or something. Kenya's coming. My mom's driving.

I pull the laptop onto the bed, type: *Do you know Jason Stewart?*

DJ: *QB? Yeah.*

Me: *I want to kick his ass.*

DJ: *What for?*

Me: *Breathing. He's a menace to society.*

DJ: *Like the movie?*

Me: *?*

DJ: *So you comin?*

DJ: *Yo?*

Me: *Sorry. I don't know. Yeah, I think. Let me make sure it's cool with my parents.*

DJ: *My mom said she could call your mom or whatever.*

Me: *No, that's okay. I'll tell you tomorrow.*

DJ: *Cool.*

Knock-knock. Dad at the door. Unlike Mom, at least he waits to open it until I yell, "What?"

"Howdy partner," Dad says, calm as can be. "What's going on?" I close my laptop and pull it out of the way before he plops parentally on the bed next to me. Snoopy noses through the door right after, so damn happy-looking all the time with that big goofy pit bull smile and wagging tongue. He's so in the moment, incapable of resentment or self-loathing or even being pissed at me for acting like a jerk. He hops on the bed, sensing I need him more than I let on.

"I don't want to talk about it."

Dad raises his eyebrows, says nothing, sits there indifferently. I see. I'm going to talk about it whether I want to or not. I make the decision not to mention Jason by name. The last thing I need is Dad calling in the Council cavalry.

"Something crappy happened at practice," I shrug.

"And . . ."

"And . . ." My brain fumbles around for the right language. "And, I don't know, just this guy was being an ass."

"How?" he asks, still calm.

"He tackled me really high, pretty much on purpose," I say, not being as clear as I wish I could. "He wasn't even doing the drill with me, I think he just, I don't know . . ."

"Well, did you tell the coach?" Dad asks, and *pow*, instantly I regret saying anything at all. I should've just marched in with a giant fake smile on my face and been like, "*Yay, Dad and Son Pizza Night, yay!*" and then I wouldn't be in the middle of a conversation I have no interest in being in with no real resolution anyway. Jason isn't going anywhere. And I am on his radar. Ratting him out isn't going to make my life any easier, that much is clear.

"No." My stomach roils. "It wasn't like that."

"Well, what *was* it like? Who was the player?" Dad asks, now somewhat worked up.

"It doesn't matter."

"It *does* matter. Who is this kid?"

"The quarterback. I don't think anybody really wants to hear about anything he's doing wrong when he's supposed to bring us to State this year."

Dad sits back. Thinks. Leans forward, hands planted on knees. "Wait. You mean the boy who tried to . . . tried to . . ." he starts, but can't finish. "The one who . . . Audrey's brother? The Abider?"

I don't say anything. Which is coming off as more affirmative than if I'd screamed, *YEEEESSSS!* directly into Dad's face.

"How long has this been going on? Is he bullying you outside of practice? Have you talked to Tracy about him? I think we need to take this to the Council." Dad is all business now, funneling his outrage into problem-solving a problem that can't be solved.

"He's not *bullying* me. Please, I don't want to tell the Council," I beg. "It's nothing. There's nothing to tell. I'm a guy now, it's totally different. I can handle him."

"Was he picking on you for being black?" Dad asks, solemn.

"No. Not really. Honestly, I don't know. I mean, he's supposed to be an Abider, right? So he's probably not down with the minorities."

"That kid is no good," Dad says, more to himself than to me. "Racism was more overt in a lot of ways when I was your age, but we can't underestimate its insidiousness—"

"Dad," I interrupt, "can we talk about this some other time? My head hurts."

"Okay, I suppose." He seems wounded, though in a different place. "I was going to share a little about when I was an African American girl in eleventh grade, but I guess it can wait."

"I love picturing that," I say, trying to get him to lighten up. "So you weren't about to choose that V?"

"I could've, I probably should've . . ." He trails off, eons away from here and now. "To be honest, if I was stronger, I probably would've. But . . ."

He falls silent for a minute. My head throbs, along with my pulse. Snoopy wet-noses me and I pet him behind the left ear.

"That was not to be," Dad pronounces. Then gets all cheery, as in fake "Up with Changers" cheery (I recognize the move from the mixers at Changers HQ). "And I wouldn't have had you and Mom had I gone that direction, so I am most certainly happy with who I am. As should you be, by the way. You're a good kid . . . Can I get you some Advil?"

I nod my head. And that's when the buzzer rings; it's the doorman, advising us that the be-hatted pizza delivery lady is on her way up to the apartment with our pies.

I ate five slices—yes, five—and the Advil didn't really work, so I took two more PMs, and now I'm lying here in bed finishing up this Chronicling because I still can't seem to fall asleep, but I need to because I want to be rested for practice tomorrow and do really well (suck it, Jason), even if it's only for the JV squad. If I prove myself, maybe I'll even get in the varsity game for a minute or two on Friday night. Why that matters to me at all, I'm not sure. But it does. Right now, it's everything.

In the first *Peregrine Review* meeting, we looked through Mr. Crowell's collection of literary magazines, like *McSweeney's*, *Bomb*, *One Story*, *Tin House*, and so on. The guy really knows how to party; he told us how sometimes a whole weekend will pass by and he will have done nothing more than curl up on his leisure chair with a new issue of one of these magazines and scarcely remember to use the toilet. Which, A) TMI, and B) I hope he knows Tracy's idea of a perfect Saturday most certainly does not involve stewing in your juices on a stained, rust-colored 1970 corduroy Barcalounger reading fifty-page interviews with obscure writers who have one foot in the grave.

Anyway, I'm at a back corner table with Audrey, Aaron, and this cute, athletic-looking freshman girl Amanda, who is wearing about five pieces of jewelry fashioned from duct tape and seems very involved in whatever photographs she keeps turning vertically between her hands and studying closely like a naughty centerfold picture.

Aaron and I are the only guys in the class, except this frizzy-haired skinny dude wearing a Neil Young tee, Brian, who is feverishly scribbling in a spiral notebook, and Mr. Crowell, whom Chloe is monopolizing by forcing him to flip through her poetry chapbook, which she wrote and hand-sewed in the eighth grade, inspired by her favorite poetess, Jewel. I think I see Mr. Crowell wince.

"Poor him," I say, and both Aaron and Audrey chuckle.

Amanda looks up too, smiles a big braces-filled smile, and goes back to dissecting the journal.

Audrey's been a tad chilly all day, probably since I was kind of a jerk at practice last night. I want to apologize, but I don't really know how I'd say it.

Aaron is acting a little weird too. Like, trying to be all butch Mr. Varsity Football Stud while simultaneously sitting here giggling at Nora Ephron. I mean, I wish I could tell the dude I know all about the little "secret" (a.k.a. Danny) he feels he has to hide from Jason and the rest of the football team, not to mention his parents and everybody else in school—but I have a feeling that would freak the poor guy out. (Probably not as much as if he knew we'd double-dated boy-boy/girl-girl on the DL at prom last year. Now THAT would blow his closet *and* his mind wide open.)

As I'm thinking of a way to show I'm "down with the gays" without appearing presumptuous or hopelessly lame, Aaron asks, "Dude, you psyched for the game on Friday?"

Audrey gets up to exchange journals from Mr. Crowell's shelf.

"I guess. I'm a little sore," I say. "I probably won't play."

"*Ploughshares* or *Granta*?" Audrey asks when she comes back to the table.

"Everybody plays eventually," Aaron says. "And if you're not sore, you're not going at it hard enough."

"Dirty," Audrey says cheekily, slapping both journals on the table. "You done with that?" she asks Amanda, who simply flips to the next page, where I think I see a little boob in an "arty" shot that's part of some photography spread.

"I kind of got nailed yesterday in practice," I say to Aaron, looking at Audrey. "And I was kind of a jerk to her after."

"My brother, your teammate and quarterback," Audrey

says, by way of explanation to Aaron. "And my personal ancestral nightmare."

"We've all had our struggles with Jason," Aaron says. "Welcome to the club."

"I was just embarrassed," I confess, mostly to Audrey.

"If that's the farthest it goes, consider yourself lucky," Audrey brushes it off. "Someone should castrate him before it's too late."

"Girl, you did not," Aaron snarks, but then tamps it down when he seems to remember my outsider presence.

"Folks," Mr. Crowell interrupts, "we're supposed to be perusing and reading for inspiration. That's what's happening over there, right?"

I start looking over Amanda's shoulder at the photo spread of some half-naked lady posing in the desert between a goat and a Joshua Tree, as Audrey and Aaron continue whispering about how much Danny was tortured by Jason over the last couple years, but how ecstatic Danny is now, to be away at school in Atlanta, a.k.a. Valhalla. They are talking all cryptically, swapping pronouns when necessary, so I won't understand what's really going on, who Danny really is; Aaron saying he wants to fly under the radar, keep his head down and post as many yards as possible, so he can get his athletic scholarship and the heck out of Genesis next year—maybe even play for a school near Atlanta (presumably so he can be closer to Danny).

"He texted yesterday—from modern dance class!" Audrey squeals. "He says he's in heaven!"

"Yeah, can you imagine how many hot girls in tight spandex he's surrounded by all the time?" Aaron asserts for my benefit. "Lucky bastard."

There is a dissonant moment where Aaron throws a

pleading look Audrey's way (which he thinks I don't see but I do), and then I offer with no sense of irony or ridicule: "I LOVE modern dance."

They do simultaneous double takes.

"I do," I insist. "Mostly because *I* get to wear the tight spandex. Why do you think I'm playing football?"

Aud snorts and Aaron laughs, which breaks up some of the tension before Mr. Crowell starts wading between tables and handing out writing exercise prompts. I get a poem, Audrey a short-short story, Aaron a personal essay. Nobody (but Chloe of course) seems happy with poetry, but I have something on my mind, and I'm psyched to get down to the business of trying to get it out in a concise, indirect way, which is what poems do, right?

I start free-associating, like Mr. Crowell has been telling us to, jotting random thoughts and images and words in pencil on a blank sheet of notebook paper. I've written down about twenty things when I notice Audrey watching me. She hasn't put anything to paper yet, nor has Aaron, who is staring out the window, likely wrestling with the prospect of writing something personal without revealing anything personal.

"It's a little odd that you're into the whole literary magazine thing," Audrey says out of nowhere.

I look up. Aaron is studying me now too.

"Maybe you shouldn't pigeonhole people," I counter. "You know, maybe let them surprise you."

"Touché," Audrey says, and then she and Aaron smile at one another, and I go back to my free-associating: *muscle, ink, extinct, lightness, soft, freedom, man, woman, secrets, lies, love, love, love.*

When people say football is a religion in the South, BE-LIEVE them.

As high up as I felt last year when I got a glimpse of life on the JV cheerleading squad? That's like being a background extra in a home-renovation show compared to playing on the football team, where everybody's the gorgeous star of their own superhero blockbuster.

I'd observed it from down on the field last year, but that didn't prepare me for being amidst a thousand-plus people in the stands clapping in unison while seventy-something pairs of cleats militaristically (not to mention ominously) march down the center metal bleachers, with boastful rap music blasting over the crappy speakers. Our names and numbers are announced, but you can scarcely hear anything over the hungry roaring of the crowd. As you pick through the manic audience all swathed in some combination of maroon, black, and white, strangers slap your helmet and hands, sometimes grabbing you by the shoulder pads and butting heads with your helmet alarmingly forcefully, with no regard for their own cerebral damage. Basically, folks just try to touch any part of you within reach as though you can bring them good luck, like one of those cats with the waving paw you see in the windows of Chinese restaurants.

It's straight-up bonkers is what it is, and I almost had a coronary the first time some burly local fan in a flannel shirt with a chewing tobacco tin–sized hole in the front pocket took it even further and slapped my ass hard as I rounded the corner and began walking the front-row gauntlet of bleachers. I whipped my head around to see what the hell had just happened, but the guy betrayed NO shame in the least, just initiated intense eye contact, pumped both his fists in the air, and yelled at the top of his register, "WOOOOOOOOO!" jutting his chin at me then toward the field. "Now get on down there and show them what Falcons are made of! *WOOOO!*"

My gaze followed his nod, where Jason and the other starters (including Aaron, Baron, and Dashawn, a friend of DJ's) were already on the sideline, bouncing up and down like boxers, loosening up, throwing and catching balls to get warm. For a minute I forgot I was also headed down there bringing up the rear of the snaking line of players (most of us back here officially on the JV roster, but nevertheless suited up for the varsity season opener).

I just kept marching, following the player in front of me. As I passed the rows I noticed a few of my teachers, some other faculty, familiar nameless (to me) students, janitors, Miss Jeannie from registration (in a foam Falcon headdress), the principal, vice principal, the French teacher, guidance counselors, even Hank our late-night doorman at our apartment building. *Damn*, who wasn't there? Everybody to a person smiling and encouraging, hollering, clapping, nonstop dapping my shoulders, my helmet—and a couple more rattling times, my butt.

The game itself was a similar blur, and went faster than seemed possible for all of the anticipatory run-up. The whole first half, I stood on one of the benches so I could see over the guys on the sideline, me and a handful of freshmen and sophomore JV guys just gripping our helmets and shifting our weight back and forth, acting like we were ready if called upon, but in fact terrified of being asked to go out there with all the lights and screams and dreams and hopes and anticipation raining down on us.

I was watching the furry Falcon mascot pretending to be bowled over by the stunning beauty of the Lady Falconettes' cheering, when this kid Damon next to me got called in on our second possession in the second half. He snapped to, but when he stepped off the bench and yanked his helmet over his head, he twisted a knee or something and crumpled to the ground. It was hard not to laugh because it was so unbelievable, but dude really hurt himself and couldn't go in. They had to carry him off in the Falcon golf cart with a platform on the back before the next snap of the ball.

The only other part I remember is the crowd went buck when Jason threw two "perfect" touchdowns, one of which Aaron caught over two defenders' heads, and the tangible pressure on the sidelines was considerably alleviated when in the fourth quarter Dashawn forced and recovered a fumble and returned it all the way, putting us up by twenty-one.

"Small!" I heard from somewhere in front of me. "Small! You're up. Gunner!"

It was the assistant coach Peters, and it appeared he wanted me to go in with special teams.

My chest tightened, all my blood felt like it was rushing away from my limbs. *Don't trip, don't trip!* I was yelling at myself with Damon's fate in my head, as I hopped down off the bench and found myself mechanically jogging over to the sideline. All the blood had seemingly left my brain too, since I couldn't even remember whether we were kicking or receiving, but then I saw our kicker run out and realized that I needed to line up on the other side of him, and before

I knew it, he dropped his hand and booted the ball and I was racing down the field full tilt toward two kids who were peering up expectantly into the lights above us like a flying saucer was about to land and perform a double alien abduction.

The guy on my side of the field caught the ball. There was a short pause and beat of silence after he collected it into his gut, and then he started kicking up dirt running toward us. I trained my eyes on him, specifically on the ball in his left hand as he pumped his arms, picking up speed. Closer, closer, closer. I launched his way with my hands outstretched toward the ball, which I TOUCHED and tried to wrap the tips of my fingers around to pry loose, but he held on too tight. I did grab hold of his other arm though, which spun and slowed him just enough for the teammate behind me to tackle him to the ground and end the play.

Whistle from the ref. Low clapping from the stands, our sideline, the special teams coach. I stood there panting, swiveling my helmet around like, *What next?* as everybody scurried off and on the field with purpose, and finally I realized that was my cue to exit. Which I did, right as Jason jogged on, absorbed by the plays written on his armband. He didn't even register my presence. Fine by freaking me.

And that's what I remember of my first high school football game experience. As a *player*.

I would stop there, but this Chronicle wouldn't comprise the entirety of my first high school football game experience unless I also include a retelling of what happened *post*-game, at the after-party at a teammate's house near school.

I walked in solo, clutching my skateboard in one hand like a blankie, and a six-pack of Dr Pepper in the other. Right when I sidle in I'm greeted by a wall of cigarette smoke (with some pot and cloves muddled in). Music's loud, crushed cups strewn about, the party already in full gonzo mode. I don't see DJ (who'd texted he was going to meet me here), just a bunch of the guys from the team and random girls hanging off them vying for attention, when all dudes seem to want to do is impress one another.

Some of the players do the head-nod thing as I wade through the living room, nice and open-faced like I am somebody or something. Like I am their equal. Some of the girls are extra smiley too, which I have no idea what to do with, but luckily I can leave that conundrum for another time because I soon find myself in the dining room and headed toward the kitchen, praying I see someone I can actually talk to before I decide it was a terrible idea to come here, and that I should instead be sitting at home eating cold pizza and watching some old-timey detective movie with Snoopy balled up on the couch next to me.

I know it's stupid because this is decidedly not her scene, but I keep expecting (hoping) to see Audrey at the party. Like last year when we went to our first high school rager together after we cheered our first JV game. Who will I have to make fun of everybody with, if not her? We get each other, not to mention everybody else. But she doesn't know that now. Or can't see it because of the shell I'm in.

"Yo, Erkel!" It's DJ, coming through the kitchen with some red punch sloshing around a blue cup.

"I was beginning to think you'd bailed," I say. "Can I have some?"

"It's just Hi-C."

"What else would it be?" I say with an exaggerated shoulder shrug.

"Kenya's here. She was asking about you," DJ shares, then adds, "for some reason I can't understand." He rummages around an open cabinet and locates a glass, pours half his punch in it for me.

We head toward the backyard. The thing I said about high school cafeterias and prison segregation? It's on full display at parties too. All the white kids are inside dancing and drinking and talking about the game, and all the black kids are outside in the backyard, kind of doing a different version of the same thing. The Latinos aren't really present and accounted for, except Carlos our safety, who's five foot two and downright Hobbit-esque, but always seems to have a bevy of hot girls of all ages orbiting around him like flirty satellites.

"Qué pasa?" he says as DJ and I pass him on the back deck.

"Damn," DJ says, shaking his head in admiration at Carlos.

"Yoooooo!" A circle of dudes is calling DJ, who perks up soon as he sees them.

"Cypher?" he asks me.

And—I'm paralyzed. Like, I've just seen a ghost, which may be a cliché but is completely apropos because despite appearances to the contrary, I am the whitest thing out here right now, and I'm being asked to do pretty much the opposite of that. Not that anybody knows but me.

"Nah?" DJ prompts, shedding his hoodie and stepping into the circle.

The extent of my knowledge of cyphers consists of 1) *8 Mile* the movie, where pale-faced Eminem playing a version of himself, blows away all of the "surprised" black people rapping and beatboxing and cutting up in cyphers outside the auto factory, in abandoned parking lots, and at rap battles; and 2) the line from the song "Vivrant Thing" by Q-

Tip, where he raps, "*You would find me in a cypher if I didn't cop a deal*," which Andy's older brother used to play in the car when his parents made him drive us to baseball practice.

All I know is: I'm no Eminem, and I want nothing to do with a cypher, even though all of these guys (and one chick) are looking at me expectantly like, *Why wouldn't dude want to join in?* I can literally feel sweat dripping under my armpits, my palms growing damp.

"Um ..." I say, but fortunately nobody can hear me, because someone is beatboxing, a few are clapping, and DJ is starting like, "Uh ... uh ... uh," closing his eyes and jogging his head and generally getting down to spit his spoken word/ hip-hop swag.

Dashawn is waving me in, sort of dancing and moving his head with the beat too, but I say, moronically, like I'm fifty years old, "I'm okay, you all go ahead," while surreptitiously taking tiny steps backward.

"*O, O, my boy, he's so shy, took him to a party and thought he was gonna cry.*" DJ points at me, then goes on: "*Skate fool, hate school, so cool, got his juice from a pee paw, he saw, up in the mall, lucky he's so small, not very tall, Oryon Small, who you gonna call? Ghostbusters, don't trust us, colored punks getting busted, don't pass muster, must be why he rolling on that skateboard, so hard, up with the Lord he a hot shot, big snot, naw, don't be scurred of us, get on the bus, but not in the back, that shit was wack, 16th Street Baptist, goddamn Birming-Ham, Ala-Bam . . . uh, Montgomery Rosa Parks and the rest of us darks, say hell no, we won't go, don't shoot me, just 'cause I wear this hood-ee, oh goodie, he's done with that surreous obit, accompanied by just a little wit, but don't forget that shit or you just might end up repeating IT—*"

"Ohhhh!" Dashawn yells, and a few others join in as DJ

finishes with a flourish, looking at me like, *That is how it's done, sucka!*

"Your turn," DJ hollers to me. "Let's hear some of that A-town crunk style!" And everybody claps encouragingly, and I'm about to buckle under my own weight when . . . my vision goes black.

"Guess who?" The old hands-over-the-eyes-from-behind maneuver, which is usually annoying as hell, but is the most welcome greeting of all time right about now.

"Kenya!" I shout, like she's Santa Claus, the Easter Bunny, and Jesus all rolled into one get-out-of-teenage-social-jail card. I turn around to face her, grab her hand, and pull her toward the house. "Get a drink with me?"

"Uh, okay," she says. "You all right?"

"Just thirsty."

I drag Kenya to the kitchen, just in time to catch half a dozen of the senior football buttholes I don't know, surrounding the king of the buttholes, Jason, as he thrusts his cup in the air, clashing it against everybody else's and causing massive waves of beer to splash all over the counter, floor, and walls.

"To all the homosexuals in the house!" Jason screams, and everybody repeats, "To the homosexuals!" And then they all drink, practically choking because they are laughing so hard at how funny Jason is.

"To all of the transvestites in the house!" Jason screams even louder next, and everybody repeats, "To all the transvestites!" And they drink and laugh even harder.

"What the?" Kenya says.

"To all the bitches!!!"

At this I see Kenya's jaw clench like she is about to march over to the butthole brigade and shut that idiot nation down, so I quickly tug her into the next room, where there's a tub in the corner filled with wine coolers and beers chilling in dirty ice.

"I don't see how natural selection hasn't kicked in on that dude yet," she says, and I pop open a wine cooler and pass it to her. "No thanks."

"Sadly, he *is* natural selection," I say, then take a big swig of the cooler myself. Raspberry, tart, strong, so surprisingly *gooood*, like medicinal lemonade. I swallow, pretending this isn't my first time drinking wine, shake my head at the feel of it going down. "It's worse than you know." I take another swig, the bubbles burning the back of my throat.

"Hey, slow up," Kenya says. "Are you sure you're okay?"

"I'm great!" I respond, feeling an inexplicable burst of energy (not to mention confidence), and pull her onto the dance floor, such as it is, where a table has been kicked over and about five girls are pelvic-thrusting to Michael Jackson squealing, "*Billie Jean is not my lover, she's just a girl . . .*"

Kenya gives in and starts moving with me, but I can tell it's against what every cell in her brain is telling her to do.

Long story short:

We danced.

She had a few swigs of my wine cooler.

I had more than a few swigs.

And . . .

We kissed in the hallway by the bathroom. It just happened. She leaned in, or maybe I did, and her lips were crazy soft and it was completely unexpected, and I'd like to say I was prepared for what happened in my brain next, but it was as if I forgot who/what/where I was for a second, just gave in to this completely foreign feeling I'd been dreaming and speculating and talking with Andy about since I was like ten or eleven, and was thus completely taken by surprise when a few seconds in to kissing Kenya, I was transported to the MetLife Stadium in New Jersey, set up for the Olympic track-and-field trials, and Kenya's there on the second platform on the podium, bunches of flowers in her arms, and a silver medal being placed around her neck, her times qualifying her to go to the Olympics in Tokyo. Her parents were in the first row behind her, filled with utter joy (with a reserve of sadness for the fourth member of the family who couldn't be there—her brother who was murdered).

"Too much sizzurp?" Kenya asks, pulling back from my face.

"What? No!" I say, coming back to the present.

"I thought I lost you there for a second," she says, smiling, so I dip back in for another smooch. Her lips part a little this time, as do mine, and my hands instinctively reach around her waist and pull her toward me, and then I sort of push both of us up against the hallway wall, and we are just kissing like that for I don't even know how long, half of me pressed up against her lips, the other half still at the stadium cheering along with the thousands of people in the crowd and sharing in the sheer pride and joy that swells around future Kenya in my Changers kiss vision.

So that went down.

I hadn't planned it. No one ever does though, do they?

After kiss number fifteen, as if scripted, my phone buzzed in my back pocket, her phone buzzed in her front: both of our parents summoning us back to our respective homes. I don't even know how Kenya talked hers into letting her out on a Friday night in the first place, but perhaps because she's a senior now they are willing to let her make some more of her own decisions in life. She'll be out there in the world next year, headed, it seems, down the path to that podium, just like she's always wanted. No one deserves it more.

We stiffly hugged before bailing on the party, waiting out front where her dad was driving to come pick her up. I asked if she wanted me to wait with her, but she said no, it was probably better if she was alone when he got there. So I skated off toward home, down the dark, windy streets of the subdivision, the occasional streetlamp dilating my pupils from the flood of light.

A small part of me knows I shouldn't have kissed Kenya. That my heart is really with somebody else. But Audrey seemed out of reach, and Kenya was very much in reach, and I guess I could blame it on the al-co-hol, but that would be a lie. Maybe life was simpler when I was Drew, even with all the mixed-up feelings around Chase, back when he wasn't such a self-righteous drag.

Damn, why am I being so serious? It was just a party make-out session. That's what kids do, they have a drink or two, kiss other kids (and more stuff), no big deal. Right? I'm not a user or anything. I'm not that guy. Besides, as my nana always says, "You can't put the shit back in the horse now."

I skate faster, just me and the sound of my kick-pushing down the street, the gentle roar of four wheels beneath me. The beat of a pebble here, a shard of twinkling glass there. Not many lights are on in the houses, just a few blue TV screens glowing from the front rooms like eerie, fishless aquariums.

CHANGE 2-DAY 20

Today I stepped into a universe I previously had no idea existed: teen poetry slams. We drove to the Tennessee Titans'-sponsored Youth Urban Poetry Slam finals (YUPS), which is about a forty-five-minute drive from Genesis, during which I was squeezed between DJ and Kenya in the backseat of DJ's mom's 1989 cream Toyota Camry. DJ's mom Emebet was at the wheel, with nobody in the passenger seat, because there is no passenger seat (for a reason I never really ascertained and didn't feel comfortable inquiring about).

When I climbed into the Camry in front of Central (of course I couldn't be picked up at home per Changer rules), Kenya was already in the backseat next to DJ. We both said "Hey," as she scooted over to allow me to wedge into the center seat, after which we didn't say another word to each other for the length of the trip. I tried to flash her a solicitous smile, but she jerked her head away and rolled the window down, turning the whole backseat into an ear-battering wind tunnel.

So much for a few harmless kisses.

DJ also seemed tense, pushed against the rear door while flipping through his notebook, which was filled with maniacal scribbles like that scientist who went to MIT and everybody thought was crazy but was actually a genius. He didn't really talk on the ride to the Slam, except to shush his mom after she looked in the rearview mirror, waited to lock down some meaningful eye contact with me, and said, "DJ shared with me what happened to your biological parents, and I guess I just wanted to say, I am so sorry for your loss. That shouldn't happen to any child."

"Mooooom! Jesus Christ!" DJ shouted over the roar of the wind.

"Language, Dee!" his mom cut back.

"I told you not to say anything," DJ returned. "Damn."

"It's okay," I said to him. "It's okay," I repeated to her. "Thank you though." I felt like such an asshole, a sentiment it seemed Kenya was onboard with, given she was still turned toward the window as if actually catching sight of me would cause her to instantly projectile-vomit.

"Well, if you ever need anything," Emebet started, as DJ made pleading eyes at her to no avail, "you just say the word, and we'll do anything we can. Right, Dee?"

"Wow," DJ said, then went back to flipping through his notebook. Nervous.

We exited the highway. Kenya's long legs were folded into the small space behind DJ's mom's seat, and I felt our thighs sweating against one another. We kept pulling them apart and readjusting while DJ's mom commenced grilling Kenya about her college track prospects, which schools' coaches were scouting her, what were her favorites.

I sat and watched the city go by as we got closer and closer to downtown, past the warehouse district, where I briefly wondered what the newly buff Chase might be doing at that moment at the RaChas HQ—plotting, scheming, practicing his abdominal planks. We screeched into the parking lot beneath the Holiday Inn, where Emebet leaped out, all apologies, and tossed the keys at the attendant, because we were running late for registration.

Up in conference room 2A with the green, red, and black floral carpet and heavy emerald drapes separating it from conference room 2B, a Titans player in a loose-fitting jersey was already up onstage welcoming everybody to the event. I think he was the third-string kicker or something, because nobody really cared he was there.

DJ pointed Kenya and me to some seats in the rear while he looped the Titans lanyard with plastic-covered ID over his head and around his neck and stood to the side of the stage with about twenty kids who had also reached the YUPS finals. It was about 80 percent girls, and 70 percent black. Mostly juniors and seniors. The girl who came up second actually reminded me of Drew. Her poem was about a sailboat ride on the coast of Maine with a now-dead grandfather who fought in the war. And some other stuff, but a lot of "salty sea reclaiming the bounty" and naval war imagery.

Another girl got up when (not) Drew finished, a black girl with straight hair under a (I swear) raspberry-colored beret. She was the previous year's champ, and as soon as she took her place in front of the tarp painted to look like a graffitied brick wall, she began pacing and angry-talking about her daddy only being invited to attend her high school graduation if he could correctly tell her the name of the school she was graduating from.

"This ain't no multiple choice, it's my life!" she spat, as the audience waved and whistled, clapping at practically every line. Her poem seemed to strike some chords.

Raspberry Beret's face was screwed up with rage. And sadness. She finished by suddenly stopping her manic ranting and pacing and standing frozen in the middle of the stage, face toward the audience, her mouth open as if she were screaming, with no sound coming out.

I noticed a lot of women in the crowd shaking their heads and murmuring things like, "Preach, girl," while the Drew-looking kid stood off to the side, tears streaming down her face. No wonder Raspberry won last year. She was stupid good. I snuck a glance at DJ, and I could tell he was even more apprehensive, but he was keeping it together, clapping really loudly for her.

Sucks to be him, I thought. But soon enough it was his turn, and holy crap did he throw down. Less frenetic than the other competitors, DJ kept to one small section of the stage and somehow sucked all the energy toward him. I'd never seen confidence like that before, not even from Kenya when she's on the track. He was so still and thoroughly absorbed in his own moment that it made all of us watching feel like we were seeing something we shouldn't, like this was a spontaneous eruption of confessional intimacy we just happened upon and could not turn away from.

"My heritage needs my greatness. Stained, but enlightened. Wrinkled, not worthless. Did I forget how to fit the mold?"

DJ sounded so wise and passionate, like a prophet or one of those guys who starts cults and gets all his followers to do whatever he wants just with the power and intention of his voice. It was all I could do to stay in my seat. I clocked his mom, and saw that her eyes were squeezed shut. Then I looked at Kenya and she was smiling so big I was surprised her cheeks didn't cramp.

"I am a living canvas. I am the reason. I am running past guilt. I am sprinting to glory. I am where I belong. I am my own story. I am my own story. I own my own story. I am."

When he finished, the room was silent for a beat, then exploded with applause. He ended up defeating Raspberry

Beret. She was runner-up, looking sort of shocked at her loss. DJ was awarded a Titans jersey with *Slam Champ* and the year of the event as the jersey number, a Titans ball cap (which I know he'll never wear as a lifelong sworn Atlanta Falcons fan), an inspirational-looking signed hardcover book he'll never read, and a gold-painted trophy of a hand grasping a mic, *YUPS* etched on the plaque.

The organizer asked him to put on the hat and jersey and hold up the trophy and pose with the third-string Titans kicker, who had left for the poetry part of the event but magically showed up just as DJ was being crowned winner, handing him a scholarship check for $1,500 as the cameras flashed, local news cameras rolled, and his mother gleefully hugged herself in her seat. DJ is so getting a full-ride scholarship to any college he even remotely thinks he may want to attend.

When DJ's name was announced as the champion, Kenya and I had spontaneously embraced, but suddenly snapped back rubber band–style to our silent awkwardness, which I don't even know what to say about. I mean, half of me wanted to just be like, *What the hell was that about at the party?* to relieve the tension, but the other half was straight terrified of her, wondering if I'd hurt her somehow, fooled her in some way I didn't know, and her dad was going to give me a beat-down, or DJ was, the minute she told him what happened. Luckily there was a lot to distract us onstage, as DJ shook hands and answered questions, just generally beaming like mad up there.

We went for pizza after, DJ on freaking cloud nine. Dude was psyched, and I'll probably never forget that image of him in my head, in the millisecond before he knew he won, when the cheesy local weatherman acting as the YUPS host was holding DJ's and the other girl's forearms like they were boxers who'd fought all ten rounds without a knockout. He was peering down at his feet, rocking slightly, the lights low, breathing kind of hard, just like that boxer who'd made it through. But there was this halo vibrating around him too, a total contentment with where he was, with what just happened. He was wholly pleased no matter which way this was going to go, peaceful and calm and satisfied that he'd done the best he could possibly do.

Now back home on my bed alone, I keep thinking, *What a feeling that must be*, as I toss the football DJ didn't want with the Titans logo in the air above me and catch it over and over. His bone-deep contentment when he finished performing his poem, clear even though he tried to front and act chill, not wanting to seem gloaty or unduly proud. I've seen Kenya with that same contentment after certain races now that I'm thinking of it (even though I know she cares more about winning than just about anything).

I wonder what that's like, to be totally happy doing something you love so much. I'm psyched for DJ and his golden mic and all, but it also makes me a little depressed to be sitting here alone wondering if I'm ever going to find my thing like he and Kenya seem to have. I mean, even if it doesn't work out for them, at least they'll have tried their best at something, and maybe that's enough. Or close to it.

What am I supposed to do? What am I made for? If I am my own story, unlike DJ or Kenya or Tracy or Chase, I don't know how to write it. And I sure as sunshine don't have a clue about the ending.

Today sucked dirty diaper juice.

I woke up feeling like a phantom. Like I didn't even know who I was anymore. I stared at myself in the mirror as I do every morning, when I decide I'm *this* (fly skate rat) or I'm *that* (bookish literary geek) and head out to face the bad old world, just as I have for the last twenty days. But today I came up short in the invent-a-personality wheel of fortune. I had no answers. Not even pretend ones. It hit me like a bowling pin to the face that I'm really not anybody at all. I'm pieces of people, *ideas* of people. I have no identity, secret or otherwise. I'm water, sloshing around into whatever form is presented to me. But the me that exists without a container has no substance, no heft, no realness.

Keeping it real? What even is that? Why am I so quick to get pissed about being misunderstood? It's like I want everyone else to solve the puzzle that is me. Because I fracking can't.

I don't even know what I'm trying to say, except that nobody knows me and why should they, when I don't even know myself?

Right when my eyes opened this morning all of this depressing stuff from the night before started flooding in. I went to the kitchen to distract myself, to see whether Mom and Dad wanted to do some corny family activity like we used to when I was younger, when I was Ethan. You know I had to be desperate if I was game for bowling, or going to one of those cloying "make your own pottery" places, which is really just painting somebody else's pottery *mold*—an irony not lost on me at this moment.

But when I got out to the kitchen it was empty. On the counter was a hastily scribbled note with eight dollars stuck under the paper towel roll:

We went to Costco and some other places. Know how you hate errands! Should be back by 4 or 5. Treat yourself to lunch. Take Snoop for a long walk. We have our cells. Text or call if you need anything.

Love you,
M & D
(even though it's Mom who always writes the notes)

Yes, Mom, I need something. I need not to be such a loser that my own parents don't even want to hang out with me on a Sunday.

With nothing to Chronicle, nobody calling me (not even Tracy, who is likely baking blueberry scones in an ruffley apron for Mr. Crowell this very moment), and no homework either (I guess so everybody could focus their juju on the big Falcons win instead of Algebra), I decided to be a good son and walk Snoopy and "treat myself" to a corn dog at the Freezo.

Which, it turns out, was an epic mistake. Not the corn dog. The walk.

Let me explain.

I somehow manage to haul my gloomy butt out of bed, put yesterday's clothes on and pull a hat over my head, and then dress Snoopy in his harness. We go downstairs, and I hop on my board, figuring I'll let Snoop pull me toward the park that's about a mile away. When we skirt by the dog run, Snoopy puts on the brakes, all eager to chill with some canine friends.

"Okay, boy," I say, picking up my board and asking Snoop to sit while I take off his leash, make him make eye contact with me, and then repeat, "Okay," to release him into the dog run, just the way I was taught when we went to puppy kindergarten back when he was an adorable fur ball everyone cooed at on sight.

As soon as Snoopy runs into the park and starts happily wagging and sniffing all the puppy butts, two different people (two!) come running over to their smaller dogs and scoop them up. This causes some other canines (not Snoopy, mind you) to start jumping and barking and aggressively trying to snatch the two picked-up dogs out of their owners' arms. Which. I'm fifteen and even I know that if you make something look like prey, predators are going to come calling. It's High School 101, people.

So now the owners of the aggressive-acting dogs scramble over and start trying to drag their pups away from the people clutching their fluffy smaller dogs in the air. No one is connecting the dots that their panic is the reason those dogs are snapping like sharks, trying to get their jaws on what is being telegraphed to be the most irresistible treat ever. Meanwhile, Snoopy is just standing there smiling with his fat tongue wagging like, *Let's play*!

"You shouldn't bring dogs like those in here," I hear from behind me. "They're born aggressive."

I turn around to see who is talking to me, and it's a long-haired lady in a prairie skirt and tank top, yanking on the collar of a Rhodesian ridgeback that's easily ninety pounds and, I see when he circles, unfixed. His testicles are the size of navel oranges.

"Excuse me?" I say.

"It's irresponsible," she snarls, the ridgeback attempting to yank her arm out of its socket.

"He's just sitting there," I try, indicating Snoopy, who isn't even looking at her big-balled dog.

"The minute he came in, he got everybody riled up," she insists.

"Seriously, bro." Some hipster dad with a soul patch has walked over to add his two cents. "You know they're born to fight, right? I mean, there's kids in here."

I can't even believe what I'm hearing, can't even get a word out because it's so irrational and contrary to what is actually happening right in front of their faces, and yet they see something else. It's like the whole dog park has come down with a case of Hysterical Canine Blindness. And they are picking on my dog, who is doing nothing wrong besides being born the breed he is, and my frustration and bewilderment manifests like a giant fuzzy peach lodged in my throat.

"Their jaws lock!" the ridgeback lady screeches as she finally maneuvers all her weight to push her obnoxious dog from the park, slamming the gate behind her.

"Uh—" I start, but nothing will come out.

Soul Patch Dad idles next to me, stomach paunched out, side-eyeing Snoopy. "I mean, I got no beef with the good ones, but some people . . ." He nods at the lady leaving. "You know, bro. Just like, it's probably better if you don't bring him in here."

By now Snoopy is frolicking with another dog like a freaking commercial for organic dog food, the two of them leaping and rolling and wagging their tails so fast their whole torsos wiggle. Nevertheless, Soul Patch Dad gestures toward the gate, indicating I should follow.

"FYI, there's a no–pit bull legislation working its way through the city council," he adds, as a gaggle of other concerned dog owners sort of flank him like it's *Gangs of New York* and we're about to go at it with our manmade weapons fashioned from wood planks with rusty nails sticking out of them.

"Seriously?" is all I can manage, as I go over to Snoopy and grab his collar. He has no idea what's going on and resists at first, but then I get the leash on him and he happily trots alongside me while the assembled Dog Park Mafia silently watch us go, triumphant that they got the kid with the SCARY dog to leave them to their happy, bullshit Sunday scene.

It's only on the way back to the apartment that I think of about a million things I should've said. Like, *Their jaws don't lock; that's a myth.* Or, *Actually, lady, pit bulls are no more aggressive than other breeds like beagles and golden retrievers. And the American Temperament Testing Society research backs that up.* Or, *Get your dog fixed because, news alert: the world has too many dogs already!* Or even, *Don't you think you're being a little intolerant?*

By which I mean, unbelievably, irrefutably, cripplingly intolerant. Maybe even a little racist. Okay, very racist. Against Snoop—and me. I mean, when I used to walk my dog last year when I was a cute, nonthreatening blond girl, people would be all over him and letting him kiss them and slobber on them, and they'd be scratching his butt and just having a general love fest. And people would be like, *What is he, a hound-lab mix?* And then I'd correct them and say he's a pit bull, and while of course some people might recoil, mostly they were obviously assuming he was one of the "good ones" because he obviously was living with a good family—a.k.a. white.

And now folks just assume he's a pit bull right off the bat, and even though he's the same dog, people don't pet him as much when I'm walking him. And look what just happened. We were basically run out of the park like the Elephant Man with his Elephant Dog.

Needless to say, I lost my appetite for Freezo, and for stupid dog runs. Snoop can walk on a treadmill like on the *Dog Whisperer* for all I care. Or sit and watch dogs playing on TV for socialization, because we are not ever going out there and facing the awful world like that again.

By the time I moped home, Snoopy's usually irrepressible spirit was also completely squashed, and he seemed almost as down as I was. We both plopped onto my bed right after we got inside the nice, cool apartment. My parents still weren't home. The sun was low, and it was dark in there, but I didn't feel like turning on any lights.

It was hard to let go of the fury in my chest. I could feel my pulse was still elevated, my skin sticky. My brain doing that exhausting circular logic thing where you try to find answers to things that have no answers.

Snoopy chose that moment to fart and then look around with confusion as if the smell and sound had come from someplace else. He crawled closer to my lap, then laid his giant, heavy blockhead on my legs with an exaggerated exhale. Yeah. Cold-blooded killer. Of air quality, maybe.

For distraction, I opened up my laptop, logged onto Google, and typed, *how to beatbox*. I watched a handful of videos on YouTube, and started reading about how to simulate a kick drum by repeating the letter *B* over and over, like in *Bogus*.

I do it myself: *Buh, buh, buh.* Snoopy rouses at the racket, then realizes I'm not calling him and falls instantly back to sleep. His nose whistles like an old man's, the sound providing a steady background rhythm. I move on to the hi-hat, more of a *tst* sound with my teeth closed. *TST, tst, tst,* I say, loud like a tire bleeding out air in staccato.

I click on an NPR link, which suggests I say, "Baboons and pigs, baboons and pigs," and, "Bouncing cats, bouncing cats," over and over. Which, okay, I'm all alone here and Snoopy can't tell anybody, so I start doing it, cupping my hands over my mouth as I spit it louder and louder, and it really sort of starts sounding like a beat, and—

Knock-knock-open.

"Are you okay?" Mom, panicked.

"Ma, what the H?"

"I thought you were choking," she says, all worried-faced.

"Come on, can I get some privacy?" I am thoroughly embarrassed.

"I just wanted to let you know we're back," she says, adding. "You had privacy all day."

I slam my laptop shut.

"Are you okay?" she asks suspiciously.

"Yep. Fine," I say flatly, praying she doesn't stick around.

"Sure?" she asks after a few more excruciating therapy-like seconds.

"Yep." I don't even bother meeting her eyes.

"Oh, you know I love a *Yep*."

"*Yes*, I'm fine," I snap. "I'm just tired."

"Okaaaay," she says, drawing it out like I'm crazy.

I get it. I'm being an evasive brat. I don't care. I mean,

I don't necessarily *like* speaking the way I do sometimes, "with an attitude" or whatever Mom calls it, but I swear it just spurts out like a snotty geyser. *Meh. Bleh. Yep. Wah.* The words sound the way I feel inside. Which, when I can't describe my actual feelings, is a relief, even if it pisses off my parents (and, when she's paying attention, Tracy).

Mom leaves me to marinate in my crappy attitude. I open my laptop back up, look at the screen as the rapping story reloads, and recommence feeling entirely lame, when out of nowhere, well, probably from the depths of my subconscious that was tapped the second Kenya's lips touched mine on Friday and I saw a flash of her future, it hits me all over again—my kiss-vision from last school year of Audrey being harassed by some thug named Kyle. I shudder. Then wonder, who the hell is this Kyle creep, what's going to happen to Audrey when she meets him, and what the hell am I going to do about it?

I know I need to get as close as possible to her so I can do everything in my power to protect her when this a-hole shows up in her life. Maybe instead of rapping, or football, or drums, or whatever dumb hobby I stumble onto, that can be the thing I try hard and get really good at.

Maybe *that's* why I was born.

Baboons and pigs, baboons and pigs, baboons and pigs . . .

"**D**as *racist*," DJ pronounces at lunch, as soon as I recount my dog run debacle. "No, for real. You think they'd be schooling you if you were some suburban white kid with a labradoodle?"

"I guess not," I say, even though I know he's right.

I'd woken up this morning thinking maybe I had over-reacted yesterday, you know, just a bad time of the month (ha!). But DJ's rage makes me feel nearly justified.

"No, that is some bull-*crap*," DJ says again. "You should write a rhyme about it."

I laugh in his face.

"Seriously," he says, staring dead sober into my eyes. "Or I will—" DJ interrupts himself like a record-skip, drops a forkful of coleslaw onto his plate, and frowns a little. He surveys the table. "Wait, where's Kenya?"

A cyclone breaks out in my stomach. "I don't know."

He cocks his head, studies me.

"What?"

"She's always at this table at lunch," he states factually.

"Maybe she's at extra help."

"Kenya doesn't need extra help."

"I don't know, maybe she went home early."

"What happened between you two?" DJ asks bluntly.

"Nothing!" I practically yell. "What do you mean?" My voice has gone up like two octaves, so there's no way I'm pulling this off.

"You barely talked Saturday," he says, slowly piecing it together: the party, the car ride, pizza after. "No, seriously, what happened?" He's staring at me like a menacing big brother. Worse, a menacing big brother and a shunned ex-boyfriend all in one. "You can tell me, whatever it is," he tries, acting casual. Like he's an old-school exterminator, luring me under the propped-up box with a hunk of cheese before pulling the stick away to trap me and starve me out.

That said, it's sort of working. And, I figure, maybe DJ can shed light on why Kenya's avoiding me. Or if I did something wrong I have no awareness of. Maybe then I can just fix it and we can all go back to how we were, shooting the bull over lunch and goofing on each other with no hurt feelings.

"Uh ..." I start.

"Uh ... what?"

"We kind of. We sort of." I just gotta go for it: "We kissed."

His nostrils flare. "Oh." Muscles along his jaws pulse. "When?"

"Uh ... at the party?" I say, reverting back to my old up-talk tic.

"Hmm," he says, crossing his arms. "That explains it."

"What?" I ask, but DJ is already wadding his napkin, throwing it onto his tray, and shuttling his dirty dishes to the drop-off line.

A t *Peregrine Review* today, we waded through submissions for the Fall issue.

"This one's not bad," I say, holding up a pencil drawing of a bespectacled and backpack-wearing falcon in midair, grasping a bunch of pens with one talon, while writing on a scroll of paper with a quill in the other.

Audrey squints across the table, pinches up her nose.

Aaron glances over, does the same.

"And that's a no," I say, mostly to myself, tossing the cover illustration hopeful in the reject pile.

"I vote we stay classy, maybe go with a vintage photograph or something?" Audrey says like she's asking, but I know better that she means it as a statement. As in, that's what we're going to do, no use arguing.

"I was thinking more along the lines of an airbrushed mountain-stream scene, maybe with a grizzly bear clenching a trout in his jaws, like on the side of a van," I joke.

"Next issue maybe," Audrey says, and goes back to reading the short story she's in the middle of.

Aaron pulls out another submission from the pile. I notice the name: *Michelle Hu.*

"Oh, she's a great girl," I say to Aaron almost like a reflex, and Audrey lifts her head, curious. "Michelle Hu, you know her?"

Audrey nods and Aaron sort of nods too, but it's clear he doesn't actually know Michelle.

"You know who else is a great girl?" Aud asks suddenly, eyeing Aaron like they have some giant inside joke.

I glance back and forth between them.

"You?" I exclaim after a couple beats, totally serious.

Audrey half-smiles. "That's not who I was thinking, but . . ." She trails off.

We all go back to perusing our submissions for a few seconds. I take a deep breath. Exhale. Ready, set, go: "I was sort of hoping to do this privately, but since you two Wonder Twins seem to have no secrets . . . I would like to ask if you would accompany me to a movie and dinner this weekend. What do you think?"

"Me?" Audrey spits, then starts cracking up in her endearing way.

"Uh, of course you . . . What? Did I not ask right?"

"No, that was fairly smooth-under-the-guise-of-being-humble. It's just, my answer is no."

"Ouch," Aaron says.

"You have a girlfriend," Audrey adds then, flatly.

At first I don't know what she's talking about, because I have never had a girlfriend, unless you count Audrey herself, but that was last year, when I was an entirely different person and can't possibly be the reason Audrey has essentially shut me down from even a harmless movie and dinner out.

"I don't have a girlfriend," I finally say.

"Not what I heard," Aud practically sings, shooting a glance at Aaron, who shrugs like, *Don't ask me*, which makes it abundantly clear that he is in fact the source of her information.

"I don't even know what you're talking about," I say, feeling a little creeped out that anybody has said anything about me to anyone. Not as creeped out as last year when Jason was spreading rumors about "that slut Drew" around school, but something along those lines.

"You're not seeing the track star?" Aud asks.

What the hell? My brain is grinding gears trying to figure out exactly how we got here, how one person knew, and now it seems like everybody knows.

"Kenya? No. She's a good friend, but we're not going out or anything." As the words come out I'm realizing how pointless they are. Audrey thinks what she thinks, Aaron thinks what he thinks, heard what he heard from Dashawn, from DJ, from the GD homeroom announcements over the PA this morning. *Good morning, Central Falcons! Lunch today is pulled pork and beans. The Books and Blues fundraiser is coming up in two weeks, and, oh yes, Oryon and Kenya are totally a thing!*

Audrey seems to sense she's struck a nerve. "She seems really nice." She's trying to be cool, but it only serves to make me feel even more misunderstood than before. If that's even possible for a Changer.

"She is," I say. "But we're not going out."

Audrey just raises her eyebrows at me—like, what was that supposed to telegraph, that she still doesn't believe me?—and then Mr. Crowell calls our attention to the front of the room where Chloe and Amanda are presenting some poems (mostly Chloe's) for us for consider, so the matter is put to bed. For now.

When I got home, my folks asked if I wanted to go out for Indian after I finished my homework. Sure, why not. I couldn't really ponder anything except Audrey, and her misconception about me and Kenya. I can't believe all of the issues that arise from one random moment at a party. It's making me crazy that Audrey thinks something that's not true, and Kenya obviously thinks something *else* that's not true, and there's nothing I can do about any of it.

Chicks, man.

Yeah, I said it.

Before I checked my Chem homework online, I made a little deal with myself to log on to my secret e-mail account, or Drew's e-mail account, for just thirty seconds, to see whether Audrey had written me/Drew back. She hadn't. But I did, however, notice Aud was also logged in at that very moment. My hand and heart trumped my head and gut.

I opened an instant message and wrote: *OMG. I've been looking to see when you'd be on here. You really there?*

Audrey: *Drewwwww!*

Me/Drew: *Yes it's meeeee.*

Audrey: *How's your new school? Central is sort of blowing, but there are a couple rays of light.*

Me/Drew: *It sucks. Completely. Without you.*

Audrey: *Have you made any friends?*

Me/Drew: *One or two. Not really. You?*

Audrey: *When I'm not cheering and he's not playing football (which is almost never) I mostly hang w/Aaron. He's so sad and lonely without Danny Boy.*

Me/Drew: *How are they doing?*

Audrey: *Good. They're attempting an "open" relationship while Danny's in Hotlanta. We'll see how long that works out.*

Me/Drew: *Lol! Do you like anybody?*

Audrey: *Like-like?*

Me/Drew: *Yes, like-like.*

There was a long gap in messaging, but I could see she

was typing the whole time. *Dot-dot-dot.* I was prepping for a long response, but then finally:

Audrey: *Kind of. Maybe. I'm not sure.*

Holy shit. Who does she like-like? Maybe by some miracle or chasm in the universe, it's me. *Oh my god.* But if it's not me, even more *Oh my god.* Who is it? I have to know.

"Baby!" my dad is suddenly calling from the hall. *Wow,* I hate when he calls me that, a little habit he started last year when I was Drew and hasn't really dropped since Oryon showed up. I mean, it's a little disturbing for a dad to call his fifteen-year-old son *baby.* "Let's go!"

"One sec!" I yell back at him through the door. *Dang.*

Me/Drew: *What do you mean you're not sure?*

Audrey: [again after a long pause that practically kills me] *I don't know. It's just weird, you know, with you, and us and stuff. I mean, it's probably nothing. Just someone seems to sort of like me.*

Me/Drew: *Who is it? A guy? Or a girl?*

"O!" Mom is now shouting from the hallway. How the heck am I supposed to care about naan and samosas when my own personal Bollywood soap opera is unfolding on a thirteen-inch screen right before me?

Audrey: *Guy.*

Me/Drew: *What's his name?*

Audrey: *Come on! I said it's not even a thing. Tell me something about you.*

Me/Drew: *Who is this guy? I want all the details.*

Audrey: *Another time. Srsly, I want to talk about you. I miss you.*

Me/Drew: *I miss you too.*

Audrey: *So what are we going to do about that?*

Me/Drew: *I don't know.*

Audrey: *Le sigh.*

Me/Drew: *Le sigh.*

Audrey: *I wish you were still at Central. Better yet, I wish I were a boarding student at your school so I didn't have to live with my family.*

Knock-knock-open: "Really? This is why you're holding up the train?" Mom asks, as I slam the laptop shut for fear she sees Drew's name and I get a spontaneous mini-lecture about honesty and authenticity and then reported to the Council for being normal.

"Sorry, just getting a homework assignment from a friend," I try lamely.

"I completely believe that. Let's go."

"Be out in a sec," I say, willing her to shut the door. Which she does after a meaningful stare that says something like, *I'm pretty sure you're lying to me, but I really don't feel like getting into it now because I want to have a nice night and we've been getting along pretty well lately, so why ruin it with a giant discussion about some tiny issue that I hope my crazed teenager is going to do the right thing about anyway, so I'll let him win this time and then kick myself later for letting it go when it comes back to bite all of us in the ass.*

And she would probably be right if she were thinking that.

Regardless, I go back to typing:

Me/Drew: *Sorry, Mom just burst in. GTG, but you're telling me about this guy some other time. At least what he looks like.*

Audrey: *Why do you care what he looks like?*

Me/Drew: *I don't. But. Is he hot?*

I quit out of e-mail, cleared my history for good measure, then ran out to join my folks in the hallway, where they were waiting for me, right at the point before their annoyance tipped over into anger.

"What are y'all waiting for?" I shout, flashing Mom a smile and punching Dad on the shoulder before blowing by them toward the elevator. "Let's keep calm and curry on!"

Today after practice I pretended to be digging for something in my backpack while loitering in front of the gym until Audrey emerged from the locker room, post-cheerleading.

"Okay, I'm only going to ask you this, like, ninety-seven more times," I announced, taking her by surprise.

She looked momentarily startled, but then smiled back when she saw me working the dimples. "The answer's still no," she said sweetly.

"You don't even know what I was going to ask," I said, hefting my backpack onto one shoulder while popping my board up into the other hand.

She gave me her best silent *Really?*

"I was going to ask why," I began, "if vampires can't see their reflections, is their hair always so freaking perfect?"

"Nice," she said, chuckling in her *har-har* way, and starting to stroll toward the parking lot. I got the vibe she both wanted and didn't want me to follow along. I erred on the side of following.

I walked beside her for a few paces. "I'm not seeing Kenya," I said.

"Okay," Audrey answered, seeming to half-believe me for the first time. "But it's still a no."

And with that, the giant ennui cloud moved in. My spirit drooped. Audrey noticed.

"Listen, it's not you or anything," she said, eyes nervously scanning the parking lot. "I mean, you seem nice and it'd be cool to get to know you."

Nice? To GET to know me?

"But I—"

The scream of tires on asphalt cut her off. Jason. The color drained from Aud's face like the complexion of one of the aforementioned vampires. She clutched her binder and books tighter to her chest as her brother pulled up to the curb in his convertible and, yes, honked.

"Your chariot awaits," I said unenthusiastically, trying not to engage with Jason, who was blasting Insane Clown Posse from his gigantic speakers.

Audrey put her hand on my back, where it was squarely out of Jason's view. She looked repentant—which was killing me because she had no need to feel responsible for anything.

"It's just not that simple," she said quietly, retracting her hand as quickly as she'd placed it there. "I'll see you tomorrow."

She smiled anemically then got in the car. Jason started pulling out before she'd even had a chance to shut the door, his eyes fixed on me the whole time he was driving away— to the point where Coach Lois in her squatty blue Prius had to beep three times to get him to notice where he was going. He narrowly missed sideswiping a parked yellow school bus with the cross-country team climbing out.

The longer part of Audrey's hair flipped around in the wind as they drove off, Jason's wide racing tires wailing and taking up way more road than they should. Which is kind of the theme of his whole repugnant existence, now that I'm thinking about it.

Seeing her with him, my body tensed. Temples throbbing, a vice grip in my neck—I felt as if I'd just geared up for some giant thing that didn't come to pass. I was enraged. Irate. Furious, seething, fuming, apoplectic, incensed, indignant. Pass the thesaurus, because I need to look up more words for "overcome with anger." I've been pissed off before, but holy crap, this was new. It was like my every cell was overstuffed with physical rage, and if I didn't do something to get it out, I might actually implode.

Chase, I thought. This must be how he felt last year, when he beat Jason to a pulp after catching him trying to assault me. I get it now. There is anger, and then there is the Hulk shit.

I just stood there, unable to move. Then, out of nowhere, I hauled off and kicked a half-empty Snapple bottle that was sitting on the curb next to me. It felt exhilarating on impact, but the bottle shattered into a thousand pieces and the next sensation I felt was rancid juice splashing on me, and a shard of glass slicing into my shin after ricocheting off a brick wall. Genius.

I remember reading in Health class about testosterone, where it said that besides making you hungry and pimply, it can make you quick to anger. At the time I thought, yeah right, another excuse for dudes who act like boneheads. But damn if it wasn't (at least for me in that moment after Jason took Audrey away, scared, and I couldn't do anything about it) completely, biologically true.

I feel like a baby back at home letting my mommy tend to my wound, which she insisted on because I was still bleeding all over my shoe, sock, and the floor when I came in the door.

"You're lucky you kids heal quicker than normal during your Cycles," she says, stinging my flesh with hydrogen peroxide. I watch as the foam turns from white to cream to pink to red, with little leg hairs sticking out the center of it. "How'd this happen?"

"I don't know," I answer truthfully. "I was overcome."

"With?"

What could I say?

"Oh, sweetie," Mom says, wiping away the bubbles with a damp cotton ball.

"I don't really want to talk about it."

"I get it, I get it," she says, dabbing the cut with some Neosporin while deftly putting on her Shrinking Cap. "Was it something to do with Audrey?"

I struggle with a Band-Aid wrapper. "Sheets and blankets, why do they make these so hard to open?"

Mom calmly takes the adhesive from me and peels the wrapper away to reveal the large perforated bandage inside. "I want you to feel like you have friends at school this year, but that brother of hers is a world of trouble. Turner, the Lives Coach, recommends it's best to distance a bit from her family, if we can."

"We? You mean *me*."

She doesn't take the bait, just sticks the "flesh-colored" (i.e. Caucasian) bandage carefully around the cut, rubs the sides down so they're nice and snug. "Audrey is a good girl. But you are my only child. And I will do anything in my power to protect you from harm. Maybe this year you could make some new friends?" She narrows her eyes in faux menace. At least I think it's faux. "Capisce?"

Oh, I capisce, I think. I capisce that when it comes to Audrey, the less everyone else knows about us, the better.

I was just about to go to sleep when my Skype beeped with a

familiar tone, even if the face on the other side of the screen wasn't. Chase V2.

"Hey girl," he says as soon as his image pops up on my screen. He's chewing gum and wearing a way-too-tight *WEARECHANGERS.ORG* T-shirt, which his pecs and biceps are pretty much busting out of like overcooked sausages. "What's the latest?"

"I'm fried," I announce, moving my laptop from my desk to beside my pillow, where I lay my head.

"Remember when we used to do this for hours?" Chase asks right off, pulling his laptop into bed with him too. At that, I realize how intimate it is, Skyping in the sheets.

"That feels like a thousand years ago," I say.

"What's wrong?"

"Nothing really," I sigh, hoping to avoid a heated head-to-head for once.

"Something's obviously up, dude," he prompts. Which makes me remember when he'd call me *dude* when I was a girl crushing hard on him, and it would basically level me because I thought it meant that he didn't want me as anything more than a friend.

"I don't really want to go into it, man," I say. "But I'm starting to catch your political drift a bit more these days."

"Ah yes, my brother," he says, smiling all too eagerly. "The angry black man can't help but open his eyes to this unjust world around him, huh?"

"That's not it at all." But it kind of is. I just don't think I've really earned it or anything. What real right do I have to be mad? I feel like a faker or—

"You know I'm right. Embrace your rage," he says, essentially reading my mind. Which really pisses me off.

"No."

"It's okay. You *are* a black man, or someone who could become a black man," he starts. "That's the point. Like Benedict says, *We are all imposters*. And the black man's struggle is the gay man's struggle is the Muslim man's struggle is the transgender man's struggle is the homeless man's struggle, is your struggle, is my struggle—"

"Dude, stop," I interrupt his RaCha rant. "Before *you* become my struggle."

"The sooner our culture grasps this, the sooner we'll all be free of the -isms," he rambles on, immune to humor.

"Yeah, well, I notice there were no women in your struggle-a-thon," I say.

"You understand where I was going with it."

"I really don't feel like doing this right now. Why did you call, anyway?"

"I miss you," he says matter-of-factly, though a wisp of sadness floats over his eyes. "I've been thinking a lot about last year. How things ended."

"Chase, it's cool. Really." I swallow hard. "I understand better now."

Neither of us knows what to say next. We stare silently into each other's pixilated faces, and it feels both comforting and lonely, like cello music or wandering around the shopping mall.

"Well, I guess I'm outie," I say finally. "Deuces." I hold up two fingers in front of the embedded camera.

"Okay," he says, resigned, returning my peace sign. He smiles at me as I click the *Hang Up* button and Chase V2 disappears; all that's left in the naked screen is the blur of my own reflection.

Well, here's a first. And what I hope is a last. I'm Chronicling from my hospital room, one bed and blue curtain over from a middle-aged Hells Angels wannabe who won't stop screaming, "I know people who know people!" at the top of his lungs. The cop stationed outside our room has not cared all night, and doesn't seem like he will start caring anytime soon. Nevertheless the guy keeps screaming. And not because of the double compound radius and ulna fractures he collected when he (allegedly) drunk-drove his motorcycle off the side of the freeway exit and onto a parked car below.

And how'd I land here in paradise with this particular roommate? Starts with the letter J—for Jackhole. I was returning a punt in the ostensibly "light" practice we were having before Friday's game, my face-mask view filled with Baron steaming toward me. As he closed in, I attempted to hurdle his back like you see in all the best NFL highlight videos, but before I could launch off the ground, dude rolled into my leg with all of his two hundred chemically enhanced pounds, and I heard a loud *pop* coming from the vicinity of my right ankle.

I didn't think it was that serious until I tried to stand up and put weight on it, at which point I crumbled to the ground like that kid Damon when he fell off the bench on the night of our season opener. I probably shouldn't have chuckled at him inside, because the Changers karma gods have obviously decided to punish me for my lack of empathy.

Anyway, I hopped off the field toward the coaches. My foot was sort of loosely dangling in the air while I held it off the ground. I don't know quite how to describe it, but it was almost like my foot was no longer fully attached to my leg. I remember reading this story in Social Studies once about this Iraq War vet who'd stepped on an IED in Fallujah and lost his foot on one leg. Not that my injury was remotely in the vicinity of that soldier's — just that I couldn't stop thinking of the uncoupling he described every time I moved my leg and felt pretty much nothing at the end of it as I was being encouraged to lie still on the turf while the emergency Falcons golf cart sped my way.

I was so embarrassed splayed out there for everybody to gawk at (luckily the cheerleaders were on an entirely different end of the field, which forestalled Audrey getting yet another look at me failing miserably at something). That said, my chagrin quickly changed to anger when I saw Jason and Baron slap hands as I was wheeled into the field house by the trainers. Like they'd planned it or something—Jason putting Baron up to the task of taking me out because Jason and I are never on the field at the same time together.

No, that can't actually be. Can it? is what was going through my head as I disappeared into the tunnel beneath the stands.

I soon forgot about Jason and really started freaking out when the trainer said he thought my ankle might be broken and I needed an X-ray, and not only were they going to call home, but also take me to the HOSPITAL. And then *pow*, at that word the excruciating pain and throbbing in my ankle magically bumped down the list of priorities, likewise all of Jason's mustache-twirling villainy, when I realized that even though I was present and accounted for at the Changers Mixer seminar about emergency-room visits last year, I couldn't remember anything I was supposed to do before the ambulance pulled up and the EMTs shoved me inside. So I said nothing. Not even a moan.

"He's nonverbal," the tech who rode in the back with me noted into a small headset.

"I'm verbal!" I shouted.

"Oh, good. We thought you were in shock and were starting to wonder about you," she said, filling out some paperwork. "You're going to be fine," she added while rubbing her knuckles on my chest bone. (*Ow,* why?)

Before I knew it, we were at the hospital and I was being wheeled into the ER for admitting. I idled there, completely helpless in the hallway, with all the other patients in waiting. There was a dude with bloodstains on his shirt, a kid with a face swollen like a water balloon, and a lady who looked like she'd seen mucho hard times with a large, pus-filled infection on her thigh. I felt beyond freaked out so I told a nurse that I thought I was fine and would prefer to come back later if my ankle doesn't feel better in a few days, but she ignored me, whisking by with some sort of machine with lots of wires sticking out of it.

All I could think was, I'm going to be "found out" for being a Changer, and, *oh my god*, what's going to happen if I'm "found out?" Are the Abider Storm Troopers suddenly going to show up and take me to a deprogramming camp and conduct experiments on me and then if I'm not deprogrammed they'll just quietly do away with me? I mean, from what Chase and Benedict say, it sort of seems like that's a distinct possibility.

I'm falling into a fear spiral when I catch a glimpse of

my ankle, looking like a tennis ball has somehow worked its way under my skin and is sitting on the outside joint, which is red and blue and so shiny it's practically reflecting the fluorescent overhead light back at me.

And then *click-click*, the wheels on my gurney are released and I'm being pushed down the hall, past a police officer loitering in front of a room, and then into the room with the aforementioned Hells Angel hollering, "I know people who know people!" when I feel this sort of *snap* at the base of my neck like I felt on C2–D1 when Tracy waved that magical fob over my Chronicling chip.

Not three minutes later, a doctor rushes in—at least I assume he's a doctor because he was wearing a white coat, had two pagers on his belt, and acted very self-important. He crosses to me, briefly looks me over, and announces to the room, "I'll take it from here," which prompts one of the nurses and another young doctor to leave.

He pats me on the thigh parentally.

"Hi?" I try.

"What seems to be the problem?" he asks, sort of leaning close and half winking. Or does he have something in his eye?

He takes what appears to be a stethoscope from around his neck, quickly slips it behind my neck, and holds it there until I feel that *snap* again at the base of my neck. Then he replaces the stethoscope, although I'm pretty sure that's not what it was because no stethoscope I've seen can listen to your heart from the back of your neck.

"I hurt my ankle playing football," I say, pointing down at the obvious.

"We're going to need to cut these pants off," he says to the remaining nurse in the room.

"NO!" I sit up and scream for fear of exposing my Changers emblem (not to mention my private regions, which I prefer to remain private). Doc plants a giant hand on my chest and pushes me back down against the partially reclined gurney.

"Relax, young man," he says through clenched teeth, again with the half wink. "We are more than capable of handling your situation." He annunciates each word clearly, like I've injured my brain and not my ankle.

The nurse tenderly handles my foot (*Ow* again), while another guy comes over and starts cutting the leg of my practice pants with a pair of those miracle scissors that can cut anything, including a penny (if the late-night advertorials are to be trusted).

The orderly stops trimming the spandex right at my hip, then carefully tucks the ripped fabric under my butt so that my cheek isn't exposed. Praise be. I try to ignore everything else going on around me (plus the periodic, jarring, "I know people who know people!" from the other side of the curtain) and explain to the doctor exactly what happened in practice, what I heard, what I felt, and the doctor calmly tells me he wants to X-ray my ankle to see if it's broken, even though he's pretty sure it's not.

"We're going to take good care of you," he adds. "And don't worry, your folks have been notified of your condition and should be on the way."

As if on cue, I hear, "Oh my goodness, oh my goodness, what happened?" from the hallway, and Tracy blows into the room wearing a floral jumpsuit from what has to be *The Golden Girls* resort collection, and yanks aside the curtain, interrupting the biker dude ("I know people who—what the?"), but then realizes her mistake and throws the curtain back, rushing around to my side of the room.

"I'm SO sorry I wasn't there for you," she practically cries. "This is all my fault."

"Trace," I say, patting her on the shoulder as she flings herself over me like an enormous quilt. "It's not life or death. I just got hurt in practice."

"Is he going to be okay?" she asks the doctor.

"He's going to be aces," the man replies. "But we have to get him over to X-ray now." He nods his head at the orderly, who comes over, unlocks my wheels, and starts pushing me out the door, as Tracy clings to the side of my gurney Italian widow–style, not relinquishing the metal guard until I'm all the way out the door.

Back in my room, we review the X-ray, which proved that my ankle wasn't broken, but I did tear some ligaments pretty severely. Like, completely off the bone, apparently. While I had some strong painkillers "on board" (medical terminology I picked up), the doctor poked around my ankle region and pointed out exactly where my ligament was, versus where it should be, and the nauseating distance between the two. All the while Tracy sat at my side like she was on deathwatch, and then my folks showed up just as the nurse was finishing putting a cast on my leg, halfway up my calf. (I chose royal blue.) Apparently the tear was bad enough that it needed complete stabilization in order to heal properly.

After Mom hugged me (crying) and Dad squeezed my good leg (stoic), the doctor, Tracy, and my folks huddled in the corner and chatted for a few seconds, after which the doctor came over and whispered, "You're going to be up and running in a couple weeks. That said, your football season is over."

Huh? If I'm going to heal in a couple weeks, why can't I play ball? I was about to ask Dr. Wink-Wink that very question, when Tracy caught my attention and mouthed, *Later.*

As I'm lying there waiting to be discharged and my folks are signing papers, Tracy's thumbs are rapid-texting on her phone.

"Anyone I know?" I ask.

Her eyes dart around the room, and she shushes me: "None ya." Then she comes back over to the bedside, where I'm sitting up now, a little dizzy from the meds. She hugs me hard, then hands me a miniature Dixie cup of water, which I finish off.

The nurse brings me crutches and asks me to stand on the good leg. She adjusts each down a notch then passes them to me.

"Good?" she asks.

I tuck the crutches under each of my armpits and grasp the handles, put some weight on them, taking some pressure off my good leg. Nod my head. I haven't been on crutches since Andy broke his leg skiing when we were in sixth grade and I used to steal them and race across the playground, hopping on two feet in between each swing.

"And we're Audi 2000," the doctor says, practically as chipper as Tracy is when she's not feeling guilty about being a lapsed Touchstone. "You've been very brave, Oryon. It was a pleasure treating you."

We shake hands and they wheel me out of the hospital to the front door, some stupid liability rule, and I feel so odd sitting there infantilized with a blanket on my lap and my leg stuck out in front of me.

Dad pulls the car around, and Tracy loads my crutches in the trunk while Mom helps me hop to the front seat. We all get in together like one big happy family, which is when Tracy explains to me how the Council's "health system response procedure" works. My chip tripped the containment plan, which is why the Changer doctor suddenly showed up and treated me accordingly. The injury to my ligament was bad enough that in normal cases they probably would've done surgery to repair it, but since I will have this body for only the year, plus we heal quicker than Statics during our Cycles, I should be able to walk just fine on the thing in a week or two. Even so, I have to leave the cast on for a month, and there's no way I could go back to playing football (or skating), lest somebody get suspicious.

"So now it's *Changers: The Method-Acting Year?*" I quip, loopy from the drugs, which are beginning to make me veeerrry sleeeepy.

No one bothers to answer, leaving me to contemplate the one upside to this whole debacle: I can quit football without having to quit football. It's like getting an honorable discharge from the military. No giant mystery that my heart wasn't really in it, but there was no way I was going to allow Jason to win by forcing me to limp off the team just because pointlessly ramming into other dudes at full speed wasn't necessarily turning out to be "my thing."

So, shout out to fate. You too, Lord King Butthole Jason. You did me a favor, brohaim. Stick that in your pipe and shove it up your bigot-hole.

It's *World War Z* at Central right now.

All because of me. Well, me and Aaron. At least that's what people are saying, though of course it all traces back to Jason, even if most folks aren't capable of seeing it that way.

Yesterday after practice, Jason and Baron were whispering in the shower about how their little plan to wipe me out worked, and how awesome it was, et cetera et cetera, on and on like a scene in a cheesy anti-bullying movie or something. There were a few other guys around and nobody seemed to care, but apparently Aaron was in a bathroom stall listening the whole time, and when he walked out and confronted Jason and Baron, they acted like he was making crazy accusations and being anti-team, and even started yanking Aaron into the shower to do G knows what, some sort of jock hazing water torture they learned on the Internet.

Aaron fought them off and escaped, but he went straight into Coach Tyler's office and proceeded to essentially put his whole college scholarship quest on the line by telling Coach what he heard and what happened afterward. Jason and Baron were called in, denied the preposterous notion that they'd somehow concocted a plan to injure a teammate, and apparently passed up every opportunity they were given to come clean and explain what their beef was with me (and Aaron). So Coach sent them home and said he'd be deciding in the morning whether the two would be allowed to play in tonight's game.

As you can imagine, the news of the imperiled starters spread through the school about five seconds after Jason got out of there and used his QB-One omnipotence to rally the lion's share of the school population to his corner.

What he didn't count on was that Baron, terrified of his father (whose only joy in his otherwise suffocating life is football), called Coach Tyler privately after they left his office and squealed. He confessed that the brutal tackle was all Jason's idea because he wanted to teach me a lesson (and scare me away from his sister), and that Baron didn't want to do it but Jason "made him." How much of a moron is Baron that he thought this story would make him look *better* than Jason?

Anyhow, Coach Tyler called an emergency staff meeting that went late into last night, after which it was decided both players would be benched for at least one game, and possibly more, depending on a disciplinary hearing that would be set up with the principal.

I wasn't even in school Thursday so I could begin recovering, but first thing Friday morning, before I'd heard anything about *Et tu, Baron,* Coach personally intercepted me from homeroom and walked with me as I hobbled to his office, where he proceeded to apologize profusely for his ignorance about the team dynamics that had gotten so out of hand. He needed to get through tonight's game, but asked to schedule a meeting with me and my foster parents first thing Monday to make sure they knew how seriously he and the school were taking this. He also inquired if I'd heard my parents say anything about "pressing charges." Knowing the Council would want less than zero part of that noise, I immediately said something like, *No freaking way, let's just drop it and move on; it was just a simple football injury, they happen all the time.*

131

The immediate outcome? Jason and Baron were suspended from play until further notice. And Central lost. Spectacularly. The first defeat in eighteen straight games.

I made the mistake of going to the game (as Coach had requested for "morale"). I stood at the end of the bench on my crutches, wearing my team jersey, sans pads. The instant the whistle blew after the other team scored a pick-six touchdown off of Aaron's bobbling a pass from QB-Two, I felt the first soda cup whisk by my head and spray the back of my neck with Orange Crush.

"BOOOOOO" in unison from a corner of the stands. "There's no R-A-T in T-E-A-M," someone shouted.

I looked behind me, and there was Jason in the stands, banned from even being on the sidelines, bookended by hostile, zealous fans. I turned toward the field just in time for a giant pretzel to bean me in the middle of my back. They are heavier and harder than you'd think.

After the game, Jason raced down to the railing closest to the field, leaned all the way over like he was about to do a somersault past it, and mouthed, *You're dead*, to me while pressing a fake two-finger gun to his head and pulling the "trigger" as I limped by on my crutches toward the locker room. He seemed drunk.

"You too, you bone smuggler," he hissed then, as Aaron jogged past me. Which almost caused Aaron to trip over a half-empty Gatorade bottle lying in the grass beneath him. His helmet snapped up toward Jason, who was now poking his tongue into his cheek and rolling his eyes back into his head. Aaron didn't respond, just kept jogging off the field like he didn't hear a damn thing, even though I know he had to be collapsing inside.

Not that I didn't have my own problems to contend

with. A few students, and even an adult—in fact I think it might've been the *WOOO!* guy who slapped my butt on the night of the first game—hissed various threats and insults at me as I went by. I texted Tracy and asked her to roll up pronto to give me a getaway lift home.

"This too shall pass," she declared soon as I heaved myself and my crutches into the passenger seat.

"How'd you hear?" I asked.

"It's on the radio."

"Great."

"You smell like a food truck," she said, flaring her nostrils.

"It's my new cologne. Eau de Pariah."

"You going to be okay?" she asked, as we pulled up to my building. "Want me to come up until your folks are back?"

I shook my head no, climbed out of her VW bug, and started limping away on my creaking crutches. But then she beeped twice and I turned back, her automatic window slowly rolling down.

"Almost forgot. Changers Mixer next weekend. Mandatory."

"Ugh."

"Dress to impress!" she chirped, and sped away.

At home, I find myself alone again, and feeling it in more ways than one. I try not to think about it, but I'm a little depressed. Or a lot depressed. Nothing like being the reason a thousand people are miserable tonight. Even if it's over a stupid game where one team just happened to carry a leather ball farther than the other one.

The *Changers Bible* says that right about now is the hardest time for being in a new V. That the adrenaline rush from the Change starts to die down, reality settles in, and you can't help but be like, *So I guess this is really happening for another, oh, 330 days . . .* A big wad of out-of-control awesome.

It doesn't help that everybody I know is on dates tonight—Tracy, my parents, even DJ, who claims he's out with some hot college girl whom he met at that slam. I don't know if I buy it though, because ever since the thing with Kenya it seems like he's more pissed at me than she is.

I'm too tired to figure it out or sweat it, and just want to curl up in my bed and binge-watch *Dr. Who* until blood starts dripping from my eyes like vampire tears.

The phone's ringing. Probably my parents checking in.

It was Audrey calling! I had no idea she had my, well, Oryon's number.

"It's me," she says right after I say hello.

"Me?"

"Audrey," she adds. "From school."

"I know," I say. *Just breathe, O. Act cool. Simply be. Simply be.* "How are you?"

"Better than you."

"You can say that again."

"Better than you," she repeats. "Har har."

"So what's, uh—"

"Why am I calling?"

"No!" I say. "I mean, I'm happy you did. But I—"

"You're wondering how I got your number," she interrupts, sounding a little self-conscious and like she might be regretting it.

"Besides the twenty times I wrote it on a piece of paper and secretly stuck it in your locker and backpack?" I say, regaining a little composure.

"It was on the team directory," she points out like, duh,

which immediately snaps me back to what happened earlier, and why she's taking pity and reaching out to me, the black Benedict Arnold of Central. "I guess I just wanted to say, I don't know. I—"

"It's okay," I say, trying to give her an out.

"No, it's not," she starts. "I mean, if even half of what I'm hearing is true . . . it's just, story of my life, I can't believe I'm related to that monster, and I guess I just wanted to see how you're doing."

"It wasn't the best forty-eight hours."

"I'm sure. Wowzers."

"But it wasn't the worst either," I add. "Especially now that I'm talking to you." I totally mean it. But as soon as I say it, I can tell I've come on a little too strong.

"How does your leg feel?" she changes the subject.

"A little better. My back, however, is still aching from the concession hail storm that rained down on me tonight."

She chuckles. I wait. The silence on the line is hard, but it's okay.

"How's Aaron managing?" I ask.

"I haven't talked to him yet. He won't answer my texts."

"It's got to be really brutal for him too."

"You're sweet," she says. And then, "Oryon?" I love how my name sounds in her voice. "When you feel better," she continues, cracking on the word *feel*, "we can go out for that dinner and movie. But just as friends."

"Is this a pity date?" I push, wanting to know, sort of.

"It's not a *date*."

"Pity," I say, and she laughs again, a symphony in my ear.

Shuffling around school today I felt slightly less hated, if only because no chili dogs or Red Bulls were being hurled at me. There were still a few sneers and threatening looks in the hallways between classes and in the cafeteria at lunch, but after Dashawn came up to me and gave me a very visible shoulder bump in the middle of the caf, before helping me carry my tray to the black table where he made it abundantly clear I was welcome to sit, the heat let up some. DJ and Kenya were seated at the far other end of the table, but both nodded my way as I sat down in front of the tray Dashawn had placed on the table.

You can tell who your friends are, or at least who knows what actually matters in life, when you are the supposed cause of a lost football game. Of course it makes zero sense that I am to blame, when if Jason and Baron had just laid off me (and not been sociopathic hate mongers), Jason would've thrown for a million yards and scored a hundred touchdowns as usual, and everybody would be happy today and all week long until it was time to start sweating the next game. But that is not the country we live in yet. Just as I learned when I was Drew, most folks choose not to wrestle with the complicated reality, when blaming the victim is so much easier.

The black (*ahem*) balling was so fierce, even Mr. Crowell took me aside at the end of homeroom and inquired as to how I was "holding up." Initially I assumed that he'd heard about all the hoopla through other faculty members, but then it seemed like there was something deeper in his apprehension, like maybe Tracy was the source of his exacerbated concern. I didn't have time to suss it out any further, as I had to get to first period—which takes a lot longer on crutches. And there are no elevators in the building, which (yes, Changer gods, I'm getting the message on the empathy front) is the first time I've considered how ridiculously hard it is just getting to class if you're, say, in a wheelchair, or differently abled in some way.

During English, Michelle Hu slyly passed me a note that read: *If you believe Everett's Many-Worlds theory, then you won the football game in an alternate universe! (Of course, it also means you are dead in an alternate universe.) Yay sports!*

Later by the lockers, I was thinking about how I wished I could carry Michelle Hu around in my backpack to cheer me up and keep me centered, when Audrey came up from behind and asked, sort of with a lilt in her voice, "How are you *feeling*?"

I started, which sent one of my crutches clattering to the linoleum floor. Aud picked it up.

"Much, much better," I said, giving a theatrical bow.

Audrey laughed as she carefully leaned my crutch up against the lockers. "Good to hear."

"*So* much better, in fact," I went on. "How's Friday night looking?"

"Can't do the weekend," she said.

"How about Thursday?" I persisted. She seemed to be wavering, so I added, "Just as friends, of course."

After a beat she said, "Sure," with absolutely zero enthusiasm. Whatever. I'll take it. It's an opening into her world, the—apologies to Michelle Hu—only universe that matters to me.

"**H**ow'd you find this place?" Audrey asks, as soon as we push through the beaded, glittery curtains and into Pho Sure, my favorite restaurant in Genesis.

"My folks and I have this thing where we make ourselves try a new restaurant every couple weeks, and this was by far the best," I say, but then immediately remember "my folks" aren't really "my folks," and I need to be on guard about that kind of personal stuff when it comes up.

I forget because I just want to be "myself" with Audrey, without always stress-balling having to keep my story straight. I guess this is one reason why we Changers are advised in the *CB* to "diversify our Static relationships." The sheer, unmanageable calculus of it all.

"Your family sounds really fun," Audrey says, snapping me back to the now.

The look on her face makes it abundantly clear that she probably doesn't try a lot of new things with her own folks, which I already know from the little time I spent with them. Boundary-pushing is not topping the list on the Stewart family agenda. Crazy how Aud turned out so different. She sure dodged both the nature and nurture bullets.

When we get shown to a table, I lean my crutches against the wall and walk around on my cast to hold out Audrey's chair for her.

"I thought this wasn't a date," she teases.

"It's not," I say, hobbling back around to my chair and flopping down. "It's called good manners."

"You're getting around pretty well on that," she says, pointing to my cast.

"Quick healer." I flex my biceps, kiss them one at a time. "Strong genes for our future children."

"Har har har." She turns her attention to the menu. "So, what's good?"

"Everything," I say, and then, "Two cafe sua da, iced, please," to the waiter, who I hope recognizes me from being here last time with my parents, so I can impress Audrey by seeming like a regular. It was uncomfortable when Dad grilled the older woman about where they lived in Vietnam (Hoi An), but now I can use the info to look worldly and connected in front of Audrey.

"You will love this drink," I say to her.

She looks a little taken aback. "Oh I will, will I?" she sasses.

Of course. As far as Audrey knows, this is the first time we've spent any time together outside of school and the *Peregrine Review*. There is no way Oryon would be aware of her chronic sweet tooth and that she'd love the creamy sugary deliciousness of Vietnamese iced coffee.

"Everyone does," I stammer. "It's kind of impossible not to," I manage, which seems to put her at ease.

"Sooooo, what would you suggest?" Aud asks, probably wishing she didn't need help.

"Well, since you're not a meat gal, I think the best thing to start off with is tofu and egg bun—it's like noodles."

"How'd you know I was vegetarian?"

Doh. "Lucky guess, I guess."

"I guess," she says generously. "What about you?"

"I used to be, but for some reason when I started play-

139

ing football, I just felt like eating ten turkey burgers a night. But now that football is no longer on my schedule, I just this very second decided that I'm going to go back to being vegetarian again. Tofu, here I come!"

"You're a goof," she says, looking at me from under her eyelashes.

I make a goof-face.

Then the mood shifts, and she mentions she heard that her brother would be back on the field tomorrow. "Honestly, you should've pressed charges."

I fan my hand like I'm swatting a gnat. "Whatever. What's done is done. You can't exactly expect high school to be the model of what's fair and right, can ya?"

Aud smiles. "No. No, you cannot."

After her rice noodles and my pho come, I raise my glass and say, "To new friends," and Aud quickly grabs her glass, clinks mine, and echoes, "To new friends."

We eat in silence for the first few bites. I can't tell whether she likes it or not, but then she chews a giant mouthful of noodles and her eyes light up like Vegas. She swallows, washes it down with some coffee, and says, "It smells a little like wet dog, but it tastes like heaven."

I laugh, almost spitting my water onto the table.

"Oh my goodness, did that sound racist?" Aud asks, clearly worried. "I was really talking about the odor, not alluding to some stereotype. Oh, *man*."

I laugh again.

"Well, I'm glad this isn't a date, or you'd be asking for the check right about now," she grimaces.

I pretend to signal the waiter, making the international sign for *Check, please,* and we both dissolve into childlike giggles.

* * *

"Thank you. I had a really good time tonight," Audrey says after the server really does bring the bill.

"Why do you sound so surprised about that?" I ask.

"I don't know . . ." she says, trailing off and sitting there silently for a few seconds. "It's really strange, but you remind me of somebody I used to know really well."

I let that sink in. It feels so good to hear, even if it makes me ill at ease to *be* that person she's talking about.

"Well, let's do it again sometime, with a movie too. Maybe next time as possibly more than friends?" I punctuate this with a nervous smile.

She doesn't answer. Which I suppose is better than a flat-out no.

"I have to get back to school, my mom's picking me up in fifteen," she says then.

"I'll walk you back."

"More like limp me back," she says with a conciliatory smile.

"Har har."

"Har har."

Back home, I text Chase: *If anyone asks, I was with you tonight.*

He quickly returns: *What are you playing at?*

Me: *Just trying to find some joy in this crazy world.*

Chase: *So, drugs then? JK! Consider your alibi tight.*

Me: *Thanks.*

Chase: *I'm just glad to see you're no longer campaigning for sainthood. Call me when you really want to kick up some dirt.*

Me: *Don't hold your breath.*

Chase: *The RaChas door is always open.*

Me: *I've got my hands full here.*

Chase: *With Audrey's breasts, no doubt.*

Me: *Dude. Not cool.*

Chase: *If any of her pillow talk is about her Abider kin-folk, you be sure to let me know. Deal?*

Me: *You're sick. Also. No.*

Chase: *Pussy.*

Me: *Sexist.*

Chase: *You seem happy.*

Me: *I guess I am.*

Chase: *But watch yourself. K?*

Me: *I thought I had you for that!*

Chase: *I'm being straight here. Keep your eyes open. I don't want anything bad to happen to you. Like last year. I should have been there. I'm not making the same mistake twice.*

Me: *Chase, you owe me nothing. Didn't then, don't now.*

The screen goes quiet. I pester him a few more times, but Chase doesn't respond. I tell him I'm going dark for the night, and try not to worry about the ominous warnings he keeps spitting out. I lean back into my pillows, exhale, and my thoughts cast back to an hour earlier, the glimmer in Audrey's eye as she sucked up her Vietnamese noodles, delirious with even that small taste of something different.

Well, so much for what I thought was an awesome date. Audrey was downright frosty in homeroom today. Standoffish, distant. We barely spoke, almost like she was trying to make sure I knew nothing had changed from yesterday to today just because of some flirty conversation over iced coffee.

Central won the game tonight, Jason performing better than ever, connecting with Aaron for two touchdown passes, both of them tabling their mutual hatred for the benefit of the win. Thus was the universe of Central High righted once again. Whatever. Most people seem to forget everything that happens the minute after it happens, so hopefully the whole hating on me because Jason wanted to snap my limbs fiasco will likewise fade to nothingness when Central still makes State with merely one negative blip on our record.

After the game, I saw Kenya waiting for a ride home by the field house. She was by herself, so I took the opportunity to talk to her alone, something I hadn't been able to do since Kiss-gate.

"Hi," I say, lurching up beside her on my crutches.

"Oh, hey," she says, not bothering to look at me.

"What's been happening?"

"Nothing. How are you?" she asks, pointing an elbow at my ankle.

"Oh, you know, nothing I can't deal with."

Kenya purses her lips, stays quiet.

"So . . ." I start, even if I don't necessarily know where I'm going, "I've been wanting to talk to you since, you know . . ."

She glowers right at me, as if challenging me to spell it out: *SINCE WE KISSED!* Which would make it real again, even though from the outside it seems like she's done her best to eternal-sunshine-of-the-spotless-mind that event from her memory bank.

I press on: "I guess I just wanted to see what's up, because, I wanted you to know I didn't plan that or anything, it just sort of happened, and ever since that night it seems like you've been mad at me or something."

Kenya's still staring at me dead-faced, and I'm wishing I'd never said anything in the first place, but that leaky ship has sailed so I may as well keep bailing. "It seems like maybe you thought it was a bigger deal than it was, or maybe you wanted it to be a bigger deal—"

"*Excuse* me?" she interrupts. Now she's pissed.

"What?"

"I don't want anything from you, Oryon," she snaps.

"Okay."

"Man, you sure do love yourself, don't you?"

"Not really."

"Could have fooled me." Beat. "Again."

Ouch. I should shut my excuse hole. But I don't. I want things to feel right again. Right for *me.*

"I really like you as a person," I try.

"Man. Really?"

"You're amazing," I just stupidly keep going on, "and you've got giant things ahead of you, like championships and gold medals, and we both know you don't need to be distracted by some fool like me."

She releases a sigh the length of an opera. Then forces a

pained half-smile. "Look, it's no big deal, okay? I gotta go, my ride is here."

I watch as she climbs in her mother's car. When her mom asks, "Who's that?" I can hear Kenya answer, "No one," and they drive away.

Twenty minutes later I run into DJ in front of the Quickie Mart, where I walked to meet my dad so he doesn't have to pick me up at school. DJ is gripping a jug of SunnyD in one hand, a Twix in the other.

"You going out?" he asks, jutting his chin at me.

"Nah," I say.

"No hot date with Miley Cyrus?" He's smiling, but not in a happy way.

"What?"

"The white hillbilly piece that's keeping you from seeing what's right in front of you."

"Is this about Kenya?" I ask. "Because we're cool."

"It is so not cool with Kenya."

"We just talked."

He laughs.

"What?"

"You're kind of clueless."

"So I keep hearing," I say, starting to get a little done with the whole drama.

"You don't know what a great girl she is."

"I actually do."

He shakes his head. "I gotta get going. You good for a ride?"

"Yeah," I say, and we slap hands twice and half-hug it out like we do, even though we're obviously not particularly feeling each other that minute.

* * *

I'm under my blankets now, but I can't get to sleep because I'm trying to go back to that night, review what happened, unravel the how and why Kenya and I ended up locking lips at that party. Maybe there is no reason. Maybe that was the whole point.

And maybe that makes me an opportunist. Like I led her on or something. But it was just fun, not really sexual or anything, just like, friends dancing and having a good time. I mean, what's the big deal?

And yet, it's obviously a big deal. How quickly I forgot after being Drew that to a teenage girl *everything* is a big deal. I should know better. I should care more. But I don't. I just want things to be easy again. Is that so wrong?

Lucky, lucky me. I'm getting dressed for the Changers Mixer, which I would do anything to avoid, when an IM pops up on the *Drew* account I've left open in hopes of catching Aud on there.

Audrey: *Hey, you there?*

Me/Drew: *Yaaaasssss! What's shakin, bacon?*

Audrey: *I went on a "date" with him.*

Oh . . .

My . . .

Freaking bloody hell.

It *was* me.

Me/Drew: *The guy who likes you?*

Audrey: *Y*

Me/Drew: *OMG, how was it?*

Audrey: *It wasn't a date-date, more like a friend-date.*

Me/Drew: *Why not a date-date?*

She's *dot-dot-dot* typing while I wait, staring at the screen, my eyes starting to water, my palms all moist and warm. The conversation feels sketchy. But I really have to know.

Me/Drew: *Hello?*

Audrey: *Sorry, the hosebeast was just knocking on my door looking for his Kenny Chesney T-shirt. Wait, what were we talking about?*

Me/Drew: *Your not-date?*

Audrey: *I don't know. Fun, I guess. It's not like I want to kiss him or anything.*

Okay, maybe *that* I didn't have to know.

Me/Drew: *Why not?*

Audrey: *I don't know. Why are you being so pro some dude you don't know?? He could be a serial killer who wants to wear my skin.*

Me/Drew: *No one could be scarier than your brother.*

Audrey: *Touché.*

Me/Drew: *IDK, just think it's exciting. If you like him and he seems like a good person. Does he seem like a good person?*

Audrey: *I think so.*

Me/Drew: *Is he cute?*

Audrey: *wtf????!!!!*

Me/Drew: *Just curious.*

Audrey: *This is weird talking to you about it.*

Me/Drew: *I know. But I want you to be happy. Who knows when (if?) we're going to be in the same town again. You know?*

Audrey: *I guess.*

One side of my brain is so happy she's being loyal to Drew, but the other side is scheming madly to figure out a way to push Audrey into Oryon's/my arms.

Me/Drew: *I don't mean to be a downer. It's just rare that you trust someone, so if you actually feel comfortable with him, then I want you to do your thing.*

Audrey: *I guess I thought you'd be a little hurt or something. This is killing me. Plus, I'm going to be late for the mixer.*

Me/Drew: *I still love you, Aud. More than ever. But real love means letting go.*

Audrey: *Sorry, can't type, too busy vomiting.*

Me/Drew: *Hilarious. Crap, I have to bolt. Will you be on later?*

Audrey: *Prolly. Have fun. Whatever you're doing.*
Me/Drew: *It's nothing fun, trust me. Aud, I miss you.*
Sorry if this is weird. I know it'll all work out. I don't
know why, but I do.
Audrey: *Bye.*
Me/Drew: *Bye bye bye.*
Audrey: *NSYNC!*
Me/Drew: *You remembered!!!*
Audrey: *Always.*
Me/Drew: *Bye*
Audrey: *Bye (bye bye)*

It feels dirty. I know it's probably immoral. But I don't know what else to do. I'm trying to be true to both people—well, more like four people (Ethan, Drew, Oryon . . . and Audrey). But it's getting increasingly difficult to keep the Rubik's Cube colors on their respective sides.

Buzzzzzz. My phone vibrates off the desk, falling onto my pillow. It's Audrey. Calling ME now.

"Hello?" I answer quickly as possible.

"Hey," she says. "How are you feeling?"

"Good *now*."

"So . . ." she says.

"So?"

"You have any interest in seeing that Miyazaki revival?"

Just got back from the Changers (Re)Mixer. During the break-out sessions, the Council facilitators said that it's recently come to their attention that some of us are not Chronicling every day like we're supposed to. How they knew this, they neglected to mention. They told us they understood how it can feel impossible to set aside time, but that it is major league critical to transmit at least some daily impression, recollection, or realization so we have the "full story of our lives" when it comes time to select our forever Mono. Like high school is really going to determine the full story of our lives. I fracking hope not.

Whatever. I choose to table the whole Mono conversation until my last V. Worry about it then. I mean, what's the use of getting all excited about being who I am now, when I could wake up next year as Thor, for example. One thing's for sure: this mixer was markedly different from last year's, when I was in awe of all the older Changers, basically trying to appear unfazed by this whole new life I'd started living, but inside I was Jell-O. I remember being so excited to meet others like me after a month of feeling like the only blue person on a planet full of reds. And then there was Chase. My forbidden Changer crush. Leonardo DiCaprio on the *Titanic*. King of the Changer World!

Chase was there this year too. I figured he'd be all rogue and out front demonstrating like the rest of the RaChas, but his parents made him toe the line. Homeschooling and adhering to the Changers Council minimum requirements were conditions he had to comply with in order to be allowed to stay in his house, which he didn't hesitate to tell me while he bitterly complained about every aspect of the mixer. I mean, he whined so much I started to defend the whole thing, even though I agreed with a lot of what he was saying. That seems to be where our dynamic has settled. Reflexively oppositional, like an old married couple.

In a seminar called "V2: The Sophomore Slump," Chase was channeling his inner Jason, conspicuously sighing and sucking his teeth and taking up as much space as possible by splaying his beeftastic arms across three seat backs with his legs draped over the chair in front of him. Everybody's chitter-chattering like it's a family reunion, only no one resembles the person they did before, it's like we've all joined the Secret Service and undergone complete facial reassignment surgery.

The side door to the stage pops open and Turner, the Lives Coach, glides in wearing some sort of loose white swami getup with a lotus flower appliqué on the front, and strands of wooden beads around his neck, wrists, and ankles. Somewhere even Gandhi is like, *Dude, tone it down*. He's followed by a handful of Council members: Charlie "Mr. Cool" exec from last year, some people I don't recognize, and Tracy, wearing full business drag, a fitted dark blue suit and skirt, like Special Agent Dana Scully on *The X-Files*, her hair all slicked back, not a pastel or flower in sight.

Chase does a spit take when he spots Trace. "Look who's giving executive ball-breaker realness. Guess she's really angling for that promotion, huh?"

His snarking makes me feel protective of her, because even though I might not love the whole Up-with-Changers mandate she's made her raison d'être, she's still my Touchstone, and a good person who truly believes she's improving the world for everyone. I mean, what are Chase and Benedict and the rest of the RaChas actually doing, besides not bathing and being really loud? I don't see them building any wells in the desert.

"A warm embrace of the soul to all Y-2s!" Turner meaningfully intones into his headset mic, adjusting the front to his lower lip. There is an enormous swell of applause, spurred on by the Council members and the Touchstones onstage behind him who wave and jump around warming up the crowd, even Tracy who pogos up and down in her pumps. "Thank you all so much for joining us," Turner says, "not that you had a choice!" He laughs to himself, but it doesn't come off right.

"He should stick to mind-numbing earnestness," Chase snits, rolling his eyes.

I do my best to ignore him, because I don't need any more Council attention drawn my way, especially not from Turner, who was inches from separating me from Audrey forever last year. I'm all about staying off his new-age radar for as long as possible.

"*Conducere*," Turner says. "As you know, it means *to bring together*." And then it is thirty minutes straight of mission talk. Change, impermanence, dimensions, purpose-driven lives, cultural medicine, integrity, denial of the self, not abusing our power. *Thou shalt not reveal yourself as a Changer to those who are not Changers.* Chase pretends to fall asleep.

"You may be inhabiting a sophomore slump, making you resistant, reactive. Don't fall prey to your lowest instincts. Rise above. But keep your feet on the ground." Turner falls silent for a moment, bows his oddly tiny head. "At this point

I know you're sitting there wishing you hadn't even come to this mixer." There are a couple sniffles and coughs before he continues, "I bet some of you even tried to get out of it by asking your parents or Touchstones if you could sit this one out. Were some of you perhaps feeling a little under the *weather* this morning? Needing a personal day?"

Turner tilts his chin toward a bunch of us as he speaks, including me. He's trying to connect, but reads more creepy.

"Understand this. It's completely normal to feel like two separate people at this point in your life. Or perhaps one person split into two, or even three. We expect you to struggle with these dynamics. Struggle is life." He sighs, seemingly exhausted from his zeal, then gathers himself up. "We are *all* everybody, even we who have chosen our Monos."

I shoot Chase a look, because that is essentially the same message he was spewing at me last week.

"Now, I want to turn our attention to a touchy subject, one that I'm fairly positive every one of you," he jabs a limp thumb at us to punctuate his words, "is processing right this very moment in your lives. Continuity."

Dead silence.

The Touchstones onstage look grave, including Tracy, who is pulling her respectful "serious" face, which I've seen on more than a few occasions.

"How do we, as people who change, continue in relationships with those who may not?"

Thoughts of Audrey flood my head, as somebody raises a hand behind me, a jet black–haired girl with straight, short bangs and thick glasses.

"It's not a question," Turner says, as the girl slowly lowers her hand and sinks into her seat. "Of course everybody—even Statics—changes all the time, though there are those intractable pockets on this planet, like the Abiders, who want to believe otherwise. But this paradox is certainly more pronounced in our Changer existence. How does love survive all the forms a person takes over our lifetimes? It is one of the universe's fundamental mysteries."

Where is Michelle Hu when I need her? I think.

"In the end, the question," Turner sums up, his reflexive self-satisfaction now in full bloom, "is irrelevant. It is the fact that we *ask* the question that matters."

"What the eff is he even talking about?" Chase whispers, but I barely hear him because onstage, Turner is leading a charge of, "In the many, we are one!"

"*In the many, we are one!*" all onstage, and some of us in the audience, repeat practically involuntarily. Turner gives a tight bow and steps aside faux-humbly, beads swinging. Everybody claps. For a long time. Like Turner is Beyoncé and we're trying to lure her back onstage for an encore.

Charlie steps up, all slick in a tight designer suit. "Hey man, hey, what's up, yo." He nods at different people he sees in the audience and apparently recognizes.

Turner and the other few members of the Council discretely file out the door they came in, leaving Tracy and five other Touchstones onstage behind Charlie.

"Welcome! How great was *that*?" Charlie hollers. More clapping. "Okay. Okay. Whew. So I'm here to lay some new info on you that's vital to Y-2 of your Cycles. Everybody pumped? Can I get a *Heck yeah!*"

A smattering of "Heck yeahs" fills the room, including one from Chase, except his sounded more like, *Eff this!*

People are anxious, including me, since the last time dude spoke to us, he basically informed us that we'd see flashes of Statics' futures when we kiss them. Now what? Are we getting X-ray vision? Because that is a superpower I've always thought was overrated. Like, so what, you see people naked or something? Who wants that? It's just embarrassing. It's not "hot," it's not anything but too-much-information, and if you're not James Bond or Jason Bourne, how many times are you really going to need to see what's inside a locked safe, or behind a closed door? Also, I just realized, if you really had X-ray vision, wouldn't you see through people's skin, through their flesh and muscles and organs, basically dead-ending on their SKELETON? Who wants that? Radiologists want that. Nobody else.

"So, we've made a few amendments to the rules," Charlie goes on, which snaps me out of my X-ray-vision reverie. "On the heels of what Turner has shared about past relationships you've had during Y-1, we've come to the conclusion that it is in the best interests of all parties if you only attach romantically with a given Static as a single V."

He looks around. I'm not quite sure what he means. Nor is anybody else.

"The lines are already necessarily blurred. And to avoid any misuse of power, as has been happening, unfortunately, we'd like you to keep the boundaries as clear as possible." Charlie looks around the room again. A few hands pop up, but he ignores them. "By all means, stay friends with the same Statics over all your Vs if you want. It is revealing and critical to see how you are treated and interpreted by the same people when you look so different externally. Those are messages we want you to absorb. However, if you become intimately involved with a Static, that needs to be a one-off thing."

He smiles all toothy, like anything he just said makes sense. People are whispering, frowning; one guy in the front row looks from the way his shoulders are bouncing like he's starting to cry.

Chase leans toward me, grouses (louder than I'd like), "See? More of their big brother bullshit."

"Are there any questions? . . . Yes, on the aisle," Charlie says, chipper, pointing to a redheaded girl in green Doc Martens.

"What if you liked someone and they seemed to really like you back, but nothing actually happened?"

"Did you kiss this person?"

"Not really."

"Not really?"

"No."

"Then you're good to go. Good luck," Charlie says, like he's answered these questions a million times. "Next?"

"What if you've kissed someone once, but nothing happened after that?" from an Asian guy in a football jersey.

"Did you see a vision?" Charlie asks.

"Yeah, he was riding the Matterhorn on his honeymoon."

"No, you can't become romantic with him this year," Charlie says, pointing to the next person.

"But what if you've kissed, but only . . ."

And on and on till the break of dawn. Basically, everything pivoting around whether or not you've had the kiss that spawns the vision. So I'm not supposed to be with Audrey. Again. Which: good luck keeping me from her.

Next thing I know, we're released from the session, and told that the official part of our mixer is over, and it's time to party. Charlie actually says, "Time to party!" And Tracy eagerly claps her hands together in a way that nearly crushes me.

Chase and I sit outside in the courtyard, me listening to

his RaChas propaganda, basically a less manipulative version of the doctrine presented by Benedict, who we can still sort of hear chanting from the other side of the bushes by the entrance to Changers HQ, where he and about a dozen RaChas are carrying on their quest to out Changers among the Static population.

"It is going to go down," Chase says, even more jittery than usual.

"What?" I barely muster, glancing across the lawn where the BBQ hoedown is getting underway.

"Benedict has zeroed in on a potential nest," Chase says, shrugging out of his jean jacket to reveal a too-tight white T-shirt with, wait, are those cigarettes rolled up in the sleeve? "Smoke?"

"Who are you, Joe Camel?"

Chase looks for somewhere private to light up. "We hear there are a couple churches doubling as Abider camps." He starts walking over to a closed stairwell, the very stairwell we emerged from last year after our Y-1 sessions let out. When I was following him around like a lost puppy. "Come on," he says, and yanks on the door. It doesn't open. He pulls harder. It gives with a loud, echocy screech. He holds it ajar for me. Against my better instincts, I go in.

I settle a few stairs above him. Chase lights up, takes a long drag, then offers the cigarette to me while he exhales. "You're getting a new body in eleven months."

"It's gross," I say. "And a little obvious."

"Calms the nerves. So much waiting."

"For what?" I ask, irritated that I'm being sucked in.

"For Benedict to decide it's time," he says mysteriously.

I try to change the subject: "Remember last year when we saw those cynical burners hanging out here?" I stand up, trying to fan the smoke away. "Now we're essentially them."

"You may be asleep, my friend," he says. "But I'm wide-a-freaking-wake."

"To what? You know, you have all these huge problems with the authority of the Council, but the way you talk about Benedict is pretty much the same thing. You're still being controlled and used."

Chase takes another long drag of the cigarette. Exhales through his nose and lips. "You don't know what you're talking about."

"Maybe not. But I know a narcissist when I meet one, and Benedict—"

"Benedict," he cuts me off, sharp. "Has my back. He has all our backs. Even *your* sorry back, which seems to be missing its spine."

Errrrrrk—the door cracks and a beam of sun cuts across Chase's face. He hops up just as everybody's favorite Lives Coach comes in, hoisting his white robes so they don't drag across the dirty cement floor.

"Extinguish that cigarette, please," Turner says. "Changers HQ is a nonsmoking environment."

Chase defiantly takes one more pull and then stubs the cigarette out on the metal handrail.

"When can we expect you souls to be joining us at the festivities?" Turner asks, placidly glancing between Chase and me, ignoring the mini-rebellion.

"In a few minutes," I reply. "Just catching up with an old friend."

Chase doesn't answer. Turner holds the door open for a few more seconds before saying, "I look forward to seeing you both there," and releasing it with a chill-inducing scrape.

It's dark again. And quiet.

"What a phony," Chase says, craning his neck up and down as if looking for spy cameras. "We shouldn't talk about this stuff here anyway."

"Or anywhere," I say, tracking his sightline and spotting nothing but cobwebs and the odd gray industrial smudge. Paranoid.

"Benedict says they scan the Chronicles for certain words and phrases," he whispers.

"I'm going to find my parents."

"You do that," he shoots back.

"What exactly is your beef with me?" I ask suddenly.

"I don't have beef with you."

"It's a full-on cattle ranch up in here, dude."

"We're just on different paths," he says, shrugging with palpable disappointment. "You're a good person. I just want more for you sometimes. I want *you* to want more for you."

"Later, Chase," I say, done now with his B.S. and his judgment and his more-radical-than-thou assessments of my character flaws. It's rich, really, given he's been a privileged white male two Vs in a row. Sure is easy to grouse from the power seat when you're literally risking nothing.

I stormed out, as well as one can on crutches, and limped across the courtyard, found my parents, inhaled a barbecue-tofu sub, and played one round of squirt-water-in-the-clown's-mouth-to-blow-up-a-balloon before we took off. I pumped and pumped, wanting nothing more than for that balloon to explode in the clown's dumb, laughing face. It never did.

"**S**omeone's in a good mood," Mom observes, as I'm silly-dancing around the house. "Anything you want to let me in on?"

"I have a date," I say, just wanting to share it with somebody.

Mom, startled by my sudden honesty, slides into a chair and pats the one next to her for me to join her. "Really? With whom?"

I electric slide over to her, grinning. "Just a girl at school," I say. (I won't be giving Audrey's name and hearing what I know will come next, especially after the Mixer.)

Mom seems genuinely surprised. "Well, that's lovely, sweetie."

"What, you didn't think I have game?"

"No, I know you have *game*," she says. "Somebody has a date," she announces when Dad comes in for some water.

"Way to go," he says. Probably because he doesn't know what else to say.

After dinner and watching a leg of *The Amazing Race* on TV with my parents, I head to my room to plan what I intend to be the date of Audrey's lifetime. Man, I wish I could drive so we could go into Nashville and not have to be limited to the offerings in Genesis. I've got to think of the best place to take her after the movie. Something fun and different, like Elks Lodge bingo. Or maybe I'll go classic, the Freezo for milkshakes and watching the planes take off and land by the regional airport. It needs to be perfect.

I'm researching movie times and restaurants and other fun things to do when Dad knocks on my bedroom door, pops his head in, and says somebody is here to see me. I shut my laptop, push it back on my desk, turn around to see Tracy looking far less chipper than she has been. I wonder if something happened between her and Mr. Crowell.

"Hey," I say, swiveling around in my chair.

She comes in, Dad closing the door behind her, and perches on the side of my bed.

"Looks like you were really mixing it up at the mixer," I say.

"We need to talk."

Which instantly freaks me out. "What?"

"I need you to stop communicating with Audrey."

"What the hell? No way," I say immediately. "I see her every day."

"YOU can see her," she says. "But not Drew."

"What do you mean?" I ask, knowing exactly what she means.

Trace screws up her mouth like she's disappointed in me. Which feels almost as bad as having my tendons torn from my ankle by Baron's cleat.

"What?" I snap, defiant now.

"We might need to go over that chapter in the *CB* together again," she says, "because maybe you missed it: you're not supposed to stay in touch with anybody as your previous V."

"I know," I respond, practically daring her to tell me I'm lying.

"Especially Audrey," she says. "The Council is still worried about her family's ties."

"You know Audrey's not an Abider!" I yell.

"*I* know that," she says, willing me to calm down. "But it's just one of those rules, I don't know what to say. And you know you can't date her or be anything more than friends, if that's where things are headed."

"What are you talking about?" I whine, my voice getting squeakier and squeakier, fending off tears. I feel so trapped and persecuted, like one of those nutso people in a movie who ends up screaming, *One day you'll all see the truth!* while being wheeled away in a straitjacket.

"Well, you were sort of *together* last year—"

"NO WE WEREN'T!"

Tracy purses her lips into a thin line. "Listen, just cut out the contact with her as Drew. It's not cricket, okay?"

"How do you know if I'm—"

"Just cut it out, okay?"

How does she know? Is the Council monitoring our every move, online and in person, just like Chase and Benedict say they are? Did getting caught hanging out with Chase get me put on some special list? Are they reading my Chronicles? Literally thought-policing? I mean, *whatthehell* is going on right now?

"I know you had the vision with her," Tracy adds somberly.

"So?"

"So . . . just don't push it," she says.

"We're just going out as friends." I'm not sure this sounds particularly credible, especially now.

"I know it doesn't seem like it, but trust me, I'm on your side," she says.

I don't want to tell her anything else because I feel betrayed. It seems like the only person who's truly there for me and always has been is Audrey, the very person I'm forbidden to be with.

Tracy hovers like there's more she wants to say until I sort of roll my eyes and she pats me on the knee, says, "Sorry," then leaves.

I can hear her whispering with my folks on the way out, but I can't make out what they're saying. I can't even tell whether my folks are in on it, or if Tracy has said it's Touchstone-Changer business or some ridiculousness. I hope it's the latter, because I can't deal with them all up in my personal life too. I wait, tense. But no one else comes to the door.

I open my laptop and log in as Drew. *Wrong user name/ password.*

I retype it the same way. Denied again.

I do this about ten more times before the system locks me out.

Dear Chronicles,
Today I hijacked the Central High PA system and made an impromptu broadcast to the whole school before the principal barged in, yanked away the microphone, and tossed me out of the booth. The speech went a little something like this:

> *Calling all the basic bitches . . . I have an announcement. You're basic.*
>
> *Also, there's this secret, ancient race of kids called Changers who transform into four different people during each of their four years of high school. Look around, kids! See that stud on the lacrosse team? He was that scrawny Puerto Rican kid whose harelip you made fun of last year. What about that girl you got to third base with this weekend behind the Yogli Mogli? She was a dude last year, a really hairy one! Oh, who am I? I'm Little Orphan Oryon, and I'm one of the Changer freaks who walk among you. I was that cheerleader girl Drew who your quarterback sexually assaulted last year! And then you decided I was a slut who asked for it. Hope everyone feels awesome about that because I know I totally did.*
>
> *Anyway, I just wanted you all to get the memo that your lives are puny and simple and we Changers are fundamentally better than the whole lot of you, but don't*

worry, we're here to walk you to your best selves, Oprah style, and lead you down the path of empathy and enlightenment.

P.S. For all you Changers in the audience right now, I'm totally going out with Chase. We are in love and getting married and getting it on ALL THE TIME. That's right. Changer-on-Changer action. Feel me? Oh, also, Audrey? You listening? I know you think I'm your potential new boyfriend, but I'm also your BFF from last year. Go ahead, quiz me. I'm Drew! And Oryon! I'm both! Best of both worlds, baby. And I've been lying to you since we met! Sorry. But them's the rules.

Oh yeah, and one more thing. Turner? You look stupid in those robes. In the many, we are . . . Who gives a shit? EMPATHY SUCKS!

[Sound of mic dropping.]

And ... twenty-four hours later, nothing happened.

After my last entry, neither Turner nor a representative of the Council nor Tracy, not even my parents, burst into my room flanked by a Changers SWAT team assembled to whisk me away to Changers jail for breaking every rule in the *CB*.

Maybe they aren't eavesdropping on my dear diary after all? I don't know precisely what's what, but I care less and less because in a matter of hours I have a date with Audrey. And being a Changer is the least of my worries.

Right now I just want to be a boy in love with a girl.

As simple and as complicated as that.

The love songs are right. Dreams do come true. They really, really, really do.

Take tonight. An enchanted, charmed night, where everything I've ever wished in my imagination would happen did happen, only better, because it was live and in person, and I was lifted so high and carried along so fast that gravity seemed somehow optional, and I swore my lungs were expanding in my chest to take in more air, more atmosphere, more everything, the world around me now so suddenly, completely, irreversibly wonderful that my body longed for nothing more than a way to inhale the entire thing.

In other words: it was my first real date with Audrey.

We talked about everything. Okay, not everything. But sharing with her came so naturally, and I don't think it's because I've known her more than a year. I think it's because we are good together. We fit. Boy, do we fit.

This is made irrefutable when, after dinner, we decide to bail on the movie so we can keep hanging out, and we walk to the outskirts of the community airport to watch the small planes take off and land. Audrey shoots me a look when I unroll a blanket, sort of bow saying, "M'lady," and gesture for her to make herself comfortable.

"Isn't this place called the kiss-and-cry?" she asks, head cocked.

"That's only when you are actually boarding a plane

167

and flying away into the sunset forever. Which is not in the plans. At least not yet."

She laughs. "I just don't want you to get any ideas."

"Oh, don't worry. I have no ideas at all. I am literally bereft of even the hint of an idea. Dr Pepper?" I ask, rooting around in my backpack for a can and the two cups I packed. Aud nods and I pour her a drink. "Here's to traveling to unexpected places." I lift my cup toward her.

"You sure like a toast," she says, tapping the lip of her cup to mine.

"Eye contact!" I chide. "No eye contact while toasting means bad sex for the next ten years!"

"I thought you said you didn't have any ideas."

I just grin and pop the dimples and try to look harmless and irresistible at the same time. "So, tell me about yourself. Are you an introvert? Do you like punk rock? Have you ever been in love?"

Audrey is quiet, then leans back on her elbows, almost completely prone, her hair hanging loose at the base of her neck, blowing side to side in the wind.

"Sometimes. Sometimes. Once, maybe."

"Wait, once to being in love?"

Another beat. "Yes."

"Who was he?" (I know, I'm an ogre.)

"It was a *she*," Audrey corrects, her skin pricking pink, I can see, even in the dusk.

"And what happened?"

"That's your only question?"

"What other question should there be?"

Aud rolls over onto her side, lowers her elbow, and at last relaxes. "You're all right, Oryon," she says.

"You're all right too, Audrey," I reply, but before I can

finish the thought, she leans in and plants a kiss on my mouth—technically our third, but it feels like our first, so markedly different from the fumbling, desperate, insecure kisses we shared when I was Drew.

She pulls back quickly, looks into the sky.

I swallow hard, clear my throat. "I lied," I murmur.

She turns her face back to mine, stern.

"I *do* have an idea." I gently grab her shirt collar and pull her toward me, cupping her cheek with my other hand until our lips meet again, soft and lingering, just barely overlapping, like clouds.

And there we stay. Connected. Together. No Changer vision haunting me. No audience at all beyond the odd tiny airplane circling above in the blue oblivion. I feel right. And happy. Nothing else. And I wonder how any of this could be wrong in any universe—mine, hers, the Changers Council's, even Michelle Hu's multitudes.

"This is weird," Audrey says after about ten minutes of kissing (not crying).

"Sorry?"

"It's weird because it's not weird, you know?"

And I do know. I feel exactly the same way. And I tell her as much, and we kiss some more, and then, only after the sky darkens and the blue bleeds to black, do we finally roll up the blanket and gather our cups and walk slowly away from the airfield, our fingers linked at the pinkies, arms swaying as if weightless.

After her father picked her up from the front of the cinema, where he assumed we'd been for the last couple hours, I flew home, actually flew, on the wings of freaking love, and called Chase to tell him I'd broken the rules, gotten romantic with Audrey again.

"And?" he half-groans.

"I'm worried. Won't I get in trouble?"

"For what? Being human?" he laughs it off. "Screw the Council. They are trying to hold sand in their fists. You can't control people, or feelings, or desire."

No kidding.

"They say they're protecting the Statics. But they're really protecting themselves and their agenda, whatever that is. I say good for you, you little rebel."

"It wasn't about any of that," I try.

"Every action has consequences, Drew-ryon."

And I think, *He's probably right*. And then I realize, *I don't care*.

If the world ends tomorrow, it will have been worth it. To know she loved me once.

To hope she might love me again.

WINTER

"Love," Mr. Crowell intones. Then falls silent. Like, for a long time. As in, everybody (even Chloe, working her best RBF) starts fidgeting anxiously.

"Hard to sit with the concept when it's right in your face, isn't it?" Mr. Crowell continues after (I swear!) two full minutes of silently staring down each of us on the editorial board. "What is love?" he asks, pointing directly at Aaron, then at me, then Audrey, then Amanda (who is rocking an awesome gold-and-silver handmade duct-tape headband, btw). "Thoughts?"

Chloe thrusts up a hand, starts talking before Mr. Crowell manages to call on her: "Love means never having to say you're sorry."

"Okay, but—"

"If you can't love yourself, how are you going to love anybody else?" she interrupts.

Aaron laughs, practically choking on the cinnamon toothpick he's chewing.

"I'm thinking less cliché, more soul, more depth. What does it mean to love and be loved?" Mr. Crowell poses, gently redirecting Chloe. (Sometimes I think he might be the most generous, patient person on the planet.) Then he goes on: "I don't expect you to give me an answer right away. I mean, you're all just barely starting down this path of life, which, by the way, I hope will be filled with great and varied loves." Which sounds vaguely Changers speak, if you ask me. Maybe he and Tracy have been reading chapters of *The Changers Bible* back and forth to each other over tea and crumpets.

"Above all else, love and our capacity to love is what makes us human," he says, a slight crack in his voice. "That's why the theme for the Spring issue of the *Peregrine Review* is going to be *love*."

Chloe perks up in her chair, saucily uncrosses and then crosses her legs, trying to get Mr. Crowell's attention. He doesn't register her. Aaron, I notice, is (like me) staring straight ahead at the blank chalkboard. If I were a betting man, I'd say the image of Danny hanging out in Atlanta with every cute guy under the age of twenty-five is flashing through Aaron's head, though he doesn't betray anything. I'm trying to appear even half as cool when Audrey calmly, slowly swivels her head around like a meerkat popping out of its hole and bores her captivating, round, glimmery eyes into my soul.

Sigh.

That face. I missed that face over the seemingly interminable winter break. We talked only what, two or three times during the entire vacation? And briefly at that. Her folks made her go to some family reunion thing in Ohio or Iowa or some other state comprised mostly of vowels. She was never alone.

Blink blink. She looks so cute, slow-blinking at me, I can barely focus on what Mr. Crowell is saying about the many forms of love, which incidentally, I'm full up on, thank you very little. Audrey's been almost all I can think about for weeks—okay, for more than a year. She seems different today, though I can't nail down precisely how. She's calm. Looser. We haven't really talked much about what we "are" after this period of what do you call it, *hanging out* over the last couple months: just this amorphously though undeniably close boy-girl friendship with lots of attraction and feelings swirling around, plus kissing (when possible), heavy petting (as the adults call it), and ever so slowly making our way around the bases.

Never kiss and tell, Nana always advised. Something I didn't understand until now. Which is why there's been little need or desire for Chronicling, lest every day be filled with the one word and one word alone that has been on my mind and likely embedded in my Chronicling chip all fall long: *Audrey. Audrey, Audrey, Audrey, Audrey, Audrey.*

Audrey.

And they called it puppy love. Oh I guess they'll never know how a young heart really feels and why I love her so . . .

Speaking of Nana's adages and her favorite butterfly-collared, dreamy singer Donny Osmond, it was really rough visiting her down in Florida over break. We all jumped in the car as soon as school let out and drove the ten hours to her condo. There, we ate many dinners at Applebees in between doctors appointments, interviews with home-care givers, tours of assisted-living facilities, and whispery debates between Mom and Dad about "bringing her home" with us.

There had been talk of maybe going down to Orlando for a day or two of roller coaster riding, but Nana wasn't feeling up for it, so basically I spent two weeks watching vintage horror movies on Netflix, or skating alone around an abandoned strip mall until a security guard would inevitably show up, make the open-palm universal *halt* sign, and say, "There's no skating here" (unknowingly quoting one of my favorite Lupe Fiasco songs).

I also took a lot of long, solo evening walks on the beach

with Snoopy, just like I did the year before when I was Drew, only this time nobody was grotesquely ogling my beach body or talking to me without my permission. It was just me and my dog and the murmur of the waves, as if I were shooting a pharmaceutical commercial for a drug that gave me the ability to go for hours without having to pee, or hike across the constantly caving sand free of joint pain.

Anyway, it was a little disconcerting and heartrending that half the time I was at Nana's she wasn't sure she knew who the black kid lounging around her condo and getting lemonade out of the refrigerator was. Dad kept explaining to her loudly, "This is Ethan. He was Drew. Now he's Oryon," over and over like a "Changers for Dummies" seminar. I'd catch Nana looking at me funny, as though she couldn't think of the right word for something and was searching deep in the recesses of her mind for it—and each time she did, I felt gutted.

Every day there was mounting evidence she was slipping away. Sometimes it was something as minor as her dropping a spoon and all of us hearing it clatter to the floor, but then watching her search for it on the table a few seconds later. Or, her shakily holding the television remote control, bracelets tinkling, while simultaneously asking me, "Where's that blasted remote?"

I love Nana so much. I can't deal with the thought of losing her. So I'm just putting it out of my mind. Mom and Dad kept insisting she's "strong as an ox," and "gonna be around bugging us for years to come," though every time they said so, it sounded more like hope instead of fact. One day over break when Mom and Dad were out at a nursing home tour, Nana and I watched *The Price Is Right* together, which we always did when I was younger (arguing over numbers, which she was inevitably correct about because of course she knew from actual shopping experience how much a can of chunk light tuna or toilet bowl cleaner cost).

"I wonder," she said suddenly during a commercial break between Showcase Showdowns, while the volume was muted, "what life would've been like had I chosen Chase."

My head snapped around to where she was sitting on her green leather leisure chair. "As your Mono? As your Static partner?" I asked, frantic.

Nothing.

"Who's Chase, Nana?" I prompted. "Were *you* Chase?"

"But love makes you do funny things, Drew—I mean, sorry, Ethan," she said, reaching for the remote control because her show was coming back on. "Ooooh! A red Ford Fiesta!"

"Nana," I shouted over the bespectacled host barking into the long, thin microphone, "what kind of funny things? Who did you love? What did you do?"

But she didn't say anything else besides, "I love *you*, sweetie!" and then laughed her old-lady laugh and nodded in the direction of the TV screen.

During the *Peregrine* meeting, Mr. Crowell handed me and Audrey the joint assignment that's going to be the main feature anchoring the love-themed issue. We're supposed to find and meet with about a dozen people "of all walks of life"—gay people, straight people, bisexual people, old people, young people, monogamous people, married people, unmarried people, people who have multiple relationships, people who've never even had one relationship—and ask them what love means to them. Get details from their lives, hopes for their future relationships, regrets about their pasts, just like Barbara Walters before she stopped being a journalist and started sitting around that table with all those shrieking women.

We are meant to get all this interviewing done in the next few weeks, so we can start compiling, shaping, and editing the copy, not to mention taking Amanda around to photograph portraits of the people who end up being in our final submission. Which is a truckload of work and means, YES, more "official" time to spend with Audrey that her parents can't cock-block, like they have been doing since the minute she laid eyes on me as Oryon. Thank you, Mr. Crowell! A box of chocolates is on the way.

Mr. Crowell was the first person we asked to speak with for our story. He was sheepish, but he couldn't exactly say no to letting us practice by answering a few of our questions, when the assignment was his bright idea in the first place.

We met at Starbucks after school, Audrey with blank notebook and pen in hand, me with a preliminary set of questions that we had brainstormed during the rest of our lit mag activity while Chloe was frenetically scribbling lines for a set of twelve love sonnets she insisted she contribute to the issue.

"What's the first thing you ever loved?" I ask Mr. Crowell soon as he sets his herbal tea on the small round table between us. Audrey is at attention, pen hovering above her notebook, another pen cutely tucked behind her ear (in case what? the other pen runs away?).

"That's a great question! My mother, probably. But as a child, I remember loving my plastic Digger the Dog toy; it walked when you pulled a string."

"When was the last time you were in love?" I ask, while

Aud flips to the next page of her notebook with a flourish. Mr. Crowell blanches. His tea bag, half-hanging over the rim of his cup, drip-drips pale green water on the glass surface beneath it, the liquid creeping its way toward his cell phone. "Well, uh, uh . . ." he stammers, absently poking a finger into the puddle.

Am I supposed to keep asking, or just listen, or—

"You could say somewhat recently," he finally lands on, after about ten uncomfortable seconds.

Audrey quickly jots down every word he says.

"I think it'll go better if you two use a tape recorder moving forward," he eagerly redirects, pointing to Audrey's notebook. "I'll try to get a loaner from the music library, or we might have some funds to purchase one for the club."

It feels like he knows that I know something that Audrey doesn't. Like about Tracy. I could be reading into it, but maybe not. As if on cue, his cell phone buzzes; he looks at it, his face sort of softening before he silences the text and wrestles the phone into his front jeans pocket.

"And?" I prompt.

"Well, when you meet someone special," he says, uncomfortably, "you just know."

Audrey finishes getting these momentous words down and looks up at me. We try not to betray our shared embarrassment, my face going hot.

"I think we should perhaps focus more on prepping you for your other subjects," Mr. Crowell suggests authoritatively, completely shaking the former business off. "My silly ramblings about love aren't going to end up in the magazine, so let's talk about the questions and techniques that are going to yield the best results for your story."

Note to self: call Tracy and tell her dude is IN LOVE with her.

Today Audrey and I met for our first interviews. We lined up four subjects for our love project, and after chai lattes and biscuits at the Dis'n'Dat Café, we made our way through town, meeting and questioning people about the most intimate details of their romantic lives, something that if you'd told Ethan he'd be doing with his only free day of the week, he would have assumed he'd lost a bet. And yet, here I was, gleefully living in my own Wilson Phillips music video.

We started with Miss Jeannie, the registration lady, who as it turns out lives in a modest ranch house a few blocks from school. When we rang the bell it played a few bars of "Grandma Got Run Over by a Reindeer." Miss Jeannie answered right away, her hair teased high, perfume thick enough to smell through the door. She'd put on bright pink lipstick and was wearing slacks and a shiny turquoise blouse, clearly flattered to have been asked to participate in the journal and talk about her life; it made me feel bad about all the times I'd mentally written her off as a dumb hillbilly.

"Come meet Red!" she gushed, waving us in like we were Matt Lauer and Diane Sawyer.

Red was in the basement, bent over a sawhorse table working on his model plane collection. He looked ex-military, which it turns out he is, as well as a former English teacher at Central prior to Mr. Crowell, until he started going deaf and was forced to retire.

"You think we got something interesting to say, son?" he shouted, shaking my hand with a death grip.

"I think everyone has an interesting story if you ask the right questions," I answered as loudly as I could without being insulting, trying not to grimace as my knuckles compressed.

"Well then, you best ask the right questions. Right, little lady?" He smiled now and turned his attention to Audrey, whose hands were trembling slightly, I noticed.

We learned that Jeannie and Red had been married forty-two years. That her parents didn't approve of Red because he was a bit older, but that Jeannie didn't care "a hoot" what they thought, and the two ran off and eloped. Though they wanted children and tried for years to have them, "it wasn't in God's plan," and they both took jobs in the school system so they could be around kids all day, every day.

"I feel like I've gotten to watch hundreds of kids grow up," Miss Jeannie said, trying not to sound sad. She dug around in her sideboard and fished out a photograph of her and Red on their honeymoon in Canada, fishing, him pretending to have caught her on his line. In the picture they are both glassy-eyed from laughing, so thin and young, almost as young as Audrey and me.

We chatted nearly an hour, Miss Jeannie serving us a snack of homemade snickerdoodles and milk. Right before we left, Audrey gave Miss Jeannie a hug, and though it was against school policy, Miss Jeannie hugged her back.

"Wow," Audrey exhaled as we walked away. "You think you know a person, and then you dig under one layer and a completely new person is revealed." I nod vigorously, too vigorously perhaps. "Is it wrong that I now kind of love Miss Jeannie?"

"So long as she isn't the *only* person you love," I joke, regretting it immediately.

Audrey pretends she didn't hear me, and we walk to our next interview, this one with a local lesbian folk singer named Annie Way—whom we read about on a flyer taped to the local coffee house bulletin board. We arranged to meet her in the park, and Audrey's face falls as soon as she notices that Annie didn't bring her guitar.

"What's up, beautiful people?" Annie hollers as we approach. "Pop a squat, and let's get to know each other."

Annie is funny and kind and brash and political. She reminds me of Chase, without the anger and the bulging quadriceps. We talk about civil rights and why she believes everyone should have the right to marry, and how when her best friend died in a car crash, his partner was unable to be at his bedside when he passed away, because they weren't legally wed.

"Messed up, right?" she says, not really asking.

I can tell Audrey is thinking about Aaron, and what would happen if Danny got sick or injured, and I can see her social-injustice wheels spinning like tops, wanting to make everything fair in a world that can never be. "Totally," she says, jaw tight.

"Well, you kids can be the change you want to see in the world," Annie suggests, giving me a playful punch on the shoulder. "Speak your truth, and you can't go wrong."

It's not that simple, Annie, I think.

Audrey and Annie exchange e-mail addresses as we get up to leave, Audrey eager to join her at the next rally for marriage equality, something I'm certain Jason and her folks will never allow her to attend if they get wind of it. But it moves me that she still tries, that she still reaches for the world outside of the bubble they keep her in, even if she can't break free just yet.

"I have a great idea!" Audrey says as Annie waves good-bye and disappears over a grassy knoll.

"You want to do a fundraising concert for Annie's best friend's partner?"

"What? No. But that *is* an awesome plan. What I was actually thinking is that we should interview each other's parents!" She beams. "We're learning so much about all these different people. Wouldn't it be cool to uncover the same depth in our own families? To put aside what we think we know and allow ourselves to be surprised? To actually change our minds about someone?"

"It is a killer idea . . ." I begin, knowing I need to dissuade her from this line of thinking without seeming like I'm crapping all over her plan. "But we already have our schedule set today."

"So we'll do it the next round. It'll be awesome!"

There are so many things about it that would not be awesome that I can't even slow my brain down enough to count them all. I wrinkle my nose, searching, searching, searching for a way to derail this train. Audrey takes in my wary expression.

"Oh my god. You don't want me to meet your foster parents," she blurts, looking like she's been slapped in the face.

"That's not it."

"Then what is it?" she presses, roughly wiping away what look like tears.

"My folks aren't super social."

"Right."

"It's complicated. But it has nothing to do with you, I promise." This, like most everything I tell Audrey, is not

183

strictly the truth. But I can't exactly say, *My parents suspect you and your family of being part of a cult that wants to exterminate people like me and, also, your thug brother tried to rape me last year.*

"Forget it. It was a dumb idea anyway." She turns so I can't see her face. "Let's just go talk to the dry cleaner like we planned."

"Audrey . . ."

"They're recent immigrants. That will be cool to learn about."

"Audrey, stop."

"I get it, Oryon. You're ashamed of me. I would be too. I mean . . . my family, they aren't sophisticated like yours probably is. My brother is a nightmare. And I know how you feel about my church. We're just not the right sort of people. It's fine. Moving on."

I grab her hand and pull her close to me. I wrap both arms around her midsection and squeeze her tight to my chest. "Audrey. You are exactly the right sort of person for me."

Her body slackens, she presses her forehead into my shoulder.

"You just have to trust me when I tell you this has nothing to do with you," I continue. "And maybe someday, when things are different, I'll be able to tell you everything. But for now, I just can't. And I'm sorry. But know this: shame is the opposite of how I feel about you. If you'd let me, I'd tell the entire world that you were my girl."

Audrey sniffles, then rears back her head.

"Let's not get crazy," she says, her blotchy-cry face breaking into a weak grin.

On the way to the dry cleaner's, I tell her I'm taking her on an extra-special Friday-night date. She agrees, with the condition that I meet her parents first, something they're insisting on if I am going to spend time with their baby girl. After what just went down, I can't really decline, so I say, "Sure thing," and we plan a midweek dinner at Chez Alleged Abider, a place I've been to before, but never like this. I feel like the proverbial Trojan horse. Also, nervous as hell.

Though it's hard, I'm sticking with my plan to keep my relationship with Audrey on the DL from my parental units. It's our own secret affair, nobody's business but hers and mine, certainly not Tracy's or my folks', who'd only worry that I was putting myself into a dangerous situation and breaking Changer rules. More to the point, why should I have to spill all the gory details about my private romance? Audrey has only ever been guilty by association, she's never been anything but amazing to me and everybody else, and I'm sick of people speculating about her loyalties because her brother is a tyrant and her parents are possibly, maybe Abider sympathizers. Audrey is my business. I have this under control. And if that necessitates some mild duplicity on my part, well, welcome to Teenage Drama Island. All kids lie. At least I'm lying for a good reason.

Thankfully, DJ has agreed to be my chauffeur and cover for the night. "I gotcha," he said when I asked if he minded helping me out. And that was it. No prolonged inquiry. I'm feeling DJ more and more these days. Male friendship, man. So much simpler than the byzantine web girls weave where you never know what's a trap until you walk into it and that sticky stuff gets caught in your hair.

For my meet-the-'rents hour of power I wear nice black skate pants, a white button-down, and a bow tie, which, on second thought, I remove just in case Audrey's folks mistake me for a member of some other religion that freaks their business out. I opt for a more traditional long tie, and knot it loosely at the top, leaving the first button undone.

On the way over I pick up some tulips for her mom and a box of truffles for dessert, the kind with a glittery ribbon around the box and the writing in liquid gold. When I get back in the car, DJ gives me a once-over and snickers. "You proposing?"

"Well, it *is* the South," I joke.

DJ laughs and says, "I hope you've got your running shoes on, case her brother objects at the ceremony."

"I was kind of hoping you'd come in with me — you know, as backup," I say, half serious.

"I think that might be two black people too many. But I'll say a little prayer on your behalf. Not that you need it."

"Don't I?"

"Nah. That girl is all about Oryon. I haven't seen a chick that happy since, well, since every chick I've ever gone out with, but you know what I'm saying."

I try to swallow my grin, saying nothing for the rest of the ride, which isn't that hard as DJ launches into a monologue about his next spoken-word event and how he wants to reinvent the genre, really shake up the whole paradigm, wake people up to the reality of race. "We are NOT a post-race culture, and anyone who believes that B.S. is either white, stupid, or both."

I don't disagree. If you learn anything as a Changer, it's that all the supposedly bygone stereotypes and prejudices are far from bygone. But tonight my mind is fixated exclusively on Audrey, and impressing her parents, whom, sure, I've already met, but not as a boy, a boy who wants to, ahem, date their daughter.

"Have fun storming the castle!" DJ yells as he drops me off, giving me the thumb/pinkie *call me* sign as he drives away.

I stand alone in the doorway, breathing deep to calm my nerves, testing my breath in my palm. I'm sniffing the cupped hot air when suddenly the door opens and Audrey and her mother and father are all standing there, squashed together like a pack of Twizzlers. Her parents eye me with transparent uncertainty, neither saying a word until Audrey nudges her mom and she snaps to and says, "You must be Oreo-on."

"Oryon, yes, so nice to meet you," I gently correct, extending the same hand I just blew my possibly stinky breath into. "These are for you." I push the tulips and chocolates in her direction, and Audrey coos beside her like she's just been handed a puppy.

"My, aren't you a thoughtful young man," her mom says, embracing the flowers and truffles and finally moving aside to make a sliver of room for me to cross the threshold. Her father is still sizing me up, and I turn to shake his hand but he swivels at the last second and avoids it, pretending not to have seen my outstretched palm—a Jason move if ever I've seen one. I guess the bigot doesn't fall too far from the tree.

The dinner was about what I expected. Stilted and knotty, with a side order of WTF. I tried to talk football with her dad, but he wasn't really interested in anything I had to say beyond my intentions with Audrey. It hit me halfway through the meal (which was delicious, by the way: creamed corn, fried catfish, tomato, cucumber, and onion salad—Abiders or not, Aud's mama can cook) that I was her first official boyfriend. And as such, they were none too pleased to see a black kid walk through the door, let alone one that (supposedly) cost Central an undefeated season. Her mom did her best to be welcoming, but it was in that Southern way where I could tell every time she said, "Bless his heart," what she really meant was, *Why in tarnation of all the boys on God's green earth did my baby girl have to pick this one?*

There was a moment as I was babbling on nervously about the *Peregrine Review* project and the meaning of love when Aud's mom sucked in her cheeks, tilted her head to Audrey, and whispered, "He's so *articulate*." All I could think was, *I cannot wait to tell this to DJ.*

Aside from that, the meal went as well as could be expected, at least until Jason burst onto the scene, just back from the gym, where I can only imagine his grunts of exertion could be heard in outerspace.

"Are you kidding me?" he snapped as soon as he saw me at the table.

"Jason, I believe you already know our guest," his mother tried. "Would you like to join us for some peach cobbler?"

"I just lost my appetite," he snarled, probably quoting a line he'd heard in some action movie.

"I should be going anyway," I say, rising and taking care to fold my napkin and set it beside my plate.

"Gots to catch the bus, right, brother?" Jason sneers. "Where do you live at again?"

"I'll walk him out!" Audrey squeals, leaping from her chair and rushing to the door. I nod to her father, shake her mother's hand again, and thank them for a "truly delectable meal." Aud's mother flushes and smiles shyly, and I can see in her where Audrey's sweetness must have sprung from before life and circumstance tamped it down into so much dust.

"Five minutes!" Audrey's father shouts behind us as we shut the front door.

"You were amazing," Aud gushes as soon as we're alone. She leans in for a kiss.

I back away. "Are you crazy? Not the time or the place. They're probably spying through the peephole."

"I don't care," she says, breaking into a daffy soft-shoe on the welcome mat. "My mama liked you, I could tell."

"Well, there's one for the plus column."

"Her opinion is the only one that matters. To me, anyhow. My dad is probably just relieved I'm not a lesbian."

"So a black boyfriend trumps a white girlfriend?"

"Depends on the day." She grins, leans in again, whispers thickly into my ear, "Come on, kiss me."

"Get a room!" It's DJ, pulling up just in time after getting my earlier text from the john.

"Against all odds, I had fun," I tell Audrey, giving her a chaste peck on the cheek. She stays in the doorway until we drive out of sight, waving as her outline shrinks and shrinks the farther we go, until she dissolves into a colorful bouncy speck.

"Well?" DJ asks. "You survive?"

"I did."

"All the fish in the sea, you gotta hook the one whose brother literally tried to stomp a mud hole in you? You must really love that girl to put up with that house of crazy."

"Everyone's house is crazy in some way."

"Not like that," he counters, and we both bust out laughing.

"Don't worry, this story is gonna have a happy ending," I say.

"How do you know?"

"I've seen it," I say—though as I say it, I remember that a happy ending isn't what I saw at all.

CHANGE 2—DAY 140

I'm shopping at ReRunz for bowling shirts, when Chase spies me and lumbers over, his arms full of denim vests.

"What's up, my man?" he says. "In the market for an eighties throwback acid-wash?" He tilts his head toward the top of his denim haul, a nearly white, frayed-edged vest with a Def Leppard patch sewn crookedly on the corner.

"I'm looking for something with a little less gonorrhea," I say, using a single finger to push the pile of grody denim away. "Got any bowling shirts?"

"For?" Chase asks.

"Got a date," I say, unable to control the smile breaking across my face.

"Ah. *Le affair*," Chase mumbles with a marked lack of enthusiasm.

"I'm taking her to karaoke night at the Bowl-Me-Over in Nashville on Friday," I keep on, even though it is clear Chase can't be bothered with the details. I make my way toward the rack of vintage button-downs. *Bingo*: I spot a row of old bowling shirts.

"You know, we could really use some extra bodies down at RaChas HQ these days," he starts in, as I flick through the shirts. "Don't know if you've heard, but a kid from my old high school disappeared over the weekend—nobody's seen him since. Benedict's received some intelligence that he's been abducted and taken to an Abider reprogramming facility somewhere south of here."

"That sucks," I say, pulling out a dark blue short-sleeved shirt with *Bud* baroquely stitched in yellow over the heart, and *AGRESTO'S STEAK HOUSE* silk-screened on the back. It's probably the softest fabric I've ever felt. "Maybe he ran away?"

"Not likely. Dude, it's getting so bad that Turner and the Council are even asking for some help intercepting communications. So we've got some recon missions planned this weekend, and we need man power."

I shrug on the shirt. "I've got plans, obviously," I say, checking myself out in the mirror beside us. It fits me perfectly. Now I just have to find one for Audrey.

"Really?" Chase chides, coming and standing directly behind me in the mirror, his body easily twice my size. "We're planning a counterrevolution and all you're worried about is bowling?"

"I'm also worried about Skee-Ball," I respond. But Chase isn't laughing. I step away from the reflection, grab a maroon shirt, pull it out, see *John* embroidered on the pocket, put it back. "Dude, I thought you understood. Not that long ago, you were all up with my breaking the Changers rules, calling me a rebel."

"Rebel lite," he corrects.

I keep sorting through the rack in front of me, where I spy a hot-pink bowling shirt with the name *Flo* stitched on the front above a black poodle wearing red lipstick. It looks like it will fit Audrey perfectly. "I don't know, man. I'm just not sure some trumped-up revolution is where I want to be spending my energy. I need to focus on *positive* elements in my life right now."

"What you need to focus on is the future. Your future, *our* future," Chase says, "instead of getting in that girl's panties."

"Screw you," I shoot back, ripping the shirt off the rack. I suddenly want to punch him. Like, hard—and right in his smug face.

He puffs up his chest a little, crosses his arms, squares up in front of me. "Screw me? Screw *you*."

Is he daring me to come at him or something? Because that's clearly not what I'm going to do, especially not with bowling shirts draped over my arm like I'm the maître d' of towels. I step back, take a deep breath. "Listen, no offense to you or your mission, but life's finally good. I'm happy. Someone seems to love me. I might even love myself a little bit." I pause before deciding to really go for it: "And as you know intimately, that's not something that happens to me much."

Chase uncrosses his arms and sighs.

"It might be nice to talk about stuff like we used to," I say when he stays silent. "You know, stuff that doesn't involve Abiders and RaChas and the breakdown of society and my presumed higher purpose."

Chase cocks his head exaggeratedly. "What's more important than the fact that you're being a traitor to your race?" he poses in what seems like all seriousness, but can't actually be, can it? "You just enjoy your passing privilege. And let the rest of us worry about making the world safe for people like you to *love* yourself in the first place." He practically spits on the word *love*. It feels like a knee to the groin.

"What do you want from me?" I growl, feeling stupid now about the bowling, about my happiness, about everything that minutes ago seemed like it mattered. I struggle to catch a breath. "What do you freaking want, Chase?"

"I want you to wake up," he says with clear contempt. "There's a war going on, Oryon. And you don't even know you're on the front line."

Worst day as Oryon so far.

Second worst day of my entire life.

(Or maybe it's tied with my worst day as Drew. Jury still out on this one.)

Ethan? His worst day was probably dropping his swirly rainbow lollipop while riding a merry-go-round compared to this horror show.

Date night last night, right? I cared about little else all week. Planned everything to the nth degree, packed my backpack: the two vintage bowling shirts (laundered to get the funk of fifty million years out of them), a bottle of bubbly apple cider with two fancy plastic champagne flutes, two gothic-looking candlesticks I scored at the Salvation Army, and brand-new tall white candles to go in them. I even stuck a stick of deodorant into the bag so I could freshen up and change before Audrey's mom drove us into Nashville.

Aud had to go to a yearbook meeting, so I killed some time skating with the usual suspects who hang out at the strip mall after school. Jerry was there, as well as DJ (who can't shred but is writing some new poetry about the *utopia of the drop* or some shizz). There was also this hip fifties-looking throwback dude named Cal who's been filming us for these sick skate films he makes in different cities around the country. He was in the area for a couple weeks visiting his cousins, and asked me and Jerry to sign a release, which felt very Hollywood.

DJ and a couple friends were off to the side, him sitting on his board and them on bikes just shooting the bull or whatever, and Jerry and I kept attempting a grind off this high cinder-block wall and onto a handrail behind the Toot N Tote-um convenience store. I'd fallen about a dozen times, checking my watch between wipe-outs for five o'clock when I could meet up with Audrey.

I tell Cal to start recording because I'm going to stick this next one . . . which I do. Spectacularly. DJ launches off his board, shrieks, "Sexxxyyy!" and comes hopping over, patting me on the top of my head in celebration.

"Did you get it?" I shout to Cal, breathless, as he gets up and dusts off his stiff jeans and crisp white T-shirt, resmoothing an errant strand of hair into his always on-point pompadour.

He nods, like he knows exactly where that clip is going to go in his next film.

Jerry comes over, slaps my hand too. "Sweet. I'm parched." He nods toward the convenience store doors, where these three kids I vaguely recognize from our school just entered, rowdy in the way teenagers always seem to get on Friday afternoons.

So Jerry, DJ, and I go inside the Toot N Tote-um, which is packed with about twenty kids from school, all running amok, some squirting fake runny cheese over stale corn chips, others serving themselves Coke and cherry Icees, others trying to convince older people to buy them cigarettes and chaw. I head for the cooler, grab an orange Gatorade for me, a blue one for Jerry, tossing it to him soon as he rounds the corner already munching from a bag of spicy Cheetos. DJ is scanning the electronics aisle for a charger for his cell.

I gulp down half the bottle, and it splashes on the front

of my T-shirt, but I've got a clean white undershirt and the bowling shirt to change into, so I just keep chugging. I'm reviewing everything in my head, checking if I have everything I need, and then it dawns on me that I forgot a lighter for the candles. So I head over to the checkout counter, sort through the lighters beside the register. There are red ones, blue ones, yellow ones, and of course the ever-popular around these parts camo-colored lighters, because a lighter is definitely something you want to have to search really hard for when you need it.

"He'll take this one," DJ says, plucking a Confederate flag lighter from a different carton and adding it to my pile of items. He smirks at the cashier, his oversized *Only Tupac Can Judge Me* T-shirt on full display beneath his unzipped hoodie. The dudes from our school leave then, along with three girls who had been eating in the store. They make a giant racket, pushing one another, tossing food back and forth, generally being obnoxious. Even the girls. The clerk squints at them while beginning to ring me up.

"You must be eighteen to buy cigarettes," he says in a thick Indian accent, but doesn't even look at me.

"I don't want any cigarettes," I say, puzzled.

His eyes dart toward a different group of kids, Icees splattering on the linoleum tile beneath the machine. "Dennis!" he calls to the bored-looking kid in an apron who works in the store. "Mop in beverages!"

I pay for all my things, including Jerry's Gatorade (because I owe him one), and then stuff the lighter into my backpack, plus the Hershey's bars I tossed into the pile at the last minute, in the event Audrey wanted a little chocolate with her "champagne."

Behind me DJ pays for his charger, tucks it into the

pocket of his hoodie, and we walk out, Jerry trailing close behind, skipping his board on the ground with every other step, like a cane.

"So what you got on tap tonight?" DJ asks knowingly, digging into Jerry's Cheetos. "Or should I ask, *who* you gonna tap tonight?"

"Suck it," I say.

"Bet you'd like to say that to *her*," DJ counters.

"I don't know how you landed Audrey Stewart," Jerry chimes in. "I thought she dug chicks."

"*My milkshake brings all the girls to the yard,*" I start singing, and DJ punches me hard in the shoulder. I check my watch. "I gotta split!"

It is then that I spot over DJ's shoulder the dude from the Toot N Tote-um running out of the store, yelling, "You stole! You stole!" He's pointing at me and DJ.

We start laughing.

"What?" DJ asks, like, *This has got to be a joke.*

"Let me see what's in your pockets," the guy demands. "I called the police."

"I'm not showing you what's in my pockets," DJ says. "I just paid you."

"You with him," he says, pointing to me. "Open your backpack."

Which I reflexively start doing.

DJ grabs my arm to stop me. "Excuse me, but we just paid two minutes ago," he says, completely reasonably.

"I called the police," the guy says, the kid working for him now appearing behind him with a sheepish expression.

"This is crazy. You saw, we just paid, right?" DJ says loud and clear to the kid, who grimaces weakly like, *I just work here, bro.*

Another rowdy group of kids blasts out of the store, and the clerk goes running back toward them. "Did you pay?" He seems really stressed.

DJ starts walking back toward where we were skating, where Cal's setting up another shot on a tripod. "Come on."

I follow. So does Jerry.

Then the clerk comes out again, yelling, "Stay right there!" but we keep walking.

"This is some SWB shit," DJ says, shaking his head.

"What's that?" Jerry asks, slapping his board down and giving a little pump.

"Shopping while black," DJ explains flatly.

Jerry laughs, and I'm about to laugh too, because it seems like I'm supposed to be in on the joke, but next thing I know, a police cruiser has screeched up in front of us, blocking our way, with the clerk closing in on us from the rear.

"What seems to be the problem?" the first officer asks jovially as he gets out of the passenger seat. He must be Good Cop.

DJ is about to respond, but the clerk interrupts, "These boys shoplifted from my store, look in their backpacks."

"I didn't take anything, sir," I try.

The second cop comes around the other side of the cruiser, looking mean, hand resting on his pistol. And this must be Bad Cop.

"Search his pockets," the clerk commands, indicating DJ.

"Here we go," DJ says to me, looking aggravated now. He turns toward the cop, talking as calmly as he can. "Sir, there must be some confusion. We paid for our purchases. There were about ten other kids in the shop, and I saw one of them pocket two beers and some chaw."

"There's no need to start pointing fingers, son," Good

Cop says, eyeing our boards and clothes like they might spring to life and bite him on the face.

"There's need to clarify if there is some confusion, sir," DJ says pragmatically.

"Over there, move it!" Bad Cop barks at him, indicating the front end of the police car. "You too, the other side," he adds, pointing me over.

I comply, terrified. I feel like I could pee my pants.

"Let's see what's in the bag."

I take my backpack off, hand it to Good Cop, who places it on the hood of the car and starts unzipping the top.

"Sir," DJ shouts, "I can verify that I watched him pay for all that!"

"Son, that's enough," Good Cop says to DJ. "Now place both your palms on the vehicle. Leave them there until I say you can move."

Cal comes over palming his large camera and starts discretely shooting the action as Good Cop yanks things out of my bag: two Hershey's bars, the flag lighter, deodorant, breath mints, the bottle of apple cider.

"Quite a haul here," Good Cop says, now onto the champagne glasses and, finally, the bowling shirts, which I'd carefully rolled up, tying Audrey's with a red bow. He unwraps the shirts, holds Audrey's up, eyes the front and back suspiciously, then tosses it into a pile on top of my shirt, further down the hood. He spots Cal. "Turn that off now or I'm confiscating it!" he snaps, roughly pushing the camera down. Cal steps back, reluctantly clicks the off button.

"Are these items from your store?" Bad Cop asks the clerk, waving at the contents on the hood.

He nods. "Everything but the glasses. And the bottle . . . and the candlesticks."

Good Cop turns to me as if resting his case, while Bad Cop has moved on to pawing through DJ's hoodie pockets.

"Uh, excuse me, sirs?" Jerry interrupts from aside. "I was with them, and I can vouch that we all just paid for our things and left." He sounds more upstanding than I've ever heard him, his stoner demeanor totally absent for the moment.

"Thank you for your input, but we've got this covered," Good Cop says.

Bad Cop produces the new cell charger from DJ's pocket, tosses it onto the hood with the rest of my things.

"I just *bought* that!" DJ says, his voice clipped, incredulous.

"It's true," I add, lackluster.

DJ is growing enraged, I can tell, his model-citizen approach breaking down, whereas I feel like I'm someplace else entirely, existing in a hypnagogic time-space-continuum hiccup, because the current circumstances are just too unreal to believe.

"Where's your receipt?" one of them asks.

"I didn't keep the receipt," I shrug.

"Where's *your* receipt?" to DJ.

"Where's yours?" he shouts.

It was no use. You could see the exact point at which both Good and Bad Cops had made up their minds.

Still, I yammered on frantically, over-explaining that I had a date in half an hour, and that's why I had all the stuff in my bag. That I wanted to have good breath, make it romantic, you know? We were going bowling. Both cops rolled their eyes at that.

"Why don't you check those white kids' pockets!" DJ yelled as he was being cuffed and shoved into the back of the police cruiser. The heavy door slammed shut with a jarring crunch. I was certain the same fate was coming for me, but tried to nut up and make confident eye contact with DJ through the window. He just tapped the crown of his head repeatedly against the seat divider in front of him.

Good Cop confiscated all my things, including my phone, my board, my belt (*why?*), and put me in handcuffs and told me to stand by the hood of the car. Then he crossed the parking lot to speak with the store owner out of earshot.

I tried to turn my head so that I could hear what the they were saying, but . . . nothing. The owner was gesticulating wildly, pointing back at the store, at me, at DJ. My legs started to shake in earthquake-like waves every few seconds; I couldn't stop them. After what seemed like a year but was probably only a few minutes, another police cruiser showed up, and Bad Cop came back over and guided me into the backseat of it.

"Am I getting arrested?" I asked before he closed the door.

"You're being detained under suspicion," he replied dully. "Your parents will be called when we get to the station." He slammed the door. And that's when I just let it go, tears pouring down uncontrollably.

The cruiser DJ was in started to leave, cutting a tight circle to pull onto the street, and as it did, I noticed the bowling shirts sliding off the hood into a puddle in the middle of the parking lot.

At the Genesis police precinct, I was asked to write down my name, address, birth date, and the names and phone numbers of my parents.

"They're my foster parents," I manage to remember to add, "but they're my legal guardians." This seems only to make me seem guiltier, being a castaway that nobody wants. Stumbling on remembering Oryon's birth date didn't help either.

Then I glance at the clock above the front desk: *6:03*. I realize Audrey and her mom have been waiting for me for more than an hour. If they haven't given up already. I can't believe I'm sitting here in handcuffs when I should be sitting across from Audrey at the Cuban restaurant behind the bowling alley, feeding sweet plantains to her one after the other and surprising her with "champagne" and chocolate after dinner.

"Can I make a call?" I ask a desk cop sitting a few feet from me.

"What's the number?" she says, pressing the speaker button on the messy-with-paperwork table between us. A loud dial tone moans from the tinny speaker.

I dictate Tracy's number, and she punches it in, lifting the receiver to my ear.

Ring. Ring. Ring. Ring. Riiiing . . .

"Hi, this is Tracy! Hope your life is ticketyboo! Leave a message at the beep. *Beeep!*"

Great.

"Trace, SOS. Genesis police station. PLEASE come and get me. And PLEASE stop by school and tell Audrey I got held up—well, worse—and I'm so sorry. I'll explain later. Come now. PLEASE."

The officer drops the phone back in the cradle.

"I don't suppose I can try another number?" I ask, trying to make myself look pitiful, which is easy.

She sniffs, then goes back to filling out paperwork.

After twenty minutes or so, Good Cop returns and takes me to a room where he un-handcuffs me before shackling my ankle to the table just as in every prison documentary I've ever watched. Only now *I'm* one of those guys accused of stealing, drug dealing, grand theft auto, conspiracy to commit murder. Guilty because I'm male and black, and someone who wasn't said I was.

I feel a rush of grief pass through my body. The kind that comes with every horrible recognition, like when I first learned about the Holocaust, or saw a kid get smacked by his mother in the grocery aisle, or an angry guy twist a woman's arm on the street. A hole opens up that can't be filled. I didn't know something, and now I do—and it feels like nothing will be the same after.

Good Cop leaves the room, then comes back popping open a can of 7-Up. He places it on the table in front of me, then exits again. I take a sip, because what else is there to do? The bubbles make my nose twitch. I worry about Audrey, where she is. What she's thinking. Is she assuming I stood her up? Is she freaking out that something terrible happened? (Not wrong there.) I wonder where Tracy is too, whether she got my message. If my parents have been called yet, when they'll get here. What's going to happen? Will the Changers Council get wind of this? Am I going to Changers jail after regular jail?

I see the top of DJ's head through the high window as he's being led past the room I'm in and seemingly put in the one next door. I wonder if they're going to lock him in a leg cuff too. Then I wait. And wait. And wait and wait and wait and wait. Two hours go by. If they are trying to scare me and teach me a lesson, then I am officially learned. Though I'm not sure how I can prevent this in the future unless I never shop at a store again, or wear a hoodie, or show the color of my skin to people who have already decided it's a threat.

I finish off the 7-Up just as the door clicks open. In comes Good Cop, followed closely by a fuming Tracy, who is followed by . . . Mr. Crowell.

The hell?

"Why on earth is he MANACLED like this?" Tracy demands, angrier than I've ever seen her. She stomps over, stands beside me. "Don't you think this is going a little overboard?"

"We treat all suspects the same, miss," Good Cop says in a monotone.

"Oh, I believe that!" Tracy shoots back sarcastically.

"Officer," Mr. Crowell breaks in, more calmly, "I'm an English teacher at Central High School. This is my student and advisee. He's an A student, has never been in any sort of trouble. I'm sure there's been some sort of misunderstanding."

Tracy makes a strange *humph* sound, which I assume is supposed to serve as punctuation to Mr. Crowell's vouching for me. "When can we take him home?" she asks.

"We can't release him to anybody but legal guardians."

"I'm a relative," she says. "His aunt."

The officer looks at her askance.

"His parents are also on the way and will be here any minute. With their attorney," she adds officiously, which seems to motivate the officer. He lopes over, and after thinking about it some more, finally squats and releases me from the leg cuff. My ankle is sore and raw, even though it wasn't very tight around my jeans. Good Cop says he'll go get the necessary paperwork and to stay put as he leaves the room, squeezing by Mr. Crowell, who, I notice, doesn't move aside for him.

Tracy catches me eyeballing Mr. Crowell. "He knows. I'll explain later," she says. "Now, how did this happen?"

"Uhhh," I stammer. *Knows what?*

"I am *so* sorry I missed your call," Tracy says, as though it's completely normal that a Static has been let in on my "situation"—not to mention hers. "We were in the middle of *Lord of the Rings.*"

"Precious," I reply.

Mr. Crowell sits down across from me. "We'll go to the Toot N Tote-um to clear things up with the owner," he says gently.

"I didn't take anything—"

"Of course not," Tracy interrupts. "Don't say another word."

Which makes me want to cry again. Like really, really want to cry. Which I decide I'm not going to do, no way will I let those officers see me cry, but as soon as that decision is registered and sent to my brain, I see the tops of my parents' heads through the window, and in no time I'm blubbering in my mom's arms saying over and over, "I didn't do it," as she shushes me and shushes me and whispers, "I know, I know."

The next thing I hear is Dad telling Good Cop that they'll be lucky if we don't press charges, that this is not due process, that "if my son says he didn't steal anything, then he didn't steal anything."

"With respect, sir," Bad Cop blows in saying, looking a bit taken aback that my parents are white, "but given his, uh, *foster* background, I'm not sure you can speak for this kid's whole life before he came into yours."

To which Mom pipes up, miraculously maintaining her shrink voice, though I can tell she's straight enraged: "Surely you are not suggesting he be prosecuted for crimes you *imagine* he might have committed in his past?"

"We're going to head out now," Mr. Crowell interjects

in his warbly voice. He puts a palm on Tracy's shoulder. "To talk with Mr. Chandra."

"Well, it's this kid's lucky day, because I just got off the phone with Mr. Chandra, and he's not pressing charges," Bad Cop says, radiating disappointment.

"Let this be a lesson to you," Good Cop adds.

"Oh, we've learned from the situation, all right," Mom snaps.

"I'll call you first thing in the morning," Tracy whispers to my mother, then she hugs me again, as she makes her way to Mr. Crowell idling uneasily in the hallway.

Soon after that, my belongings are returned, and Mom and Dad sign some forms at the front desk. DJ's mom hurries into the station just as we're headed out. I try to smile and half-wave at her, but she's not having any of it. I'm so tired I don't even have room left in my head or heart to worry whether she thinks I got DJ into trouble or something.

Driving to our place, both Mom and Dad dove into full-on social-justice diatribe. Dad, especially, seemed shaken and incensed, yelling about how he'd hoped notions of equality had taken deeper root in our culture since back in his day, but it was obvious that wasn't the case. Mom said it was clear this world needed Changers now more than ever. Both seemed deflated and depressed.

"I'm so sorry this happened to you," Mom said.

"I'm not," Dad interjected. "Because now we know. Now we see how bad it really is."

"It could have been so much worse," Mom said under her breath.

When we arrived home, I told them I needed to lie down and relax, and both nodded, *of course,* but what I really needed was to check my phone. As I feared, there were three voice mails and six texts from Audrey. The voice mails progressed like this:

Voice mail #1 (5:17 p.m.): "Hey, Oryon. So, did I screw up and get the time or night wrong or something? I thought we were meeting on the front stairs at five? Are you on your way? See you soon. I'm here. Looking forward to it."

Voice mail #2 (5:29 p.m.): "Hey, you all right? I'm starting to get worried. Or maybe you just forgot or something? My mom's here, she's waiting to drive us to Nashville and meet her friend and then drive us back after. Call me. Okay?"

Voice mail #3 (6:03 p.m.): "Can you just call me and let me know what's up? It's been an hour, and my mom's really pissed, so I guess we're going home now. Bye."

They were nearly too painful to listen to. Especially the last one, which it turns out she was in the middle of leaving for me at the very moment I checked the clock in the police station and was thinking of her.

The texts progressed in much the same way, the last one coming in just about the time I was being released from the police station:

I've got to be honest, Oryon. My feelings are really hurt. I can't believe you couldn't even at least do me the courtesy of calling or texting and telling me what even happened. It's really not like you. Or maybe it is. How would I know? Whatever. I'm going to sleep.

It was obviously way too late to call Audrey's cell, so I texted back:

Audrey, I'm sorry. Something really horrible happened.

*Out of my control. I'll tell you tomorrow. Please call me
back or tell me when I can call you. I hope you can accept
my apology. The last thing I ever want to do is disrespect
you or hurt your feelings. I really miss you and hate that
I missed the opportunity to spend time with you tonight.
It was going to be so perfect . . .*

I copied it and e-mailed the same message. I debated
writing more, but in the event that her parents (or, G forbid,
Jason) were monitoring her phone or e-mail, I didn't want
them made wise to the fact that I had been arrested. That's
the last thing I needed if I have designs on ever going out
with Audrey again.

Knock-knock-open. Mom comes in and quietly sits by my
bed.

"Can't sleep?" she asks.

"Nope."

"Want some water?"

"No thanks," I overshake my head like a toddler.

"Scotch?" she jokes.

I roll over and she tickles my back like she used to when
I was little. When I was Ethan. When I wasn't making her
get called to the police station late on a Friday night to bail
me out after getting arrested for shoplifting. I mean, all kids
steal, that's what everybody says, right? But I have never, not
once, stolen anything in my life. Not an eraser. Not a piece of
candy. Not a comic, or a bottle of water, or a roll of toilet paper
from the gas station stall. I'm the bonehead who returns the
dropped dollar bill to the cashier. *Somebody must have lost this.*

"I love you," Mom says softly.

"I love you too," I respond, finally feeling a wave of
sleepiness.

"Let's do something fun this weekend." She pats my back twice and stands up. I hate when tickles are over.

"Okay," I say, doubting I know what fun even is anymore.

"Sleep in," she says, pulling the door shut.

"Mom," I call after her, though I hadn't planned what more I was going to say.

"Yes, sweetheart?"

"Thanks for believing me."

On the way to school this morning, I skated by the "scene of the crime" to see if I could rescue the bowling shirts. Sure enough, there they were, lying in a grease puddle, squashed down by the force of a hundred tire treads into a revolting, flattened heap. I took a deep breath and picked them up by my fingertips, then carried them into the restroom of the Donut Shoppe next door, where I squirted some liquid soap and scrubbed the fabric together in the sink as best as I could, before wringing them out and sticking them in a plastic bag and stuffing them into my backpack.

Audrey was not in homeroom, which I knew couldn't be good news. Maybe she just came down with a cold. Or had a periodontist appointment. She wasn't back for lunch either, though I kept double-checking where she normally sits, just in case she turned up. I wasn't super keen on eating anyway. Neither was DJ, who was trying to organize a protest at the police station. (His mom never doubted his innocence either, having been raised in the South and experienced far worse in her youth.)

"Straight profiling," DJ spits, his rage palpable and infectious. "You *think* I'm an angry black man? Okay. I'll *be* an angry black man. Right, O?"

He nudges me and I nod in agreement, but say nothing. It's not that I'm okay with what happened. It's more that I'm disheartened the way I was after that Sunday at the dog park with Snoopy. People are going to see and believe what they want. So far in my experience, it seems prejudice withstands even the harshest onslaught of fact, and I don't see how a protest at the police station is going to do anything but get us all arrested again.

"I'm in," Dashawn says.

"Me too," says Kenya.

The bell rings, and I dash toward Audrey's locker. I dial her combination, pry open the lock, pull out the still-damp bowling shirt from my backpack, and hang it inside her locker on the coat hook just as Audrey rounds the corner, her face swollen like she's been crying for hours.

I don't know what to do or say, so I do nothing, just wait for her to notice the shirt. She turns to me, then her locker—the bottom hem of the shirt leaking a couple muddy drops onto some of her books—before falling into my arms.

"I heard everything," she says, suddenly squeezing me, breathless. "Jason told our parents you got arrested."

"How in the name of Kanye did *he* find out?" I ask, squeezing her back.

She shrugs. "They said I can't talk to you anymore. They took my phone, laptop, everything. They didn't want to hear any details. They basically forbade us from being together."

"It's okay, Audrey, it's okay," I say, doubtful.

She pulls back, her face wet with tears. "How? How is it okay?"

My mind spins, grasping and searching for something to offer that might comfort her before settling on the one remaining unassailable certainty I have left. "Because I love you, Audrey Stewart. And I have loved you since before you even knew who I was."

That much, at least, I know is the truth. One that nobody can take away.

SPRING

Kenya was a ballerina. She moved so precisely, so effortlessly, with just the right amount of energy expended, not too much, not too little, a solo virtuoso performance that left a razor's edge of space to clear each hurdle without grazing a single one. Her grace was a marvel to behold, a sharp contrast to the huffing-and-puffing theatrics of her competitors, who seemed ready to burst like shaken soda bottles.

During the last race, Kenya was two full lengths ahead of the next runner when she cleared the final jump and tilted toward the finish. The crowd started with a low hum, but as soon as she ducked her head forward for that extra tenth of a second and crossed the line, everybody in the stands erupted in a full-fledged roar, even visiting families who'd come to see their kids from other schools compete in the Middle Tennessee regional track championship.

Kenya's time was projected on the scoreboard, the letters *SR* right next to it, meaning she'd just set a new state hurdle record. I wanted to jump up and down just like DJ and Dashawn and Kenya's parents and some of the other kids behind the roped-off bench, but Mrs. Barnes-Wilson was tapping the mic to get our attention, and we had to start playing "Beat It" in celebration of Kenya's record.

I popped the rim of my snare, busted out my beat, and then everybody else came in, clarinets buzzing, trumpets blasting, trombones blowing, tom-toms holding us all up from below. It felt powerful being the heartbeat of a musical operation again, like when I played drums in The Bickersons last year. A few seats over Audrey was robot-dancing to our song, but soon enough the number was totally drowned out by the din of the crowd, which had gone full-on bananas. Back on the track, I saw Kenya had broken down, crying in her parents' arms.

She already had the scholarship to Florida on lock, but all this was just icing, and further proof that she was right on "track" (ha) to that vision of mine coming true. After our song faded out and Herr Conductor let us put down our instruments and chill for a beat (ha *again*), I tried to find Kenya to congratulate her, but I couldn't make out where she'd gone off to. *Left us all in the dust*, I was thinking and chuckling to myself, when I felt a tug on my uniform sleeve and spun around to see my DL cheerleader love looking as alluring as ever.

She snuck in for a quick kiss, which set the tall feather atop my hat trembling.

"I miss my band-nerd boyfriend," she said, shoving a folded note into my hand and closing my fingers around it.

I couldn't believe she was risking having her brother catch us and pummel me into a fine powder then grab her by the hair and drag her back to his car like his parents had essentially given him authority to do any time he saw his sister consorting with Public Enemy Number One.

"We should really stop meeting like this," I said, pocketing the note and passing one I'd written into her sweaty palm. "Where are you going to put this?"

"I'll find a place," she said in a breathy Marilyn Monroe baby voice, miming slipping it into her bra.

"This is killing me," I said, meaning it.

"I'll see you in school Monday," she said, then added,

almost conspiratorially, "I think I found a way to get free Thursday night."

My knees buckled in my polyester maroon suit. I growled, grasped her by the waist.

"Got to go!" she purred, then swiveled and practically sashayed back to the rest of her squad.

I reached in my pocket to make sure her note was still there. We may have been thwarted by no electronic or auditory means of communication, but the haters can never stop the free flow of good, old-fashioned, pen-on-paper love letters. I couldn't wait to get home and read this one in the privacy of my own room.

Damn. How am I supposed to survive two nights and a full day before seeing her face again on Monday? Her note better be a good one. I know mine was. I even got a little saucier than usual. But that's all I'm going to Chronicle about that—a gentleman never tells, right, Nana?

Luckily (I guess), three hours of the forty-eight I have to grit my teeth through until I can see Audrey again were munched up by the "engagement party" Mom insisted we throw at the apartment for Tracy and Mr. Crowell, who, Tracy notified us on a gilded card embellished with Swarovski crystals, were officially going to be married.

As in Changer-Static married.

As in, Mr. Crowell and his perpetually stained, misbuttoned thrift-store Oxford shirts had to go down to Changers HQ and attend Nondisclosure and personality-testing sessions with Tracy and Turner, the Lives Coach, as well as Marybell the Static-Union Coach, before signing a binding (and punitive, if the rumors are to be believed) contract as a forever-friendly Static, before they could be allowed to marry.

The same Mr. Crowell from whom I have studiously hidden my relationship with Tracy for the past two years, lest he wonder how we know each other. And yet, the fourth wall was well and truly broken, like Humpty Dumpty–never-gonna-get-put-back-together-again style, when he came over tonight. He and Tracy just left, in fact, after gushing to all of us about their plans to marry this summer. (Wedding theme: *Excalibur*.)

Now me and Unckie Crowell are inextricably linked for at least the next two and a half years that Tracy is my Touchstone—and probably much longer than that. Yeah, that's going to be a little creepy. Not that I don't like and respect Mr. Crowell. But the whole worlds-colliding thing is kind of freaking my Changer shizz out.

"Tell me, Oryon," Mr. Crowell inquires, innocently enough, when we're left alone in the living room after Tracy went to get more hors d'oeuvres from the kitchen, raving about what a good cook Mom is (I didn't have the heart to tell her Mom got them at Trader Joe's), "where did you attend school last year?"

Oh my god, she hasn't told him everything.

"Uh, Central," I say.

"Really? They do that?"

"I was in your English class."

He toggles his head that way he does, some hair flopping from one side of his part to the other. I can tell he's reeling back through the class rosters in his brain. *Tick. Tick. Tick.* Nada.

"Drew?" I say after a few more seconds of this, my voice involuntarily raising, some sort of muscle memory in my vocal chords or something.

"Drew!" he yells, louder than he probably meant it, which Tracy clearly hears from the kitchen, because she comes bounding over, mouth full of stuffed mushroom caps.

"You didn't tell him?" I ask sotto voce.

"No," she says. "That's *your* story to tell."

"Well, I wish I'd known!"

"I *loved* Drew," Mr. Crowell says clumsily. "I mean, I, I mean, you know, as a student, she was—*you* were—such a great girl."

"It'll take some getting used to," Tracy says, brushing a crumb from her fiancé's chin.

219

"It was horrible what happened last year to her—*you*," Mr. Crowell added. "I felt so helpless."

"But *that* you told him?" I glare at Tracy.

"Of course not," she says, popping another mushroom from her cocktail napkin.

"Teachers know far more than you think we do," Mr. Crowell offers. "I wanted to reach out to Drew, to you, but, you know, boundaries and legalities."

"Isn't he the sweetest?" Tracy says, stretching up to kiss Mr. Crowell on the neck.

Gross.

"He's okay."

Unckie Crowell smirks at me. "Well, it's good to know in retrospect you were in such capable hands." He gapes longingly at Tracy as if her face is the mystical map that holds the secrets to unlocking the hands of time. Tracy returns in kind, and now I'm watching a Nicolas Sparks movie minus the clotheslines and spontaneous rain showers. (OMG, is this what Audrey and I look like to other people?)

"I should've done more for Drew," Tracy says after they break their nauseating eye-lock. "From now on I'll be more on top of it."

"You've been great, Trace," I assure her. "Then and now."

"I've been a whittle bit distwacted," she says, which makes Mr. Crowell flush, and me feel like I need to spend less time playing *Minecraft* and more time building a time machine so I can travel backward and erase these moments from my consciousness forever.

"I'm going to get some more ginger ale," I say, but they've already forgotten I exist.

Homeroom this morning: no Mr. Crowell.

It's hard not to get a little paranoid, like, now that HE KNOWS about me, and he learned ABOUT ME just over the weekend, and then for the first time in almost two years of school he misses homeroom and we have a hating-her-life substitute who's taking attendance and failing miserably at keeping the room quiet. We can barely hear the school greetings over the speakers.

"*Ladies and gentlemen, we have a special announcement today. A very, very proud moment for the Central community,*" the principal begins. "*To tell you about it is our very own Mr. Crowell . . .*" And then there's a nails-on-chalkboard feedback scream that makes all of us recoil in our seats and gasp in unison.

"*Uh, uh—good morning, Falcons!*" the voice starts, more tremulous than usual.

I look over and notice that Chloe is ferociously flipping through the brand-new issue of the *Peregrine Review*, which I'm not even sure how she got her mitts on until I spot a few large cardboard boxes behind Mr. Crowell's desk, one of their tops ripped into like a rabid badger got a craving for something literary.

Mr. Crowell continues: "*I have the pleasure of announcing— I have the* honor *of announcing—that two of Central's very own are being recognized by the Tennessee State Literary Leaders Council and awarded with the Excellence in Reporting Award at the high school level for their series of interviews on love in the spring issue of the* Peregrine Review. *It's a first for Central High, and a first for these two talented students. So let's all join in heartily congratulating . . . Miss Audrey Stewart and Mr. Oryon Smull!"*

The hell, the what?

"Woo-freaking-hoo," Chloe immediately slurs, giving the world's slowest hand clap, which is our first indicator that this isn't a dream and is actually happening. A few of the other kids start to genuinely applaud and toss out an "All right!" or "Sweet!" and seem if not impressed, then at least sort of happy for Audrey and me (as we sink lower and lower into our chairs in embarrassment). Jerry raises the roof and whistles, which prompts Chloe to petulantly toss her copy of the *Peregrine* onto the floor and continue rolling her eyes so far up into her head that it seems like they might never come back to center.

A few minutes later, Mr. Crowell slips back into class, giving the relieved sub a head nod, and proceeds to elaborate on our award, explaining that we'll be featured in the *Nashville Times* newspaper—interviewed and photographed later this week.

"What about me?" Chloe cuts in.

"What about you?" Mr. Crowell asks back, brow knit.

"What about my trophy for poetry?" Chloe presses, a lifetime of being told she is amazing at everything doing no favors to her worldview yet again.

"Well, there isn't an award for poetry," Mr. Crowell responds, generously.

Chloe snarls, her lip lifting in the right corner as if snagged by a fishhook.

"Yeah, that's why," Jerry says, clapping me on the shoulder on the way back from collecting his copy of the magazine from Mr. Crowell's desk where he is stacking copies.

Later, between classes, some *Peregrine* members set up tables to hand out the new issues. Aaron, Audrey, Chloe, Amanda, and I are stationed on the first floor hall. The announcement of our win caused a line, which felt cool and meant way more to me than I expected it would. DJ stopped by and snagged two copies, giving me a high five and Audrey a salacious appraising *Hmmm mmm*. "Literature is dope!" he shouted over his back as he passed by Jason, who was sidling up to the table.

"Hey, faggots," Jason opens, pretending to flip through a journal and winking at Chloe, who waves and then continues to just sit at the end of the table, stroking her bangs like a pillow pet.

"Sudden interest in learning to read, Jason?" Audrey says, a familiar shadow darkening her face.

"There are people waiting," Aaron adds, standing up and squaring his shoulders to match Jason's.

"For what?" Jason sneers. "Love advice from my sexually confused sister and her eggplant crush?"

Aaron clenches his jaws, and I stand up when I realize I'm the eggplant.

Jason leans across the table closer to Aaron, so close their noses almost touch. "Want to know a secret?" he hisses.

Aaron is motionless, unblinking, silent.

Jason runs his tongue over his front teeth. "I'm the captain now," he barks in a mock–Somali pirate accent, then reels back and laughs, repeating, "I'm the captain now!"

Chloe giggles conspicuously, while Audrey and I exhale,

relieved no one is bleeding on top of our pile of journals. But then we notice Aaron isn't budging. He's still frozen in fight mode, the veins on his neck popped, every muscle tense, his breathing deep and steady behind the table.

"Hey Jason," he says, his voice firm, unafraid, "I have a secret too. Wanna hear it?"

"Ooooh, scary," Jason buffoons, wiggling his shoulders.

"Whatever you're doing, don't," Aud says softly to Aaron, wrapping her fingers around his rigid forearm, his palms pressed nearly white onto the folding table. The other students waiting in line take a few steps back, forming a haphazard semicircle behind Jason.

"Come closer, I'll tell you," Aaron tells Jason. He is determined, his tone almost hypnotic now. Jason snaps to attention, never one to back down from a perceived threat.

"Oh yeah? You got something to tell me, Oklahomo? Because that's not exactly a secret," Jason says loudly as he tilts forward toward Aaron's face. "Are we gonna go?" he taunts.

It's at that precise moment that Aaron nods yes, says, "Oh, we're going," and, with everyone watching, bracing for an epic alpha football jock throw-down, flings his arms around Jason's shoulders and kisses him full and wet on the mouth.

Jason recoils, sputtering and spitting and pawing at his lips, trying to rub off the contact (like that can even be done, outside of cartoons), and then starts leaping around, pointing at Aaron, and shrieking to everyone in the hall, "Did you see that? I knew it! I knew it! Freaking fairy! Donut puncher! Knob jockey!" But no one is really listening, instead they are cracking up, jeering at Jason, who looks more the absurd clown than ever.

"Those are some soft lips, captain!" Aaron shouts over the din, saluting, inspiring even more laughter. Audrey is beaming, and I'm a little high myself, so proud of Aaron for finally caring more about who he is than what everyone else wants him to be.

By now, the teachers have heard the drama and are pouring onto the scene, pushing kids aside and trying to get everyone to calm the heck down. Before they can reach us, though, Jason clambers over the table, *Peregrine Review*s flying left and right, and punches Aaron so hard in the teeth that he flies back and thuds against a row of lockers like a giant sack of flour.

Aaron slides to the floor and Audrey races over, dropping to the ground beside him, as a giant, unlikely grin spreads across his bloody face.

"Oh my god. Are you okay?" Audrey moans.

"Totally worth it," he mumbles through cracked and red lips.

After school, Audrey and I went to the Freezo to celebrate. Our award, yes, but also her brother's at-long-last suspension from school for the rest of the week. And Aaron's de facto coming out. And each other.

I won't lie. I did think for a minute about last year around this time, sitting in the same booth at Freezo across from Chase. It seemed so long ago. Lifetimes. I was lost in the memory when I heard Audrey's voice bringing me back.

"Did you hear me?"

"What?"

"Did you hear what I said?"

"Of course," I lie.

"What was it?" She wipes the corners of her lips, licks her dip-cone.

"Ice cream is awesome?"

"No."

"Well, it is," I say, leaning in for a kiss.

It is just as I am pulling back that she says it. "I think I might love you," she murmurs, unable to look me in the eye.

I am so flooded that even right now as I'm trying to recall them, I can't be sure those were the exact words she used. But I am choosing to believe they were.

CHANGE 2—DAY 220

Nana fell in the bathroom of her condo this morning. She fractured her left wrist and cracked her head on the side of the tub, sitting there for an hour before she could make her way to a phone to call for help. An ambulance finally came and took her to the hospital. She needed three stitches on her head, but luckily they could just set and cast her wrist without having to perform surgery. It turned out to be just a concussion—no internal bleeding inside her brain—but her doctor wanted to keep her in the ER so they could keep an eye on a "small spot" that came up in her CAT scan.

What a "small spot" is, I don't know. But it doesn't sound great. Spots rarely are.

The thought of her lying there bleeding on the bathroom floor for a whole hour confused, scared, more alone than perhaps any other time in her life, it makes my chest ache. I feel my own helplessness about it, realizing I'm impotent to do anything about her falling, getting older, suffering, dying. I just have to sit back and watch what happens.

Sometimes I wonder how any of us walk around *without* fixating on the inevitabilities of life. It's a miracle we manage to shove all that reality under the mat and worry about tank tops and touchdowns and haircuts and homeroom and other pointless crap instead. At least we do until something like this happens, and it cracks a hole in the wall, and the light floods in and it's like, oh yeah, I see it now, there's the stuff that counts, the stuff we can't do eff-all about.

Mom and Dad just left to be with Nana; they're driving all night. It was all a chaotic blur as soon as the phone rang from the hospital, but while they were throwing bags together, I overheard them talking seriously about trying to bring her back with them. She doesn't want to go into a nursing home, or an "assisted care facility," as Dad keeps calling it. She also doesn't want to leave her apartment complex—and certainly not Florida, because all of her friends are there. And Burt Reynolds, or so she thinks.

It's all up in the air now though, because first things first: she needs to get well and out of the hospital. I wish Changers had the magical quick-to-heal thing going for their whole Mono lives, and not just during their Cycles. Because Nana could really use that power now. She'd be up and playing canasta with her blue-haired buddies in a couple weeks instead of, well, I guess we don't know. Thinking about that makes it feel like a giant lump of clay is stuck at the base of my throat and I can't cough it up or swallow it down.

"I'm really going to need you to step up to the plate," Dad said right before he and Mom took off.

They left me home alone because the *Peregrine Review* newspaper interview is tomorrow during school, and both were so proud when they heard about the award, the last thing they wanted was for me to miss the opportunity to celebrate my hard work. (They were slightly less thrilled that Audrey was my partner on the project, but they understood that it was an "official school activity" that we of course couldn't have assigned to ourselves. I told them to blame Unckie Crowell.)

"I'm counting on you to do the right thing," said Dad, really working his parental clichés.

"I *will*," I promised, trying to wriggle out of his vice grip on my shoulders.

"No, I'm serious," he said. "This is the first time you'll be on your own like this, and we need you to take care of Snoopy and the apartment, and handle your business." (I was going to make a dirty joke about that last bit, but I could see in his eyes how uneasy he was about Nana and that this wasn't the time or place for masturbatory humor.)

"Tracy's here if you need her," Mom piped in, a squeaky wheelie bag rolling behind her. She collected her date book and laptop from the kitchen table, adding, "And Dad and I will be back this weekend to get you, or maybe only one of us will be back. I don't know, we have to see what the situation is and, well, you get it, right?" I could sense she too felt anxious and also guilty for leaving me behind.

"Got it," I said, hugging Mom and then taking her bag from her and rolling it out to the hallway.

"Don't forget to take out the trash," Dad added, scrunching up his nose, purportedly about the reek of the trash, but his tone made it seem more like I'd done something wrong before I'd even had the chance to prove myself worthy of all this new responsibility.

"And *bathe*," Mom said. "I don't want you smelling like a goat when I get home. There's forty bucks on the table. Be good. Eat something besides frozen pizza, an apple, something . . ." she continued rattling off as Dad picked up his briefcase and duffel, glancing around the kitchen as though he was saying goodbye for a long time.

A moment that, to tell the truth, chilled me. I felt sixteen years *young* in that second. I mean, I'd stayed home when they'd been out to dinner here and there, or even spent whole solo weekend days in our old house when I was Ethan and every neighbor in a five-mile radius was on a first-name basis with my mother, but this was the first time they'd left me overnight and gone so far away.

"I love you," Mom said when she joined me in the hall. "You okay?"

"Sure," I fibbed. "I'm just worried about Nana."

Dad pulled the door behind him, nudging Snoopy's nose back into the apartment so he could shut it all the way. "We all are."

"Call me and tell me how she is?" I asked.

"Of course," Mom said. "Keep your phone on you. If I call or text and you don't answer, the National Guard is going to be banging down this door—and trust me, you don't want any part of that."

"And do you two know from personal experience," the reporter asked, "what true love is?" She quickly glanced down to make sure her recorder was indeed taping for what she seemed to hope would be the juiciest part of her *Nashville Times* interview with us in Principal Redwine's office.

Audrey and I made eye contact for a split-second before both looking away.

"Uh," Aud groaned.

"Uh," I grunted at precisely the same time.

Then the three of us—Audrey, me, and the nice reporter with the long (fake) eyelashes and meticulous bob—all laughed nervously together for way too long.

"Well?" she prompted us again, not letting it go. "Do I take that as a yes?"

"Off the record?" I thought to ask, voice warbly.

"Well, that's not my preference," she replied, and I could feel Audrey's eyes boring a shame hole into the side of my face.

"Yes, go on, by all means," Aud finally said, making a point of kicking back in the principal's cozy leather recliner and knitting her fingers together behind her head.

"Off the record . . ." I started, but just couldn't seem to finish.

And mercifully, after a few more uncomfortable wordless seconds of Audrey and I squirming and giggling and being worse interview subjects than Justin Bieber, the reporter moved on to some other topic, something bland and generic and way easier to blab about than our FEELINGS FOR EACH OTHER. That's why the greeting card industry exists, lady. Geez.

Later we were excused from class so a photographer could pose us awkwardly in various staged settings: Aud pointing at a list of literary terms on the chalkboard and me sitting on a desk in front of her clutching a clipboard and pen; us walking up the front steps of school, me toting my skateboard, Aud with a backpack slung over her shoulder acting like I'd just uttered the funniest quip in all of high school-dom; and finally, the two of us juggling giant stacks of the Spring edition of *Peregrine*—passing out issues in the hallway to a handful of preselected kids supposedly living for it. (A bit of a departure, obviously, from the less family-friendly reality of what went down when we actually distributed copies of the magazine in the hallway a few days earlier. On that note, with Jason banished from campus for his suspension, it was as though a foreboding, Axe body spray–scented fog had completely lifted from Central High, and both Audrey and I could breathe completely unencumbered for the first time all year. Maybe ever, at least on campus. Man, that felt good.)

But none of that is what I want to be Chronicling about right now. Maybe I'm trying to get it down and out of the way because it's concrete, it actually happened. I saw the shots on the photographer's digital camera, and the reporter confirmed that her story would indeed appear in next Sunday's Education supplement of the newspaper.

While what's happening NOW, as I'm thinking this, as

I'm Chronicling this, is completely UNREAL and abstract, even though I'm awake living and breathing it, lying here trying to be completely still while holding her so close to me, hearing the ever-so-slight whistle of air rushing in and out of Audrey's adorable nose which is currently hovering over the general vicinity of my right pectoral muscle. I'm trying not to twitch or stir or even look down so as not to wake this perfect angel who is sleeping so peacefully with her cheek against my bare skin.

Hold up, back up, rewind, right?

Let me try to unpack the whole wonder of it all. Deep breath. And . . . here . . . we . . . go!

Basically: Dad called and said Nana was out of the hospital and resting comfortably in her condo. She told them she "didn't want to croak anywhere but my own bed," which, while dramatic, definitely shut down the assisted-living conversation. I assured Dad I'd be fine staying alone through the weekend. Mom got on the line and equivocated, worrying that I'd be bored, scared, or possibly feel abandoned. I insisted none of these things were the case, that I was fine, was really enjoying some time alone, Snoopy was watered and fed, I'd eaten two bananas, all was under control and would remain so. If I felt lonesome I'd have dinner with Tracy and Mr. Crowell. (There was no way the latter was happening, but saying it seemed to make Mom feel better.)

They promised one of them would be back by Sunday night, Monday at the latest. So I was going to be on my own until then. Or was I?

Feeling high after Audrey's and my Central High literary victory tour earlier today, I scribbled a quick, reckless note and passed it to her after school when we were saying goodbye:

My parents are gone this weekend. I'm all alone. [Sad face] Can you make an excuse to sleep out tonight? Not assuming anything (I'll stay on the couch!), just want to cuddle up with you and my dog and about a hundred bags of mildly burned microwave popcorn with the fake butter and watch the shizz out of some old-time movies. Whatdya say, little lady? [Hopeful face]

She scanned the note quickly in front of me, both of us by habit keeping watch around us for fear of Jason or his crew popping up and running their redneck interference. But nobody seemed to pay us any mind during the rush of the Friday-afternoon jailbreak, and then, to my incalculable surprise, as soon as Audrey finished the note, she folded it up and stuck it back in her pocket and said quietly, "Okay."

Just like that.

And, just like that, I was on the verge of breaching yet another Changer tenet, and this one's a doozie: *Don't bring anybody to your place of residence, because that may be your home for all four years of high school, and you need to be on the DL, since four different people can't be living in the same house or apartment now, can they?* (That's my paraphrase of the tenet, anyway.)

Oh well, I quickly made a deal with myself, *I'll just not bring her home any other year.* Who even knows if she'll want to be friends with me as my future Vs, and to be honest, who the heck cares? We could all slip in the bathroom and have brain aneurysms or get hit by the proverbial bus and there I would be, skipping the dessert cart for no good reason. There was no way I was going to consider anything but the present, and how Audrey's face betrayed just the hint of a mischievous smile when she whispered, "Give me a couple hours to figure it out. Meet you at Starbucks at seven."

Which is how I've ended up where I am right this second, with Audrey pressed up against me in my bed, the room completely quiet, still, and dark—but for the occasional passing headlight I can spot through the slits in the blinds. Snoopy's curled at our feet, snoring, as though it's the most natural thing in the world for Audrey to be sharing the bed with us like this.

Please note: I shall be following Nana's afore-Chronicled gentlemanly rule to the word here.

But . . .

OH MY FRACKING GOD, it felt good. To be so completely and utterly—so undeniably—close to Audrey. Nobody, nothing between us.

Sure, neither of us knew what in Yeezus's name we were doing, but once we admitted that to one another and starting laughing our butts off instead of trying to take every little maneuver and moment so seriously like they do in the movies, simply put: Audrey and I fit perfectly. Like I knew we would from the second Drew set eyes on her in homeroom last year. Together we made a new color. And that transcended who I happen to be right now, a guy who was a girl who was really a guy who was in love with a girl.

It's getting downright Shakespearean in here, but my point is that love is not about gender or sex, or whatever you want to call it. As in, Mom was kind of right, Tracy was kind of right, and I'm sure *The Changers Bible*, in its way, is right, though they probably wouldn't exactly approve of how I'm learning the lesson.

It's almost eerie: I'm not Oryon or Drew or even Ethan as I'm with Audrey right now, and she isn't really Audrey either. I mean, don't get me wrong, she *is* Audrey, which makes me feel all manner of things I never knew imaginable in one body, much less three, but I guess what I'm saying is, what I'm thinking as I'm lying here next to her with my arm hooked around her like this, is

Wait, what am I thinking?

What am I doing thinking at all? I'm just *feeling*. Feeling the most satisfied I've ever felt in my life.

Who cares whether I feel like Drew or Oryon or freaking Ryan Gosling holding Audrey?

Oh man. She's stirring now. *What do I do?* She jerks, as though awakening from a nightmare, then rolls to face me.

"Are you thirsty?" I ask super quietly, like I'm green-side at a golf tournament.

"A little, I guess," she whispers back, her voice scratchy.

I gently pull my arm out from under her neck and she rolls in the opposite direction so I can get out of bed and scramble to yank on my crumpled boxers.

"Shy," she says.

I stand up and look back down at her, just her face on the pillow visible beneath the covers she'd yanked up after me.

"You are the most beautiful perfect thing I've ever seen or known of in this world," I say.

"Shut up!" she chides, and for a second I am crushed, but then she's laughing again, and I'm laughing again, and bounding off toward the kitchen to fetch her a nice, tall drink of water.

"What happened to your butt?" she shouts when I reach the door.

Oh shite. My Changers emblem.

"I bit it skating the other day," I recover. "You know, ripped my shorts."

God, I hate lying to her—especially after . . .

"Be right back."

"I'll be here," Audrey answers, turning over to make kissy-face noises at Snoopy, who wags his tail while commando-creeping to the warm spot I just vacated beside her. I certainly can't blame him.

"What the hell is this?" I heard, shrieky and terrifying, the second I walked into the room holding a glass of juice and a glass of water. Snoopy leapt off the bed and skittered out the door. For a second I thought there had to be a mouse or cockroach or something, or that Audrey was messing with me; I couldn't imagine what she could be talking about.

But then I saw it: looped through her fingers was the silver bracelet with a drum-kit charm on it, the one she'd given me at the end of last school year when I was Drew.

Oh crap oh crap oh crap oh crap oh crap oh crap . . .

"What are you even doing? That's my stuff," I stammered, noticing the top of the ceramic coil pot I'd made in sixth grade to keep my treasures was lifted.

"Where did you get this?" she pressed.

"My grandma, my—you know—I—"

I could tell some serious math was computing in Audrey's head, with no apparent solutions, no matter how many times she went over the problem. She looked at once scared, angry, confused, betrayed, embarrassed; you name the emotion, it was on her face. I set the sweating glasses atop my dresser, carefully walked over to her, tried to pull her into a hug. She stepped back, balling up the chain in her hand.

"If this is some kind of sick joke . . ." she started, but didn't finish, opening her hand again and taking another look at the now-knotted bracelet in her palm.

"Aud, *please*," I tried, keeping my voice low and calming. "Can we just sit down and talk for a minute?"

"About what? I can't even imagine. I don't want to imagine." She looked completely rattled. Then, as if she suddenly realized something, she flung the bracelet onto the bed behind her and started stooping to collect her things, throwing on a sweatshirt and stomping into her low-top Cons with the heels crushed down, one of which was sticking out from under my comforter. "I need to get out of here," she said, frantic. "I need to get out of here NOW."

"Audrey wait," I pleaded with her, but by then she was dressed and shoving the rest of her things into her backpack.

"Where's my phone?" she screeched.

I looked around, saw it peeking out the top of her jeans pocket. I pointed at it. She looked down, pulled it out, and immediately started typing furiously into the screen.

"Please," I said, trying to figure out whom she might be texting. Aaron? A girl from the squad? "I promise this'll all make sense if you just give me a minute to explain."

"Explain *what*?" she replied, hefting her backpack over a shoulder. "How do you know her?"

"Who?" I said, a reflex.

Her face darkened further.

I didn't know what else to say. I didn't want her to leave. I knew it was a false promise; no matter what I did, it would not in fact "all make sense." I couldn't tell her. But I couldn't not tell her. So I just stood there frozen, half naked, my mouth hanging open like a monster.

She blew a long breath through her teeth, then turned and left. By the time I realized what was happening, I could already hear the apartment door slamming.

I quickly scrambled to throw something on, but all I

could find was a pair of cut-off, ripped sweat shorts and a
stinky skate tank top, which I pulled over my head while
launching after Audrey through the kitchen. I got out to the
hallway as the elevator doors closed and beeped, so I blew
down the stairs barefoot, bursting into the side lobby just as
Audrey was stepping through the revolving door and out
into the night.

"Audrey!" I yelled after her, but she didn't turn around.
Hank, our night doorman, looked at me askance, as if to let
me know he was watching me. Audrey ran to the curb; I
followed close behind.

"Please? Please, just stop," I begged her.

"Get away from me," she hissed, and the tears were pouring now. She checked left and right for traffic, then sprinted
to the median of Ninth Avenue between a car and a motorcycle that had to slam the brakes to avoid clipping her. I
waited, then dashed to her, grabbing her wrist to prevent her
from running across another lane of traffic.

"Don't touch me!" she screamed, loud enough so a dude
putting air in his tires at the gas station across the street
looked up to see what was going on.

She twisted her arm away from me and ran toward him.
After another couple cars passed, I trailed behind. Fine if
she didn't want to talk, fine if she wanted to leave, but there
was no way I was letting her wander the streets distressed
and alone in the middle of the night.

"At least let me call you a taxi."

"I said leave me ALONE!"

"Dude," the guy called out, then stepped toward us. He
was white with a scruffy beard, about thirty, wearing con-
struction boots caked in mud.

I knew I had to back down. I knew what this looked

like. In fact, I knew from both sides of the equation.

"Is there a problem, miss?" the guy asked Audrey, planting himself between us. The bill of his CAT tractor hat was curled tighter than a paper towel roll above his forehead, a wad of dip tucked deep into his left cheek. He had six inches on me, and at least sixty pounds.

"It's fine, it's fine," she said, wiping her eyes. Humiliated.

The guy gave me a once-over. Noted my bare feet, my shredded hobo shorts.

"We just had a little misunderstanding," I said, slouching nonthreateningly.

Audrey huffed.

"Well, I'm right over there if you need anything, miss," he said to her, but gave me the *I don't have gun racks in my pickup for nothing* look, as he turned and plodded back to his truck.

Audrey stood there, her back to me. I walked around her other side, and she pivoted again.

"Are you not going to let me explain?"

Silence.

"I'm not leaving you alone," I said. "It's unsafe."

"I don't care *what* you do." She finally swiveled to me and glared straight into my eyes. "I truly don't."

She meant it. That's it. It was time to come out.

"I need to tell you something, something crazy, but it's the complete truth," I started, but just as I did, I heard a familiar engine approaching from down the block. I had to strain to see past the blinding headlights, but yep, there he was, rolling up in his 'stang convertible, creeping slowly like a patrol car looking for a fugitive.

"I'd get out of here if I were you," Aud said in a flat voice, and stepped into the street, holding up her hand to flag him down.

I ran over to a row of shrubs, jumped behind them, then turned back around to peer between two bushes as Audrey threw her bag in the back and silently climbed into the passenger seat beside her brother. Jason's head was swiveling around everywhere, scouting the scene. I could hear him ask, "What happened?" but Audrey didn't answer.

"What the hell happened?" he repeated, even louder. "Who is it?"

Audrey stayed silent. She slumped in her seat, and it looked like she was starting to cry again as they pulled off.

I ducked. But I'm pretty sure Jason spotted me before screeching away.

So now I'm back in my empty apartment, lying in bed next to Snoopy, with nothing but the scent of Tahitian Vanilla body mist and a little indentation in the pillow to remind me where Audrey had been not half an hour before. I can't text, I can't call. I tried her parents' phone line but there was no answer. I don't know what to do. I feel like I might go crazy. Certifiably 5150 shave-your-head-and-check-into-the-nut-house crazy.

Should I call Chase? But I don't want to tell him what happened; it feels like a betrayal of Audrey and weird anyway, with our history and his attitude.

What about Tracy? I have a feeling she's not going to understand this one. Not unless I can convince her that the way I feel about Audrey is the way she feels about Mr. Crowell. That she is my "one," the way he is hers. The Static who I know I'm meant to share the real me with.

The Council forbids Changers from choosing Static mates until after our Cycles are complete. But what if I KNOW? There have to be exceptions when Changers' lives crash into people as lovely and wonderful as Audrey.

I'll just find a way to tell Audrey everything, and then promise her I'll choose Oryon as my Mono, if she can just bear to live with whomever I'll become over the next two years. Sound reasonable? Sure it does. If you're on your third-day acid trip at Burning Man.

I don't know. I don't know anything.

This feels horrible. The worst I've ever felt. So much worse than the previous worst. It's torture not to know what she's thinking. Torture that I suspect I do know. That she hates me. That I've lost her.

—

I don't know if this is even Chronicling. My head hurts, I'm so dopey.

Woozy and tired.

Where am I?

My eyelids feel heavy and droopy, all I see in my brain is Audrey's lovely face; but where is she, what happened?—

... hello? Is anybody hearing ...

                       ... this?

Hello? *Please*—somebody.

Is my damn chip even working? I'm really hoping the Council *is* tapping our Chronicles. Because I really need them right now. Really need YOU right now. Please, if you're listening, we need help. Quick.

I've been abducted. Kidnapped, I guess.

I don't know where I am, don't remember anything, but I do know that there's another Changer here with me—can't tell whether that's a coincidence or what. But there are definitely two of us. One is, well, me, Oryon Small, and the other is this kid named Alex who I saw in the locker room that day when he tried to hide his butt cheek after PE. He's a freshman, and it seems like he might've gotten hit in the head or something. He doesn't remember what happened to him either. He's been weeping pretty much nonstop since I woke up here a few hours ago. Alex says he regained consciousness about twelve hours before they brought me in.

I know we're downstairs in a basement because Alex said he spotted a short hallway leading to a narrow staircase when they opened the door and brought me in and dumped me on the floor. It's damp and cold. And there are no windows, little light, just some ambient glow from the cracks around the metal door that's penning us in. I tried slamming into it, pulling the handle, pushing it a few times. It won't budge—seems like a padlock's secured on the other side.

I don't know what else I can tell you by way of details.

The floor is cement and cracked in thirds diagonally across the space, which is about, what, fifteen by twenty feet. It feels like a standard rectangular basement type of room, the ceiling above is about seven feet high, and there are cinder-block walls on all sides, a few low wooden benches, some plastic buckets—for toilets, I guess—and a handful of wad-ded towels and trash scattered about. It smells like bleach and propane.

Somebody tossed down some granola bars and two bot-tles of water earlier. Alex said they gave him a peanut butter sandwich the day before. He also said I slept restlessly for ten or so hours before waking up one last time and remain-ing conscious, which is when he just flat-out asked if I knew what a V was, if I know who the Council is. Which is when we figured out we're both Changers.

Wait, somebody's coming down the steps . . .

CHANGE 2–DAY 223, PART TWO

Two guys just came in, one in a black hood with eyeholes cut out, the other with a black bandanna covering half his face, both clad in black long-sleeved shirts and pants. Brown work boots. They carried in an unconscious girl and deposited her limp body on a towel in the corner, while Alex and I shrank from the light that suddenly flooded in from the hallway.

I considered rushing them, but realized I'd have no chance, feeling as weak as I do. I need to gather my strength. Take notes. Man, I wish someone would hear this.

The creepy dudes exited as quickly as they came, slamming the door shut and padlocking it on the other side. They left two sandwiches and a half-empty bottle of water on one of the benches.

"Hello, hey?" I try in the girl's direction after I can no longer hear footsteps on the other side of the door, but she is out cold. She's nail thin, looks to be about seventeen, with wavy light-brown hair with a streak of purple in it and pale skin. She has a red scratch on her left cheekbone, with tiny dots of dried blood running the length of it.

I get closer and nudge her shoulder. Nothing. Nudge it a little harder. Still nothing. I try to feel for a pulse, poke around her soft neck beneath her jaw. It takes me awhile to feel it: slow and steady pumping. *Phew*, at least she's alive.

"They're going to kill us," Alex says, and starts sobbing again, balling himself up in the opposite corner.

"They wouldn't give us food if they were planning on killing us," I respond authoritatively, tossing him a sandwich, which he catches against his chest. "We aren't Hansel and Gretel."

I'm not sure I believe it myself, but it seems like the right thing to say. Unwrapping the bread from the cellophane calms him down some.

We eat silently and quickly, chewing like cows blinking into the darkness in the general direction of the girl. After we finish eating and split the little bit of water, we start hearing a distant but loud, repetitive banging noise coming from upstairs, followed by more silence.

"What do you remember?" I ask softly after probably another fifteen minutes.

"I don't know exactly," Alex starts, coughing twice. "I was waiting for my mom to pick me up from swim practice behind the Y. Next thing I know, I woke up here with a massive headache."

"Did you see anybody?"

"Not really," he says fuzzily, his speech slightly slurred, as if he's tipsy from downing a couple beers at a keg party. "What do you remember?"

"Less than zero," I say, but then I'm unexpectedly flooded with images. "Wait, I, I was walking my dog in the morning . . . the morning after I—"

Oh my god, Audrey. What must she be thinking?

"I was walking Snoopy, that's my dog, toward the park, first thing in the morning," I slowly continue, reaching for every word, doubting every one even as I manage to grab hold of it. "A couple trucks screeched up on either side of us . . ."

And Snoopy, what happened to Snoopy?

"Some guys jumped out, and, and—"

"You don't remember after that," Alex finishes for me.

"I guess I don't," I concede, recalling then that my plan had been to take Snoopy for a quick walk before skating over to Audrey's to try and force her to talk to me in person.

Alex and I both fall silent again, seized by our own thoughts and memories, all of which are suddenly suspect, constructions and imaginings, trauma-tainted. I realize I don't know what time it is, or what day, or how long I've been here. I am petrified that Snoopy was hurt or taken by the same psychos, or maybe he ran away when those guys jumped me. But if he gets picked up by Animal Control and taken to the pound, he's not going to last long, since they don't keep pit bulls alive much more than twenty-four hours if nobody comes to claim them.

I think Mom or Dad was supposed to be back by Sunday—is it Sunday?

How will they know what happened? What will they find that might tip them off? Even if they find something like the locket by the bed or the condoms I hid at the bottom of the trash or, I don't know, my collection of letters from Audrey—how would that lead them to me here? Wherever *here* is.

Did anybody on the street see what happened? Did the daytime doorman see me and Snoopy leave and not come back? Could he have notified the police? Could the police even help?

Now I'm the one crying. But I cheat to the side so Alex can't tell. It's dark enough to hide.

The girl started stirring a few hours ago. It seemed like she might be waking up on a few separate occasions, and each time her eyes opened, Alex and I went over to try to be there to comfort her, but out she went again for another spell. It wasn't until the fourth time that she actually woke up, and grew instantly terrified that there were two strange guys at her side. She crawled as far away as she could in the cramped space, pressing her back up against the wall, fists balled tight.

It took some convincing before she accepted that we were not her captors. And man, even under duress, this girl was a good Changer, not betraying that she was one until it was completely undeniable that Alex and I had too much insider Changers info not to be Changers ourselves.

Her name is Lynn, and she's a junior at a high school in Nashville. She had been at a graffiti-art gallery show and all-night party in 12 South with her girlfriend when some guys suddenly rushed her as she was having a quick cigarette in the alley out back, and then she woke up here, similarly unable to remember anything after that moment.

She was confident, brassy, and, even in this crappy situation, funny every once in a while. She was raised a boy, and had been a boy for her previous two Vs—but insisted fervently she would be picking a girl for her Mono, regardless of who she turned into next. She'd been having the best year of her life—even though she said she despised her name and every instance that she heard people calling her by it.

"Why?" I asked.

"It's neither here nor there, sounds like a menopausal, Midwestern, thick-around-the-midsection church lady," she said, finishing off one of the protein bars that were tossed through the cracked door into our basement before Lynn awoke.

"I think we're supposed to wait until our Cycles are complete before picking," Alex said earnestly.

"*Oh, Lynn, we've run out of frozen cookie dough for the youth group fundraiser,*" she ignored Alex and continued, droning on in the voice of precisely the type of lady whom she was just describing. "*Lynn, meet you at three at Lucille Roberts for Zumba class. Gotta tone those glutes!*"

"So change your name," I said, chuckling.

"Yeah," Alex agreed.

"To what?" she replied, as though it was the first time she'd ever considered such a thing. Which is hard to believe. This girl seemed like she did pretty much whatever she wanted, whenever she wanted, and didn't worry too much about what anybody thought about it.

"What's a name you like?" I asked.

"My best friend's middle name," she said, and then seemed instantly sad. "Elyse. I always thought it was a really pretty name . . ."

Alex and I stayed quiet.

"She died," Lynn (Elyse) added.

"I'm sorry," I said reflexively. "When?"

"Right after we moved here, before my Cycle started," she said. "Drunk driver plowed into her on the interstate, came across the median."

I didn't know what to do or say, so I just repeated, "Sorry," a couple times, while Alex sat in his corner and cleared his throat to break up the silence.

"Well, *Elyse*," I said after a while, "awesome to meet you. Come here often?"

She gave a weak laugh.

"Right, Alex?" I prompted.

"Yep, Elyse," he echoed, but you could feel the hope evaporating with every passing second.

After we took turns napping, I came up with an idea, even if it was a Hail Mary at best. I told them about Benedict's theory of how the Changers Council monitors our Chronicles for suspect incidents and conduct. (They were both impressed that I even knew a RaChas member.) My little test Chronicle about doing drugs and telling everybody at school that I'm a Changer might've missed any random scanning, but perhaps if Alex and Elyse did it, our chances would be better that the Council would catch something—if indeed they were trying to catch something.

I asked them to Chronicle some crazy, made-up stuff of their own, in addition to reporting what I've been observing closely about the space, to give hints as to our location. I mean, if Mom and Dad are home, and now I've been missing, what, about two days, and they tell Tracy I'm missing, and Tracy turns it over to the Council, maybe there's a situation in which our Chronicles can be accessed in an emergency capacity? And if three of us are missing from the region, maybe they'll notice a trend and send a search party or something?

Damn, I wish I'd listened when Chase was blabbing on about Abider deprogramming camps. Speaking of which, none of us—Elyse, Alex, nor I—have even dared utter the A-word aloud, though I know we're all thinking it.

* * *

An update from the Department of Futility, here are some more things I've noticed: I believe we are somewhat near a railroad track, since I can hear trains sounding their horns twice a day, about eight to ten hours apart. Maybe twelve hours. I have no idea how much time is passing for sure, but I've been watching how the line of light under the door moves across the floor, which leads me to believe there is a window at the top of the staircase on the other side of the door, and that we are possibly in a building that runs north-south, since that strip of light seems to move from right to left, which if it's the sun rising in the east and then setting in the west means that the window is facing south . . .

Or maybe I'm getting it backward. Who even knows if that'll help? . . . I can't think straight, and here's another thing I'm choosing *not* to mention to Elyse, and especially not Alex: I keep hearing voices. Or thinking I'm hearing voices, when I'm pretty sure nobody's talking.

To fill up the space I ask Alex about his past, which is one of the only things that seems to make him stop crying. He was a girl living in Northern California before his family moved to Genesis and he woke up as a boy named Alex at the beginning of the school year.

"What kind of stuff did you like to do?"

"Riding horses."

"That's cool," I said. "I've never ridden a horse."

"It's the best feeling in the world sitting on top of all of that power," he told us, his tone almost relaxed for the first time since being stuck in here together.

Normally I'd tease the guy about being the type of person whose parents are so fancy they own a horse and give him riding lessons (and I could feel Elyse thinking the same thing), but these were not normal times. And really, who was I to judge?

"Here's something I never understood," I offered. "How do you make a horse change which foot gallops in front?"

But Alex didn't answer; he'd fallen asleep.

Then it was quiet but for Alex's heavy breathing through his perpetually congested nostrils.

"Who's the girl?" Elyse suddenly asked out of nowhere, from across the dark. It had to be the middle of the night, as there was only the tiniest sliver of light coming from around the door, seemingly from an artificial source, like maybe an exit sign in the hallway.

"What do you mean?"

"Your girl," Elyse said flatly.

"How do you know I have a girl?"

"Really?"

"Audrey," I conceded, even though it felt wrong to speak her name, to bring her into this hellish place.

"Now, *that's* a pretty name," she said. "What's her deal?"

"What do you mean?"

She didn't answer, just said, "Man, I could use a cigarette right about now."

Everything with Audrey rushed back, and I started feeling that stinging sensation in my chest that comes on suddenly when you try to hold back crying but you know you're never going to be able to.

"You're being nice to Alex," Elyse said, exhaling as though pretending she was smoking a cigarette. "I can see why that girl likes you."

And at that I lost it, just started sobbing into the sleeve of my stinky shirt, which was way overdue for the long-lost luxury known as a washing machine. (If I get out of here I'll never complain about having to wash, fold, and put away laundry ever again.)

"Oh, I'm sorry . . ." Elyse said when she realized I was crying.

"I messed up," I managed. "I really messed up. Not that it matters now."

I could hear Elyse coming over to me, picking her way through the dark. Her hand found my head, and the next thing I knew, we were hugging. It felt so good: the first time any of us had touched except for accidentally while passing around food and water.

"It's all gonna work out," she whispered as we rocked back and forth. "I promise."

It was the kindest lie I'd ever been told.

A few minutes ago three guys pushed through the door, the bright light like spears into my eyes, which have gotten so adjusted to darkness I may as well be a mole person like those subway tunnel dwellers I used to hear about in New York.

They were wearing the identical garb as before, black bandannas and hoods covering their faces, black clothes. They rushed Alex, picking him up by the legs and arms like a farm hog. He immediately started struggling and screaming, which prompted Elyse to launch onto the biggest guy's back and begin punching him in the ribs. I tried tackling the second guy but it was no use; they shook both of us off like Taylor Swift's boyfriends. A stale protein bar a day does not Superman make.

"Try that again," one of them growled, wolflike, before dragging Alex out of the room, "and you'll be sorry."

I'd only hung on a few seconds before I was tossed to the ground, but I did manage to pull up the shirt on the guy I'd jumped. In the light I could make out a small tattoo: the ancient symbol of a Roman numeral I, the Abiders emblem!—and, not for nothing, the same tattoo that I noticed on Jason last year.

"Am I going to say it, or are you?" Elyse asks, as soon as the thugs depart and Alex's screams die down. "Abider deprogramming? Or worse."

"Let me just think for a minute," I say tersely.

"No need to get snippy with me, Kid Cudi. It's not like you believed they Changer-napped us to take us for ice cream."

"Aren't you even worried about Alex?" I snipe.

"Dude, you need to get it together, because if we aren't a team, we are never going to make it out of this rat hole."

Just then, two protein bars, half a bottle of apple juice, and a bottle of water are tossed into our cell. We eat the bars, even though neither of us have much of an appetite.

"I'm sorry, Elyse," I say, pocketing half my ration for later, optimistically presuming there will be a later. "I'm just not sure what to do anymore."

"Man, you think I am?" She laughs, takes a swig of juice. "Well, one thing I know for sure: this is not the end of my story. I didn't come this far up the Changer ladder to get snuffed out now. No way I'm letting a bunch of yahoo Abiders decide my destiny. I have earned that frigging right myself."

I listen, and I think about Nana, and Audrey, and Snoopy. And I realize: *No matter what we tell ourselves, no one decides anything in the end. We are all being carried on the current, mistaking rafts for shores.*

CHANGE 2—DAY 226 *(I THINK)*

Some strange organ music has started, likely from a boom box or speaker placed on the other side of the metal door. There is faint narration beneath the music, but I can't quite make out what it's saying. Or maybe I'm imagining it.

Elyse is asleep in the corner. There's not much else to do.

I don't really know what day it is, and I'm not even sure how long I've been in here. How many nights do I have to be gone before my parents give up hope I'm alive? On the cop shows it's always forty-eight hours until the odds of finding a missing person drop to nearly nothing. I know it's been longer than that.

I wonder if Snoopy was found, or is he stuck in some prison cell like I am, both of us paying for my recklesness?

I guess I kind of brought this on myself, being a selfish teenager, worried about *me me me* and nobody else. This is the last thing my parents need to deal with when they're already stretched to their limit with Nana. I can only imagine how crazed my mother must be. She's always been so reasonable, shrinky-chill, except when it comes to protecting me. Then Mama Bear Banshee comes out, and G help anyone she perceives to be threatening her baby. What I wouldn't do to see her bust through that door . . .

The music's still playing, in fact is getting louder, the voices chanting more insistently. The only words I can make out are, "*Stay one, stay strong . . .*"

Or maybe it's the voices I was hearing before the music

even started. I can't tell; it's all running together.

Is Tracy looking for me? Is Mr. Crowell helping her? Is Audrey worried since I haven't been in school? Or just relieved . . .

The bandanna brigade just came back, huffing as they heaved a big dude by his arms into the room, his legs limp and dragging heavy behind them. His face was still covered by a hood, his muscled arms bloodied and dirty, tied together so tightly it was cutting into his skin.

In the light Elyse and I exchange a look, tacitly deciding whether it's worth trying to rush these guys again. I mouth, *Not yet*, and she scratches her nose in agreement.

The Abider goons drop the unconscious guy's arms, twisting him so he lands on his left shoulder and side on the cement floor, head lolling to the ground, causing the dark hood to inch up his neck. I frantically scan our captors while there's light, try to find something, anything notable about them that might help us escape. Where is Sherlock when you need him? He could probably make out their life stories from the scent of their farts.

"Good catch," I hear one of them say as they leave.

The music swelled when the door opened, and now fades as they exit, like a waltz in hell. The zealots slam the door shut, padlocking it on the other side, as has become the routine.

"One strong!" They shout to each other in the hall. If one of the voices belongs to Jason, I can't tell.

Elyse and I are silent as our eyes readjust to the dark, the outline of this burly passed-out guy a linebacker-sized clump on the cement between us. I'm so hungry, but I don't feel like rooting around like an animal to locate a crappy sandwich. It seems like such a giant task in the dark.

We wait. The music surges, the light around the door probably at its brightest point (high noon?), but I don't really care to Chronicle many of these details anymore. Why bother? They don't matter. We don't matter. Nothing does.

The guy on the ground stirs a little, flops onto his back from his side, wrists still bound together. He must have put up a serious fight. I wish I'd been able to.

I scoot closer, Elyse approaching him from the other side. It seems like he's having trouble breathing beneath the fabric, so I reach out, grab a corner at the top of his head, and yank. It's pinned where the crown of his head is heavy against the concrete. I yank harder, twice, and finally the hood pulls frees, sliding off.

I blink hard, lean in closer. His head seems to be bloodied and badly beaten, swollen and misshapen around both eyes, which . . . are starting to flutter open. I dip my head toward his, inches away now.

OH M—

"Chase?"

His eyes snap wide, a lopsided grin breaking across his broken face. He lurches upright. "Fancy meeting you here," he slurs through wobbly teeth, as I smother him in a messy embrace, just as his head snaps forward and he slumps over, oozing back to the floor.

"Chase," I say.

Nothing.

"Chase!" I shout. "Wake up, buddy!"

He doesn't stir. I poke at his shoulders. Elyse grabs his legs and shakes. Pinches his skin.

"Come on, Chase, come back!"

I strain, but I can't see any more details in this dark. Not his eyes. Not his expression. I put my ear to his chest but I can't hear anything, no heartbeat, no air passing through, no sound at all beyond the chanting on the other side of the door: "*Stay one, stay strong, stay one, stay strong, stay one, stay strong . . .*"

(NOT) THE END

wearechangers.org

ABRIDGED GLOSSARY OF TERMS

(*EXCERPTED FROM* THE CHANGERS BIBLE)

ABIDER. A non-Changer (see *Static*, below) belonging to an underground syndicate of anti-Changers, whose ultimate goal is the extermination of the Changer race. The Abider philosophy is characterized by a steadfast desire for genetic purity, for human blood to remain unmingled with Changer blood. Abider leaders operate by instilling fear in humans, for when people fear one another, they are easier to control. Abiders sometimes have an identifying tattoo depicting an ancient symbol of a Roman numeral I (*Figure 1*), the emblem symbolizing homogeneity and the single identity Abiders desire each human to inhabit.

I

FIG. 1. ABIDERS EMBLEM

CHANGER. A member of an ancient race of humans imbued with the gift of changing into a different person four times between the ages of approximately fourteen and eighteen. (In more modern times, one change occurs at the commencement of each of the four years of high school; see *Cycle*, below.) Changers may not reveal themselves to non-Changers (see *Static*, below). After living as all four versions of themselves (see *V*, below), Changers must choose one version in which to live out the rest of their lives (see *Mono*, below). Changer doctrine holds that the Changer race is the last hope for the human race on the whole to reverse the moral devolution that has overcome it. Changers believe more Changers equals more empathy on planet Earth. And that only through empathy will the human race survive. After their Cycles (see *Cycle*, below), Changers eventually partner with Statics. When approved by the Council (see *Changers Council*, below), Changer-Static unions produce a single Changer offspring.

CHANGERS COUNCIL. The official Changer authority. The Changers Council is divided into regional units spread out across the globe. Each Council is responsible for all basic decisions regarding the population of Changers in its specific region.

CHANGERS EMBLEM. A variation on Leonardo da Vinci's *Vitruvian Man* drawing, dating to approximately 1490 CE (*Figure 2*). The Changers Emblem contains four bodies superimposed in motion, instead of two (as portrayed in da Vinci's composition), and appears to the eye as both four bodies and one body at the same time—though all sharing one head and heart. An emblem of the Changer mantra: *In the many we are one.*

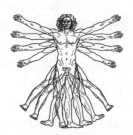

FIG. 2. CHANGERS EMBLEM

CHANGERS MIXER. Required events for all Changers to attend, during each of the four years of high school. Council rules and regulations are emphasized at mixers (see *Changers*

Council, above). Mixers sometimes require classwork and formal discussions, but mixers are primarily designed to offer more informal camaraderie and problem-solving techniques, both of which help Changers address some of the difficulties that frequently arise during their Cycles (see *Cycle,* below).

CYCLE. The four-year period of different iterations, or versions (see *V,* below) that a Changer goes through between the approximate ages of fourteen and eighteen. One V per each of the four years of high school.

FEINTS. The story a Changer family tells the non-Changers (see *Static,* below) in their lives, to explain each V's (see *V,* below) absence during the following year of school. The specific details for Feints are provided by the Council (see *Changers Council,* above), unless a Changer and her/his parents submit a formal request for an alternative Feint, which is necessary under certain circumstances (i.e., when Statics are especially integrated into a particular V's life, or when a particular Feint will better protect the identity of the Changer and her/his family).

FOREVER CEREMONY. Regional "graduation" events held on the day after high school graduation for every Changer within a designated region. A joyous though private (from Statics—except parental Statics; see *Static,* below) occasion, as each year of ceremonies initiates more and more Changers to migrate into the world and eventually find a Static mate, with whom they will start a family and raise Changer offspring of their own. At the Forever Ceremony, Changers are introduced one by one, and each speaks a little about each of her/his V's (see *V,* below) before declaring in front of both the Council (see *Changers Council,* above) and their community whom they will live as for the rest of their lives (see *Mono*, below).

MONO. A Changer's "forever identity," a.k.a. the V (see *V*, below) a Changer ultimately selects for her/himself after living as each of the four different assigned V's. A Mono cannot be the individual a Changer lived as during the approximately fourteen years before her/his Cycle (see *Cycle*, above) began.

RACHAS. Common term for "Radical Changers," a small but growing splinter group of Changers who seek not to live in secret, as the Council (see *Changers Council*, above) dictates. RaChas are freegans, anarchist free spirits, often living in the margins, surviving on what human society at large throws away. RaChas philosophy calls for living openly and demanding liberation and acceptance for all, Changers and Statics alike. RaChas have adopted the ancient Roman numeral IV, rotated on its side (*Figure 3*), as an emblem, symbolizing their desire to shake up traditional Changers philosophy and call attention to the limitations of the four-V Cycle (See *V,* below; see *Cycle*, above) each Changer must go through. RaChas have been known to recruit Changers with the intention of indoctrinating them into RaChas activities. RaChas have also been known to battle Abiders (see *Abider*, above) and even stage missions to rescue Changers who have been abducted by Abiders and held in Abider deprogramming camps. [*Nota bene:* While the Changers Council is at odds with the RaChas movement, it can also no longer deny its existence.]

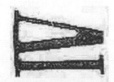

FIG. 3. RACHAS EMBLEM

STATIC. A non-Changer (i.e., the vast majority of the world's population). Particularly sympathetic Statics are ideal mates for Changers later in life. Once a Changer has completed his or her Cycle (see *Cycle*, above), s/he will be fully prepared to assess various Statics' openness and acceptance of difference. When a Changer feels certain that s/he has found an ideal potential Static mate, s/he may, with permission of the Council (see *Changers Council*, above), reveal her/himself to the Static. [*Nota bene:* This revelation can occur only after a Changer's full Cycle is complete, and s/he has declared his or her Mono (see *Mono*, above).]

TOUCHSTONE. A Changer's official mentor, assigned immediately upon a Changer's transformation into her/his first V (see *V*, below). The same Touchstone is assigned for a Changer's entire Cycle (see *Cycle*, above).

V. Any one of a Changer's four versions of her/himself into which s/he changes during each of the four years of high school. Changers walk in the shoes of one V for each year of school (between the approximate ages of fourteen and eighteen).

Acknowledgments

Thanks are due to a great number of folks who helped *Changers* evolve from a lightning-bolt idea in the park to an actual book series we are proud to have our children (and others) read. The love and kindness of the following friends, family, and colleagues can be felt on every page of *Book Two* (and beyond):

Johnny Temple, Johanna Ingalls, Aaron Petrovich, Ibrahim Ahmad, and Susannah Lawrence at Akashic Books; Jason Amon of Chocolate Shores, for "Change Is at Hand"; Kaleb Anderson, for contributing writing to DJ's slam poem in the *Change 2–Day 20* chapter; Karl Austen and Ryan LeVine at Jackoway, Tyerman, Wertheimer; Kate Bornstein, for everything; Kevin Buchmeier, Nick Gotten, and John Chaisson of the *Changers* band, The Bickersons; Sarah Chalfant and Rebecca Nagel at the Wylie Agency; our families; John Green; Laurie Hasencamp and Mike Lurey; Tom Léger; Téa Leoni and family; Jennifer Mencken and Ben Pivar; Misty Travis Oaks; Langley Perer and Dawn Saltzman at Mosaic; Alex Petrowsky; Spencer Presler; Amy Ray; Scott Turner Schofield; Zac Simmons and Dana Spector at Paradigm; Doug Stewart at Sterling Lord Literistic.

And to the seventh grader at Middle School 378 in New York City who asked, "Are there Changers in the real world?" *Yes!*

T COOPER and **ALLISON GLOCK-COOPER** are best-selling and award-winning authors and journalists. Between them, they have published seven books, raised two children, and rescued six dogs. The **CHANGERS** series is their first collaboration in print. The two also write for television and film, and they can be reached at their websites: www.t-cooper.com and www.allisonglock.com.